Please return this book on or before the date shown
above. To renew go to www.essex.gov.uk/libraries,
ring 0845 603 7628 or go to any Essex library.

DS12 4005

Essex County Council

GW00775765

30130505230738

THE SAMURAI KITES

When two Australian nurses, Mae Winters and Sally Brandeis, crash-land after a mercy mission in the New Guinea jungle, they are the only survivors. As they wait for rescue, their would-be liberators are massacred by a Japanese patrol, leaving them in the hands of the modern Samurai, Lieutenant Oshima, and his sadistic Sergeant Nagato. So begins a long march to the Japanese encampment, and as pity for the two women vanquishes the code of blood, their captors are at deadly odds with each other in the torrid heat until they kill and are killed in a ghastly struggle...

To my wife, Diana,
and mentor, Tom Hungerford.

THE SAMURAI KITES

by

William Warnock

Magna Large Print Books
Long Preston, North Yorkshire,
BD23 4ND, England.

British Library Cataloguing in Publication Data.

Warnock, William
      The Samurai kites.

      A catalogue record of this book is
      available from the British Library

      ISBN   978-0-7505-2813-9

First published in Great Britain by Sphere Books Ltd., 1981

Copyright © William Warnock 1981

Cover illustration © Charles Pino by arrangement with
Temple Rogers

The moral right of the author has been asserted

Published in Large Print 2008 by arrangement with
The estate of William Warnock, care of Bryan Drew

Magna Large Print is an imprint of Library Magna Books Ltd.

Printed and bound in Great Britain by
T.J. (International) Ltd., Cornwall, PL28 8RW

It's quite another thing to capture it one's self. I trembled with excitement when I saw it coming majestically towards me ... to gaze upon its fresh and living beauty ... to feel it struggling between one's fingers.

From the diary of naturalist
Alfred Russell Wallace (1823-1913)

Kocho
rakka eda ni
Kaeru to mirebo
Kocho kana

Fallen petals
rise back to the branch
I watch.
Oh! ... butterflies!

Moritake

Part 1

THE SHOOTING GALLERY

Chapter 1

The woman, the older of the two, leaned back on the hull of the Dakota, her fair hair bright against the olive skin of the broken plane. She had not moved for an hour.

The port wing had fractured on impact and, half severed from the fuselage of the plane, reached up towards the sky in an ironic salute.

Lieutenant Oshima swung his binoculars slowly sideways seeking out the younger one. He felt omnipotent: fascinated by this strange power of command; this ability to summon up such thrilling images at will; to pin these exotics to a ground glass display of his choosing.

There the girl was, by the tail of the plane which had broken off and lay about five yards behind the fuselage. She was standing looking anxiously straight at him. Oshima knew he was in deep cover, but wondered if the lenses of his field glasses had caught the light. He stopped breathing.

At length she turned away and walked nervously a few yards back towards the plane. She peered fixedly in the opposite direction; directly towards where Squad Leader Nagato lay hidden somewhere over there with the others.

Oshima let his breath out slowly. It was as though the girl knew she was being watched. She reminded him of the goldfish in his father's study, peering anxiously into the distorted world outside its glass prison sphere: a carp pool perhaps, where, for sport, you could drag glittering prizes up into the light with barbless hooks.

But she was not prey. She was bait, for there still could be a rescue party. His stumbling on the wreckage last night had explained the sound of the enemy spotter plane they had heard overhead, droning unseen, back and forth across the valley, since dawn.

Oshima sniffed the air. The gagging smell of death had subsided with the rain. He wondered how many had died in that plane.

He had watched these two women tend a third survivor all through the morning. Only a couple of hours ago they had ceased stooping over the prone figure; a man, or another woman, it was impossible to tell. They had distanced themselves from what was now just an anonymous bundle under a blanket dragged out of sight behind the plane hull. Whoever it had been, had died.

The woman had comforted the girl for a long time, holding her in her arms like a child. Since then they had been staring out into the jungle, across the narrow and temporary space that had been scythed flat by the disintegrating wreckage of the plane.

Since first light he had studied them ceaselessly, riveted by their beauty. The sense of elation at their discovery was still with him, but now Oshima felt drained from staring through the powerful lenses. It was as though his eyes were being sucked out by the power of those fascinating images.

This fatigue fused with the depthless exhaustion he felt always, now. It seemed to Oshima sometimes that no amount of sleep would ever be enough to cure this tiredness.

In last night's brief dusk they had all heard the voice close to the edge of hysteria, calling out, wildly, over and over again. Then silence.

He had sent Moritoh and Wasumi to reconnoitre. They had come back excited by the discovery of a crashed plane a quarter of a mile from where the Section had bivouacked. It had been too dark to see who had made the cries. Oshima had posted a guard on the wreck and made camp a hundred yards away.

At first light he had scouted the area suspicious of a possible ambush.

Nothing. It should have been a simple matter of going in, killing any survivors, and looting the wreck for the mine of intelligence information it would yield. Then, hurrying on as before, back to base camp with his disturbing report of the unusually high level of enemy activity.

His men had been excited, as though it were to be an archery contest with a fixed target to aim at, and a competition amongst them to see which of them would hit the most centres. Nagato, for whom there could never be enough killing, had relished the prospect.

From a fork of a tree overlooking the broken plane Oshima had watched as the light had made slow sense of shadows. Gradually the wreckage had taken shape, then, astonishingly, from the cocoon of the wrecked tail plane, had emerged two women. The younger had appeared first, followed almost immediately by the other.

The sight brought Oshima an intense and complex excitement: part exhilaration, part apprehension, part wonderment. He had found himself overcome by curious trembling as he gazed upon their fresh and living beauty, amidst the gloom of the dark and tangled forest. His heart had begun to beat violently; the blood had rushed to his head.

In that moment, Oshima was overcome by a compelling and obsessive desire to capture these women alive; to possess them. The women triggered, in Oshima, a thousand unsettling memories; long-suppressed feelings that now rose up like disturbed ghosts in an empty and shuttered house.

For over an hour he had sat staring at them; hypnotised; oblivious of time; his job of intelligence gathering forgotten. He was but a few yards from them, so close, in fact, that through his powerful lenses he could see the very texture of their skin.

At length, Squad Leader Nagato, puzzled by his officer's failure to return from the reconnaissance, silently joined Oshima, jerking him out of his trance.

Nagato's eyes had flashed with anger and frustration when Oshima had held back the assault on the survivors, especially when he had seen that they were a prize of flesh.

His anger had increased when Oshima, in order to delay the inevitable death of the women, ordered the setting up of an ambush to trap any possible search party.

The slow morning had passed, a cocked, silent trap. No rescuers appeared. Now time was running out. Oshima knew that, before long, he would have no choice in the matter. Then, inevitably, these women would die.

He would give it another hour, he decided. Or, perhaps two.

Oshima brought the older woman back into view and adjusted the focus, the better to look at her compelling, troubled face.

He could almost taste the old thrill of the capture with her; some storied creature of velvet wings, black and brilliant green, a golden body and a crimson breast, struggling between his fingers.

Winters opened her eyes and watched Brandeis padding about; like a panther in a too-small cage, back and forth, back and forth, staring hopelessly beyond the impregnable bars of the trees.

The sun was hot now and lanced down through the trees. She could feel the sweat trickle down her neck.

Winters was filled with remorse about the previous night; so brutally shutting up the frightened girl when Brandeis had begun to shout out hysterically into the silent, menacing blackness of the jungle. But the anger remained, too.

How could Sally have said those awful things?

Hypocrite. Tight-arsed bitch.

Ach, but what did all that matter now? They were finished anyway. Winters wondered what it would be like to die out here in this forest. To be so much fuel for this voracious place that subsisted on death.

She had not spoken to Brandeis about the way their supplies were running out. They had been in the jungle two days and two nights now. There was little water and, apart from some biscuits and a few emergency rations, there was not much food left either. She would have to broach the subject sooner or later.

Could you live off the land in this place?

Brandeis paced, from the tail plane to the

14

wing and back.

Maybe Sally had been right, Winters allowed – crying out. At least it was positive; taking action. Maybe they would have been heard by Australian soldiers, or at least by natives who, Winters had heard, hated the Japanese and might have helped. And what if it *had* been Japanese? Wouldn't that have been better anyway? To be found by anyone rather than simply rot here hundreds of miles from anywhere?

Winters' stomach writhed. It was fear. And the smell; that nauseating miasma of corruption. What buzzing horror there was now inside the wreckage! She could hear the disgusting drone as the humanity and the last shreds of human dignity was stripped from those in there. That hideous metamorphosis had begun at once and, last night, just before light failed, Winters knew that she could never again go back inside the plane.

They should have dragged the bodies out and buried them, she knew that now. Everything rotted so fast up here. Resolve dies; energy fades. They hadn't even buried poor Chuck; just dragged him out of sight behind the fuselage and covered him over with a blanket, and a thin token layer of soil.

Merciful release was the trade term. Poor bastard. Not all the king's sutures and clamps could have put him together again. They couldn't have saved him even at base hospital in Lae.

Winters had seen enough of death to be hardened to it, but always she was staggered when the broken, torn and maimed young men clung to life so uselessly. *They* hoped. The despair was always in the eyes of the onlookers.

How, in God's name, do they hang on so long and how could anyone still believe in that bastard, indifferent God?

Private Moritoh spotted the first one edging out cautiously from the far bank. A black. Then another, and after them, four soldiers stringing out in a diagonal line across the river. Adrenalin pumped. The lieutenant had been right! A rescue party.

He sighted them along the barrel of his rifle and thought how easy it would be to squeeze the trigger one ... two ... three ... four times ... and four lives would end as tributaries of blood merging with the water of the river sparkling in the afternoon sun.

Four little squeezes. How easy it was! The familiar surge of elation caused him to shiver slightly.

His sights swung back on to the first soldier. He held his breath and smoothly adjusted for the man's traversing movement. How much more satisfying it would be if it were the familiar shape of Nagato he held there, one gentle squeeze away from death. Moritoh's tongue found the deep cut inside his mouth. Again his gorge rose at this potent reminder of Squad Leader Nagato. To have him in his sights, just for one moment: that smooth, muscular face, those flat lizard eyes, those white teeth he had seen bared in anger just once too often.

The first stick of the enemy disappeared beyond his line of vision, not a hundred yards upstream from where he sat in the fork of the tree.

His fingers traced the smooth, raised pattern of the Imperial chrysanthemum crest on the breech of his sniper's rifle, his solid and reassuring shield against these silent, implacable men coming at him with such deadly menace.

There! Another four of them; chilling silhouettes of man in green uniforms and cloth berets close to their heads. These were not the infantrymen he had seen, broken and rotting on jungle tracks after the big battles in the South. These did not make mistakes, nor fall easily into traps, nor make too much noise: these were special soldiers he had only heard about, fierce killers without compassion who hunted in small patrols far ahead of the regular troops.

Moritoh watched them cross, the vertical rise and fall of his foresight betraying his quickening breath.

They seemed to flow inexorably over the

river as though moving on a belt. This time out, he had seen more activity amongst the enemy than on any previous patrol. It seemed to Moritoh that, since he had come into action six months before, fresh from recruit training, he and his comrades had been killing every day. Yet there was always more. The enemy soldiers seemed to spring out of the ground, coming at him as though they knew no fear. Were they all unafraid? Did they not know the fear that dogged his every step?

How long before the killing would all be over? And, when it was, would he and all his comrades be dead? Already Moritoh harboured darkened thoughts that he would never return home again. Would the rich, glittering future he might have had, had he grown up in any other time but this, finally elude him?

Ten minutes passed, but there was no sign of any others. Should he not wait longer? He decided to give it another five minutes.

Again his tongue explored the painful cut inside his mouth where Nagato had struck him that morning for his alleged slowness to obey an order. Perhaps, thought Moritoh, it would be in this action that death would come to Nagato.

Some hope. The man was invincible. He would go on killing and bullying forever. War was his time; the time when the Nagatos of the world came into their own.

18

Even in reverie Moritoh was disturbed by thoughts of Nagato's awesome power and savagery.

Until he had run across Nagato no one had scared Moritoh. But Nagato was feared not only by him, but by all the men; even Lieutenant Oshima, who was afraid of no other man.

They were all in awe of that terrible physical strength and erratic anger. To tackle Nagato you would need a gun and preferably to come at him from behind. A couple of the old hands simply told Moritoh, after one occasion when he had been badly knocked about, to keep himself out of trouble. They were not going to interfere. Nagato was Moritoh's problem. Nagato: a textbook madman who would calm down after an action, his hunger for violence temporarily assuaged by the killing, tormenting and looting.

Moritoh checked his watch. Time to go. A last slow careful look. There was no sign of others coming across the river. It would not be long before he would see Nagato in action again.

He slipped off his perch cautiously and made his way up the long, steep slope to report.

Lieutenant Oshima would be pleased, guessing right about a rescue party. He was clever all right, Oshima, 'The Professor', as all the men called him behind his back.

Moritoh felt better. This time there were only eight of the enemy to outlive.

In fact there were twelve. Minutes after Moritoh had left, four other Australians crossed the river.

Special troops.

Moritoh's report told Oshima there would be no second chance if his ambush failed. The enemy patrol might be a small one, but it was one of the tough harassment and reconnaissance units which were causing so much havoc. Oshima had encountered them only once before, and that had been a close run thing.

They would not simply blunder into his trap.

They would send in one man to take out the women. The rest would stay back in the forest giving cover. They would move silently and fast. He would not have much time to act.

'Eight, you say?' Oshima looked keenly at Moritoh.

Moritoh nodded, his eyes gleaming in anticipation of the coming fight. He was still breathing deeply from the long pull up the slope.

Oshima regarded the handsome, eager face before him. How young he is! he thought, touched by his usual powerful sense of concern for the boy.

'You stay deep. Back down towards the river. Signal after they pass you. Don't come in unless you have to.'

'Sir.' Moritoh was disappointed by having been excluded from the action. Oshima watched him move away, graceful as a dancer.

Oshima checked his ambush with special care, disposing his men in depth, with clear lines of fire; set snipers in the trees to make sure any lookouts the enemy posted would be hit the moment he opened fire on the main force.

He was shaken. His expedient, time-buying rationale about a rescue party had come true. There was no avoiding the destruction of the women now.

It was as though his mind had split into two compartments; one, that of the professional killer going about the deadly routines of combat; the other, a man deeply anguished by the coming death of these women, whom he had come to think of as his own.

If only they had not cried out. If only he had not heard them. Oshima stared once more at their soft, blue-grey images on the ground glass. He could sense a nervousness about them now, the instinctive response of rare and fragile things. It was unthinkable that creatures so lovely should finish up being used as bait. Was everything beautiful that he touched destined to be destroyed, to be covered in dust, to decay?

Brandeis could feel a probing weight of eyes.

There is something out there, she was certain of it. *Oh God please don't let it be Japanese.* Those stories in the mess about what they had done to those poor half-caste women in Milne Bay. That awful business with barbed wire. How horrible. *Whoever it is watching out there oh please God, don't let it be...*

The trees were moving in; pressing at her. She never actually saw the movement. They edged forward only when her eyes blinked. Maybe if she could force her eyes to stay open, they would stop.

Brandeis peered out hopelessly into the shadow-tangle, but there were no definable shapes out there in the crowding jungle. Just the press of unseen eyes and everything that crept and crawled and slithered. She thought with disgust of the creatures she had seen: blood-freezing spiders bigger than her hand; hairy moths dropping obscenely under their own bodyweight, lurching blindly from twig to sinking twig.

What a fool she had made of herself last night, crying out like a hysterical schoolgirl, saying those awful things to Mae. Brandeis' face flushed at the remembrance of it.

It was no good counting the reasons. Her ancient fear of the dark, the shock of the crash and the crushing despair, punctuated by poor Chuck's piteous moans, had all fused together and flooded out. Then when Mae had tried to shut her up, getting angry and lying there, sulking in the dark until Mae had gathered her in her strong and comforting arms.

Mae. The Boss. Senior Sister Winters: holding her close and, for some reason, saying, over and over again, that all this ghastly mess was all her fault. How could it be Mae's fault?

Everyone seemed to want to apologise. Even Chuck had apologised his way to oblivion; uselessly consuming whatever remaining layers of protection against the pain he might have had with, I'm sorry. I'm sorry. He had wasted his last breath with apologies.

Hadn't been his fault, poor bastard. Flying blind; engines faltering; wresting the controls in that stomach-wrenching sideways slew as they tore, in a shriek of ripping metals, into the trees. There hadn't been a panic, only some half-remembered screaming as the wall of trees slammed up at them.

She hadn't screamed then, but last night she had; releasing her bottled up fears and panic with those weird cries. Had she really made those unearthly sounds?

She had hated Winters for stopping her; for shouting at her in the darkness; for shaking her quiet; for pulling rank. And she still did. She stared at her companion.

Look at you, you bitch. Just sitting there, doing

23

nothing. You're wrong about staying here. Wrong as hell.

Wouldn't it be better if anyone found them? Better than this, with the jungle creeping insidiously in to claim them, as it had already claimed the six others; her friends in there, dissolving like wax in a black, seething swarm of disgust. Someone must find them. Anyone. But, oh please God don't let it be Japanese.

They had argued for hours until Mae had ended it abruptly with: *We stay here, that's an order:* her face taut and angry.

To walk away was hopeless. Mae had said with her hateful logic. You could walk for a year and simply go in the wrong direction. Or walk straight into the hands of the Japanese… It was as if she enjoyed savouring the disasters that might befall them if she didn't have her way.

Oh God not them.

Maybe there will be a rescue party. That little plane. Mae said she had spotted it once high over the ridge on the other side. It hadn't come anywhere near them. Not yet.

Brandeis reached out for comforting thoughts. Surely it's looking for us. Surely. That's what Mae had said: *If we stay here at least they've got something to look for. How do you think we'd be spotted out there?* and she had pointed to the featureless rain forest partly visible, rearing up on the far side of the great valley.

They don't just write off a plane-load of nurses, she had said.

But in war time what if they did?

There! A movement somewhere at the very outer edge of her eye. Surely that had been something moving?

Brandeis stared hard at the spot feeling a chilling tremor of fear at her nerve ends. Warily she turned her head searching the patternless green tangle for movement, but everything was still. Two gigantic butterflies fluttered elegantly from left to right and settled on a bush by the tail of the plane. They blazed briefly in the sun then swooped, up and away, into the trees. She watched them go with regret. Her eyes caught the surcrease of the hard edge of the plane wing, a comforting straight line in a place where there were no straight lines, only disorder and anarchy.

There! Again a movement.

She turned to look for Winters. She was still sitting there propped against the plane, but now her eyes were open. Silently Brandeis pointed to where she had seen the movement; leaves shaking as though by a unfelt wind.

Suddenly Winters was standing with an incredulous look on her face. Running past her.

'Thank God ... thank God...'

A green-clad man had materialised on the margin of the jungle: a tough-looking, young soldier with beret and gun. Now his arm was around Winters.

Brandeis found herself walking towards him. He was smiling at her, but he put a finger to his lips.

'G'day,' said the smiling man in a nervous voice, no louder than a whisper.

Brandeis felt the tears gush as she pressed her forehead against his shirt.

Chapter 2

Oshima watched the women with awe as they swooped through the green shade to greet their rescuer. How beautiful!

He heard their greeting cries, but his spoken English was rusty. The unfamiliar rhythms of their speech and the distance denied his sharing their words. It had been five years since he had used the language except to read captured documents, and those pathetic personal letters that would never be posted.

He had seen the soldier when he had first risen up, almost invisible, on the edge of the goldfish bowl; watched him silence the women and put his arms around them.

They were either crying or laughing with relief; Oshima could not tell which.

Entranced, Oshima watched the shadow play. He felt the same fascination he had always felt in the laboratory when some exceptional specimen was dissected, or when studying his collection, like glittering and gaudy jewels, row upon row of them catching the light.

Had he felt the same detachment, he would have been less disquieted. But he was not detached. In this drama the players were now secret intimates of his.

Watching them, Oshima felt that he was observing something that involved him in a deeply personal way. He had a jealous desire to be part of the group they had so quickly formed; these women of his and their rescuer.

His men, invisible in the deep cover all around him, had ceased to exist. He felt that only he had been privileged to observe the ritual of the women's greetings, so charged with warmth and happiness, emotions he had almost forgotten, emotions he could not afford to intrude now. Unavailingly Oshima tried to block off his feverish and dislocated obsession with his prizes from his soldier's instinctive consideration of ambush; the young one with her fragile body and her shock of near-white blonde hair and the graceful woman with her tall, sturdy body and fair hair caught behind her head.

Throughout that timeless morning the inescapable fact that they would die by his action had crowded Oshima's thoughts like an unwelcome stranger, try as he would to force it away. He wanted no part of destroying such beauty. All that was behind him now, long since.

In his hours of intense, silent communion with the women, Oshima had developed a rare passion for them; not the conqueror's lust, with them as booty, some reward for military services rendered, but the once-familiar avidity of the collector, of the field trip and the laboratory; the private passion between the observer and the observed, the possessor and the possessed.

He had studied them, part by symmetrical part; anatomised their rare configuration of head, body, limbs, curve of throat; drunk them in through his eyes like some life-enhancing elixir; desired possession of them.

Oshima was dismayed by their existence, yet compelled by it. These two-dimensional images projected before his eyes, on to the smokey, blued lenses of his military issue field glasses, were destroying his steel carapace of unfeelingness. To have such feelings was a fatal flaw; even in a crime against the nature of war. He had put faces to enemies.

A slight hand-signal by the fair-haired soldier. Another of the enemy soldiers materialised on the other side of the scythed space. He joined the group and both women reached for him and hugged him joyfully. The soldiers were made nervous by this. Quickly the four crossed towards the tailplane section where the women had piled their kitbags. The women knelt down and began collecting some possessions.

The spittle dried in Oshima's mouth. His men would be ready, waiting for his first burst. He could sense the pressure of their collective force upon him, the held-breath force of them, trembling in anticipation of the kill. Still he hesitated.

The two soldiers standing above the women were looking around nervously, with the quick, anxious head movements of birds. The urgency of leaving was on them. Oshima knew he was running out of time. He covered them with the sights, taking aim at them along the short, grey barrel of his weapon. There it was, a perfect grouping; the two soldiers standing; the women kneeling.

Suddenly the two women stood up. They shifted and were between him and his targets. Annoyed, he held his fire and waited for the women to get out of the way. Why could he not simply squeeze the trigger? he wondered. They were all enemy.

Something Oshima had read once came to him: a venal early collector in these Islands, anxious to prove a new species existed, had brought down a rare giant butterfly with birdshot. This automatic machine pistol of his would damage these lovely specimens beyond any repair.

Suddenly the four turned and began to move into the jungle with the women still between him and the soldiers. Again, the momentary hesitation as he swung his gun sharply trying for a clear shot at the two soldiers. Already they were half in cover. They were half out of sight. He fired.

Afterwards, replaying the fragmented after-images of battle, Oshima was never exactly sure of what happened.

He saw the one soldier flung back by the force of the invisible lance of steel that connected Oshima to his victim. An impression of disintegration. The women, frozen figures in the sunlight. All round him the roar of weapons as his unseen men opened up. He glanced around quickly, then back.

The women were gone.

A sudden uncanny silence; the drift of cordite writhing upwards through columns of sunlight.

Oshima stared at the place where the women had been, the chilling realisation that they were dead overwhelming him. Something arched upwards; Oshima ducked instinctively. A moment later, the fearful crack of a grenade exploding, then the sound of a high-pitched screaming that chilled his blood. It went on and on, setting his teeth on edge. Another explosion; the harsh steel voice of an automatic weapon; cries and shouts. His ambush had failed.

A movement unlocked his will. Into his line of sight came one of the enemy soldiers, wounded and heaving painfully towards the cover of the plane. Oshima's gun sounded. Mud and flesh erupted. The crawling figure writhed like an ant cut in half and was still.

Behind him another sharp explosion. Oshima flinched under the chilling ricochet of steel flailing above him. He heard a babble of anguished Japanese and, a few yards from him, the undergrowth thrashed.

Oshima crawled carefully to where his own man had been hit. There was nothing he could do for him. The enemy's grenades were fearsome weapons compared to their own pathetic firecrackers.

Watanabe's eyes caught his, asking an unanswerable question, and at that moment, he died. Oshima turned away from his comrade, whose dying agonies had transformed him into a stranger. He felt sick. Poor Watanabe had died because of his officer's stupid sentimentality about two foreign women. Had he taken the enemy out with his first burst this would not have happened.

Somewhere overhead a clattering sound in the lower branches of the trees. On pure instinct, Oshima rolled over and over crashing through the undergrowth hugging the ground to avoid the grenade. An earsplitting crack. The baseplate guillotined over his head.

Over there! A movement of leaves swaying violently. Lying half on his side Oshima fired off a burst at a man in green, standing aiming down at him, five yards away. Oshima's burst caught him in the chest. The man died standing there; toppled like a demolished chimneystack, crumbling as he fell.

Behind him two sharp bursts of fire; one left, one right – by the familiar metallic rattle, his own men firing. A long, sustained burst of fire countered. A duel of steel sounds. There followed a profound silence punctuated by an occasional moan.

Oshima lay perfectly still. Slowly his pounding heart came under control. It was always like this; the excitement and terror of ambush.

He tried to judge the quality of the silence. Was it over? How many of the enemy were dead? His own losses? Watanabe and how many others? He pushed these considerations from his mine. More than anything else he wanted to know the fate of the women.

The hoarse, triumphant voice of Nagato brought him cautiously to his feet. Carefully he picked his way through the tangle of scrub past the plane wreck. For a brief moment he tried ineffectually to peer into the hull of the plane, but the loathsome smell drove him past. He passed three of his own men dead, then another. He felt numb.

Nagato was standing looking at him from a chest-deep patch of ginger bush. Oshima came close and then saw that the squad leader had his foot on the chest of the young fair-haired soldier Oshima had first seen greeting the women. He was still alive, but there was blood spilling out from under Nagato's foot.

Nagato stood like a stone colossus, his obsidian eyes on Oshima. He gave the lieutenant a thin smile then, leaning forward, jabbed the tip of his machine-gun deep into the soldier's eye socket. The man writhed and shrieked weakly. Nagato looked back at Oshima and then fired off a short burst. The man was still.

One of Oshima's men laughed nervously; it was Nakuini, grinning stupidly as always. Oshima felt a surge of disgust.

'For a moment there, sir,' said Nagato, jamming a fresh magazine on to his weapon, 'I thought you were going to let them go.'

Perhaps it was just being wise after the event, but later Brandeis felt she had not been surprised when the shooting began. Those unseen eyes whose weight she had sensed pressing upon her, had felt hostile, not friendly.

When the green figures who had material-ised from the forest had proved to be Australians, their faces yellow with atabrine, like ancient parchment, she had felt some-thing amiss, as though her instincts were giving a wrong reading.

She had cried. Perhaps it had been with joy, or was it because she had sensed that this was not to be the end of the matter?

Whatever the reason, Brandeis was to recall that she had felt no surprise when her res-cuers were cut down before her eyes. To have had only friends emerge from that malignant forest would have seemed an aberration.

She had little recollection of events: just the sight and simultaneous sounds of shoot-ing, of men dying with shocking abruptness, then a blur of leaves and branches tearing at her as she ran and ran downhill through the green wall, clawing open an escape route with her hands.

Within yards she was out of breath from panic. The sounds of killing were all around her.

She almost fell over the young Australian soldier who lay dying under her feet. There was the briefest moment, about which Brandeis was ashamed afterwards, when she might have carried on past him, but then she was beside him as he lay, face down, shuddering like a landed fish in its last throes of drowning.

Usually Brandeis saw soldiers long after the battle, when they were at least tranquil of drugs, or perhaps in a coma. This man was the raw material of her trade, bleeding and dying on this muddy ground, the thick brown hair at the back of his head dark with seeping blood. An earth tremor of panic passed over her and she steeled herself to turn him over dreading the sight of his face. Just at that moment he died and his awful shivering and trembling stilled under her hand. Automatically she took a pulse at his wrist. Nothing. Brandeis felt only a deep sense of relief.

The sounds of the firefight back near the plane entered her consciousness again. The fear flooded back. She scrambled to her feet and turned to run on. Suddenly it was as if all her organs and blood flow had frozen. Two yards in front of her was a Japanese soldier.

She had never seen one before, neither dead, nor alive; not even a prisoner. But she was familiar enough with their appearance from photographs, the incredibly untidy, ill-fitting uniforms, the floppy, alien-looking caps with the sun flap.

In front of her she could see his slit-toed boots; derelict's boots; worn and covered in mud. Some of the stitching had come apart. Above them cotton gaiters so ragged that they reminded her of the wrappings around an Egyptian mummy she had once seen in the Melbourne Museum.

Brandeis looked up into the face of her captor. She was shocked to find that his appearance made nonsense of the Japanese archetype she had in mind; cruel, slant eyes, yellow teeth, wispy beard and the inevitable archfiend's expression. Instead she found herself looking at a young man who had a level and curious gaze. She could not read anything in his dark eyes; neither hostility, nor curiosity, nor hate. Brandeis guessed that he was younger than she, perhaps nineteen or twenty.

He was not pointing his gun directly at her, but at the ground immediately in front of her feet. It made no difference. She felt deadly afraid. Her body came out of cold storage with a brutal surge of heartbeating. Her nerves and muscles trembled uncontrollably and she slumped to the ground beside the body of the dead Australian.

'Did your gun jam, sir?' Nagato reloaded showily, his personal contempt for Oshima never more obvious. A few of the men hovering within earshot, listening, were well aware of the tension that lay always between these two.

Oshima felt more strongly than ever before the brutal intimidating power of the squad leader. There are some men whose physical presence is enough to excite fear. Nagato was such a man, with his awesome physique and his pitiless mind.

'As soon as I've had a look around, Sergeant,' Oshima said, steadily, 'we go. The men'll need rations. See to it.'

Oshima turned to go, but Nagato had not finished.

'Sir.'

Oshima stopped, nausea churning his stomach.

'Don't you want to know how many men you lost?' The question was deliberately provocative. Nagato had never been the slightest bit affected by the loss of men before. The loss of men was a cost that meant little if the intelligence haul was rich enough, and they both knew that the plane wreck was likely to prove a goldmine of information. The question was not about casualties, but about Oshima's hesitation.

'Four,' Nagato sunk the needle in. 'All good men.'

In spite of himself Oshima was shocked. He had never lost so many men before by his own error. But, at that moment, the real question still had to be asked.

'The women?'

Nagato grinned triumphantly. 'Ah, the women! I thought you'd ask about them. One of them ran past me, but, since I assumed you'd want them saved for sport, I let her go. Private Moritoh should have cut her off – but no matter, if they're both still

37

alive, we'll find them easily enough.' Nagato looked at his listeners. 'They might recompense us for the loss of our comrades.' He looked at Oshima, 'Sir!' he said.

Oshima looked at the insolent, angry face, his squad leader's raw power on display to the others.

Oshima was aware of the eyes of the men on him.

'Get the men about their business, Sergeant.' Oshima kept his voice even.

Nagato stared at him for a moment, then knelt beside the body of the enemy soldier and drew his knife from the sheath on his belt.

'Yes, sir,' he said, savagely. He jerked his head at the men who hurried away in all directions.

Nagato looked sardonically at Oshima then began to hack savagely at the ring finger of the dead man.

Chapter 3

Oshima began a feverish search. As he made a wide circle around the ambush area he only half-saw the dead bodies of his own men. There was no sign of the real object of his concern: the women. He noted, without satisfaction, eight enemy dead. The survivors of Section Seven were urgently looting the corpses for souvenirs, food and information.

Oshima blamed himself. Ambushing that patrol had cost him dear. All these casualties amongst his men; all that unnecessary death, because he had allowed himself to be possessed by images.

He felt numb. This part of the jungle would wax especially luxuriant as it claimed and consumed this costly human waste that lay all around. The dead would never be buried; merely absorbed.

And how many others had died in that plane wreck, he wondered, their lives cut short by this barbarous rite of war, of which he was such an efficient mercenary? Or had been until now.

In the last few hours he, Oshima, the very shape, form and function of a machine, in all its sweet, efficient and pitiless efficiency, had felt himself come apart like a disintegrating flywheel.

Two beautiful creatures had blundered their way into his savage world and, by the simple fact of their distracting and alien presence, had wrecked it. But for his fatal hesitation about the women, his own men would not have died, Oshima knew it. Yet, he was also aware that were he to be faced with the same situation again, he would not pull the trigger. He was drawn on, frantic now, through the tangle of undergrowth, anguished to know the fate of the women. About thirty yards on the downhill side of the crashed plane he heard Moritoh call out softly. When Oshima reached him, he found Moritoh standing above the fair-haired girl.

Oshima stared at her, transfixed. A rush of intense relief flooded through him.

The girl was on her knees, crouched down beside the corpse of an enemy soldier. She knelt there, perfectly still, not looking at Oshima.

So familiar was she that he felt were she to look up, she might greet him as though he were an old friend. Seeing her close, third dimensionally; being within her field of physical force, sent a charge of excitement through him.

Oshima and Moritoh stood staring down at the girl. She was dressed in a torn shirt, trousers, gaiters and boots.

Neither of them had ever seen a woman so dressed. The sight of her body, so revealed, had a shocking impact on them both. They were acutely aware of the femaleness of her: the cinch of belt around a narrow belly, the frame of round buttocks tight under the stretch of her clothes, the mysterious sweep of her thighs and the swell of breasts almost hidden by her arms. The rent in her shirt led from the left shoulder to the middle of her back. Through it were revealed the straps of her underclothes and a glimpse of white, translucent skin that promised a softness beyond their imaginings.

The impact of her presence rendered Oshima incapable of the slightest action.

'Where is the other one?'

'I don't know, sir. She didn't come this way.' Moritoh looked uneasy. 'I doubt if she's dead, sir. Sergeant Nagato told us all not to shoot them.'

Oshima felt a sickening dread. Nagato had said that? Oshima knew then that he was trapped. He looked hard at Mirotoh who met his eye for a time, then averted his gaze. They both knew about Nagato and his treatment of women.

So Nagato had them in mind for sport? Oshima determined that he would not allow that. He would have to kill this girl. And the woman, if she were not already dead.

'Bring her.' Oshima's voice was harsh. It was as well she had not caught his eye. Killing her would be difficult enough as it was. He hurried back uphill towards the wreck, unseeingly.

A few yards from the tail plane Nagato crouched over a body like a feeding tiger, his knife at work on a dead enemy soldier's mouth. Oshima averted his gaze.

'You been inside?'

Nagato shook his head.

'Two minutes.' Oshima spoke tersely, not

41

troubling to disguise the disgust in his voice. 'Get the men ready to move.'

Nagato barely looked up from his grisly task.

Winters tried to block out the smell by pressing her hands against her face, and by breathing as little as possible. It was hopeless. The gagging stench pressed in on her, thick as formalin.

The explosions, and the screaming that had gone on and on, had ceased. The hideous drone of flies blocked off all sound from the world of men and death out there.

She knew she would have to get out of this horrible charnel house, but was immobilised by dread about what might be waiting for her out there.

Some instinct, over which she had no control, had carried her into the plane hull, this dark, putrescent bolt-hole: the one place she had vowed she would never again enter.

All this death. These bloated travesties of human beings, with whom she shared this place, had been her friends. Now she had seen new friends, those would-be saviours, die right in front of her, before she had even learned their names.

And where was Sally? Already dead? Winters felt ashamed. Just running, bolting blindly into the wreck without a thought for her.

She felt that it was all her fault. Everything was her fault. *You reap what you sow.*

She remembered the brass plaque that hung alongside her mother's kitchen stove, in the Dutch of her grandparents. *'Wie zaait zal oogsten'* and her grandfather explaining to her what it meant; the inevitability of punishment for sin.

You reap what you sow. How often she had pushed away that crude, Calvinist concept of sin and yet, she had believed the truth of it when their plane had been slammed about in the sky like a scrap of rag caught in a willy-willy. At that moment she had known it was her fault; punishment for her long affair with David. All her fault. And she knew the truth of it now.

Impatiently Winters pushed the thought away. There was nothing rational about that; nothing. Being involved with David had had nothing to do with the crash. Nothing to do with poor Ian dying a nameless death somewhere under the scour of sand and sun in that great desert battle. Nothing to do with this.

But even as she pushed the insidious guilt away, Winters knew that it would come worming back.

Who had died out there? Who was left? Was it possible the Japanese had lost that short and terrible encounter?

Winters had often wondered what it was

43

like; the fear, noise and terror of combat. Now she knew first-hand something of the secret that the wounded soldiers she had nursed had kept to themselves. It was a memory of this crippling fear she now felt that had lurked there behind their eyes like a guilty secret. Now, here, she found herself shamefully immobilised by her first encounter with it.

She made up her mind to move.

Soon. Not yet. Come on … as soon as I count to ten. One … two … three…

A black and alien silhouette filled the sun-bright gap in the fuselage. Man with gun. Japanese.

Winters felt a rush of fear and shame as her bladder betrayed her. She tried to make herself still and small; hoping the man would go away, but already he was clambering into the wreck.

Oshima ducked in through the jagged opening.

Inside the plane the appalling stench of corruption overwhelmed him. He felt a gagging rush of nausea; held his hand across his mouth and nose trying not to breathe.

Slowly his eyes travelled along the length of the narrow space. It was a mass grave. Those bloated bodies had once been women. The seethe of flies pulsed in the foetid air.

Oshima forced himself forward towards

the pilot's cabin through the jumble of broken bodies, boxes, kitbags, twisted metal, crates. He noted automatically the labels and chalked signs: 'Urgent,' 'Forward surgical area, Lae' and so on. He stopped halfway along the hull and prised open a crate with his bayonet. Blankets. Another contained cartons of roller bandages; a third, gleaming stainless steel surgical equipment.

Wedged against the bulkhead immediately in front of the pilot's cabin there was a huddled body: eyes staring. As he moved forward the last few feet Oshima was suddenly gripped by an atavistic terror. The eyes had followed him. He cried out involuntarily, drawing back in horror.

Then he saw that it was she; the woman; the precious other half of his matched pair. Oshima stared at Winters in awed silence, aware only of his pounding heart and an irrational joy that his captive had survived.

Winters crouched like a frightened child, pressing herself against the bulkhead, as far from his unnerving gaze as she could go.

Slowly, the smell and the insidious drone of flies rose again into Oshima's consciousness. He became once more aware of their grisly surroundings. He jerked his head towards the rear of the plane, watched the woman uncurl reluctantly, edge past him, and stumble back through the debris. By the opening she looked back at him questioningly, a thrilling silhouette against the bright green of the jungle outside, then she was gone.

For a long moment Oshima stood there weightless, mindless; staring blankly at her pristine and disturbing after-image. Both of them had survived. He felt whole again.

Abruptly he ducked through the bulkhead into the cockpit and began to scoop up maps, logs, and every bit of paper he could find, aware of a panicky need to escape from this claustrophobic, bloodied coffin.

A last look around, then he scrambled with desperate haste towards the light, overwhelmed by revulsion for this place.

As he covered the last four feet he heard the woman cry out. The sound of blows. He flung himself out of the plane.

Nagato had the woman backed up against the plane's hull. He was slapping her and trying to rip off her shirt. There was an expression of pure terror on her face. She swivelled her head back and forth trying to avoid the blows whilst keeping her arms crossed over her chest in an endeavour to hang on to her shirt.

A few yards away, Nagato's special cronies, Nakuini and Maro, were standing watching with lecherous grins. Despair overcame Oshima. How could it be otherwise with such men?

'Stop that!'

Nagato straightened up and, with one

46

hand still gripping Winters' shirt, looked balefully at Oshima.

'Sir?'

'We are Japanese soldiers, Nagato. We have a code of honour. We are men. We are not beasts.'

Nagato stared at Oshima for a long moment. His gaze was oddly glazed. It was as if he had not heard. He turned back towards Winters and slapped her hard; once, twice. Finally, he backhanded her savagely and she crumpled to the ground with a cry.

The squad leader picked up his weapon.

'But surely, sir, we can have some fun with them before we kill them?'

'Get the men ready to move, Sergeant.' Oshima kept his anger in check. 'I'll give you orders about the prisoners in due course.'

'Prisoners?' Nagato affected an incredulous tone. 'Prisoners, sir?' Nagato laughed derisively and winked at the other two. 'I thought we were under strict orders not to take prisoners.'

'I'm taking them along.'

'Look, sir, if it's information you want...' Nagato drew his knife.

Oshima suddenly was aware that the overwhelming feeling he had for his squad leader was one of utter contempt. He drew on the intensity of this feeling to measure his gaze against Nagato's. There was a long moment that stretched Oshima's will to

47

near breaking point, but, at last, the knife was returned to the sheath.

Oshima looked at his watch.

'One minute, Nagato, we move out.'

Nagato shrugged for the benefit of his cronies and disappeared behind the hull of the plane.

There was an uneasy silence. The other two men began to edge away. Oshima whirled on them savagely and was about to abuse them when, absurdly, they suddenly cartwheeled sideways, their arms flying upwards like mimes affecting fatal surprise. The murderous rake of fire instinctively drove Oshima to the ground. As he dived he glimpsed Inoki running into sight from behind the wreck only to crumple abruptly, in a slew of his own blood.

Oshima lay stunned, his mind racing in a disordered turmoil. A counter-attack? Had Moritoh miscounted? A second patrol? Where the hell had they come from? How could he have failed to anticipate them? Self-disgust rose up in him like bile. A lost plane, full of nursing sisters – of course there would be patrols and search parties out everywhere. Had these women possessed his wits entirely?

He had been resigned to die for so long now that, for a moment, he wanted to embrace this releasing death, but if the idea was acceptable to Oshima's intellect, his

48

instincts only seemed to want to survive. Under the frightening crack of exploding grenades and the sustained fire of machine-guns, he crawled frantically deeper into cover; trying like a frantic mole to drive himself deep into the earth.

His soldier's instincts took over, seeking to make sense of the intermittent bedlam of death going on all around him.

The firing went racketing on; screams, shouts, all interspersed with the scary, suspenseful silences of jungle combat. Over there: the familiar tin-can roar of a Nambu – at least someone was returning fire.

Another long silence. Where were the enemy? How many? He closed his eyes for a moment against an image of Inoki dying. Inoki, a boy, fresh from Japan, not three months under his care, his young blood spilling there, because his officer had been possessed by some private fascination.

There: somewhere to the left, a sustained and agonised moaning.

Oshima's mouth was dry, his heart racing. Slowly he raised his head. The moaning stopped. Nearby, the sound of metal on metal: someone changing a magazine.

With extreme caution he loosened a grenade from his belt. He edged forward: one yard, two. There, not four yards in front of him, the fragmentary view of a man in a green uniform lying half on his side with a machine-gun held like a revolver in his right hand and his back to Oshima.

Pull the pin, release the lever, count five. Oshima lobbed the grenade underarm and pressed himself flat behind the bole of a tree.

The explosion was shattering. In the ringing silence that followed Oshima waited for signs of life. Hearing none, he crawled close. The man was dead.

Oshima averted his eyes from the reeking body torn open by his grenade. To his horror he found himself caught by the gaze of a second enemy soldier on the ground face to face with him, not two yards away.

Desperately Oshima pitched sideways, anticipating the meat-hook tearing of bullets, knowing his reactions had been fatally late.

But nothing happened. He lay there disbelievingly. Charily, he turned his head. The soldier's eyes had followed him, but the man, although alive, had not moved. His back broken, he lay flat on the ground, his chin half buried in the mud as though pinned to the ground by some enormous force.

For a long moment they gazed at each other, their eyes interlocked. Oshima was immobilised by the hatred in those strange, slate-grey eyes. All his training, all his swift skills for survival, were in thrall to the hypnotic power of his enemy's gaze.

It was like being caught in that recurrent nightmare of his, in which he found himself

50

unable to move a muscle or cry out. As in the dream, Oshima knew that it would take a superhuman effort of will to move even the joint of one finger and that, until he had done so, he was locked into immobility forever.

By a wrenching act he raised his weapon and fired. The body shuddered under the brief bite of his bullets. The light went out of the eyes, but they remained open, fixed forever on the image of a Japanese lieutenant kneeling on the ground with a look of anguish on his face as though something had seized in his mind.

Somewhere out of sight above, blocked by the dense screen of jungle trees, the sun was shining fiercely. Probes of sunlight diffused in the pall that drifted slowly up from the arena. It might well have been the smoke from a funeral pyre; the silence was that of a graveyard.

The normal processes of analysis that had served him for so long were short-circuiting in Oshima's mind. The faces of the men he had commanded for the past two years, the two women, the broken bodies, sundered flesh, those staring dead eyes a yard from him, had become a series of jumbled images, destroying his objective, scientist's detachment from war and death, his apparently single-minded attention to the necessary details of survival that had stood, like a moat defensive, around himself and the men in his care.

Somewhere in front of him, out of sight, a man moaned and whimpered. Which of my charges was he? Oshima asked himself in anguish.

Where were his matched pair? Were they, too, dead? Innocent bystanders, accidental victims of the awful savagery of the last few minutes.

The silence was broken subtly by the chirr and clack of insects, the irrational chime of a bird, then another.

Oshima cursed the terrible rediscovery of his innocence.

Chapter 4

When the counter-attack began Moritoh heard the girl cry out in fear. He left her, dived into cover, then crawled carefully to the base of a giant tree, hugging his sniper's rifle to him. As he began to climb a chill overtook him. It was he who had seen the enemy cross the river; it was he who, because of his sharp eyes, had been made lookout and sniper of the squad. Had he miscounted? Would Lieutenant Oshima blame him for this terrible surprise of steel?

Bullets slashed through the leaves above his

head. He flinched and pressed himself close to his branch. Leaves rained down on him.

Twenty feet up into the depths of the foliage Moritoh found a branch that gave him a view of part of the wreck and the clearing it had smashed flat when it hit the ground. How could anyone have survived such a crash?

He thought of the girl, somewhere below him. Probably dead by now.

He had never seen a Caucasian girl before, at least not in the flesh. In a thousand greasy, thumb-marked postcards; vapid girls with pouting lips, enormous breasts and blonde pubic hair. Nagato's famous collection had been thrust under his nose on the first night he had joined the squad. Moritoh had looked through them with reluctant curiosity. Was this the mystery; these leering faces and lascivious smiles? He handed them back apparently without enough enthusiasm for Nagato's liking. He'd been jeered at, called a virgin, a homosexual. It was from that moment that Nagato had begun to hound him.

A flicker of malicious hope passed over Moritoh. With any luck Nagato would have died down there.

He felt safe and detached from it all, here in his tree. As he peered down there was a flash of an explosion exactly where he was looking. Suddenly Iwashita rose, blundered like a spastic through a patch of bamboo, then pitched forward as though tripped by a wire. The bamboo became still.

After a time subtle movement caught the periphery of Moritoh's vision. By the time he had adjusted his gaze he saw only a brief glimpse of an enemy soldier, almost invisible in his green uniform, moving a yard or two, then disappearing from sight: stalking someone.

Somewhere on the other side of the wreck there was a short burst of small arms fire. Moritoh wondered how many of his friends were still alive. The lieutenant's ambush, baited with those two women, was catching the wrong victims.

How could the lieutenant have made such a misjudgement? From the time Moritoh had joined Section Seven he had held Oshima in awe. The man, though withdrawn and introspective, had all the characteristics of a samurai. He was single-minded, dedicated and never seemed to flinch from danger. Nor make mistakes. Above all, Oshima did not make mistakes.

Without the protective spiritual armour provided by his officer, Moritoh felt vulnerable, stripped and bare as though waiting for the executioner.

There: again that movement. Moritoh aimed his rifle at the spot and waited patiently, watching the leaves stirring somewhere above the stalker.

The trembling leaves reminded him of the tickling of trout fins in the freezing snow-melt of the mountain streams where he had played as a child.

He would lie on the bank feeling for his prey under the shadowy ledges where they lurked, his fingers moving like weeds against the spotted flanks of the fish.

He nestled his cheek comfortably against the smooth stock of his rifle, watching the surface evidence of the soldier's movement. Moritoh waited, just as he had waited as a boy, for that swift movement when, with a smooth and galvanic strike, the prey would be his, struggling upon the bank.

There he was; a clear shot. Gently he squeezed the trigger. The fish was his.

Moritoh watched with that curious combination of exhilaration and detachment he had come to know. His catch suddenly surfaced above the undergrowth. The soldier was hit in the chest and yet he rose, almost in slow motion, with his weapon held above his head to help him balance. Moritoh watched the soldier stumble backwards, yard by slow yard, still upright. Finally, the man regained his balance. As he stood there swaying with his gun held above his head in an absurd gesture of triumph, Moritoh squeezed off the second shot. The man crashed backwards as though hit by a truck.

Stillness, silence. Moritoh listened to the

uneasy lull wishing he knew what was going on. Was it over? Who had survived? He peered down into the tangle but could see no sign of the girl.

When Brandeis had heard the great tearing roar she had cried out thinking her Japanese captor must be firing at her. But the gunfire had not been Moritoh's. When she had looked, he had gone.

Run? Stay?

Caught between the two options Brandeis had done nothing. She had lain perfectly still on the soft, muddy ground watching a frenzy of ants racing over the dark red patina of blood on her hands. They ran frantically up and down her forearms as far as her rolled sleeves and she studied them abstractedly, amused by their excited movement.

Brandeis thought of the soldier whose blood it was and then of Winters, whom she felt for certain was dead.

Poor Mae. She had been right about the wreck attracting attention; the men who were, even now, fighting and dying all around it were the proof of her hotly pressed logic. It was not Mae's fault that the Japanese had found the plane too. The bastards must have been waiting out there to ambush whoever came to rescue them.

Brandeis wondered how long had the Japanese watched unseen as the two of them had gone about their private rituals. No wonder she had felt so uneasy. She felt colour rise to her cheeks when she thought of how she had squatted there in the forest probably in full view of them all.

The drifting cloud of cordite had gone, but its acrid smell was still in her nostrils.

At base hospital she hadn't known about the peculiar smells of battle, nor about the look of blood fresh from steel, nor about the way the air slammed against your eardrums as grenades exploded. Nor had she known about the shouts and screams and whimperings of men locked in mortal combat.

Oh, she had seen the wounded men but, even surrounded by the latest batch of hideously broken and torn bodies, the whole thing had seemed detached, unreal, in no way telling of the thing she had just witnessed. Brandeis had often felt as though all that she saw of this thing called war was the result of something that had happened offstage; some grim charade that was taking place elsewhere.

Sometimes, dropping with fatigue, she had fantasised that it was all a hoax, that everyone would suddenly stop playing the game, wipe off the make-up, strip off their pretend bandages and go home. Now she knew differently.

As Brandeis lay there, her companion Winters crouched for the second time in the gloomy hull of the plane wreck into which she had rushed instinctively the moment the Australian counter-attack had begun. It was like falling back, for a second time, into an unbearable nightmare.

Again! Winters anguished disbelievingly. She was back in this hellish dungeon again! Had she no other response? Winters had vowed never to return to this hideous reeking place and yet, when the firing started afresh, she had bolted into the darkness without thought. She knew now there was no solace to be found here.

Sow and ye shall reap. The phrase hammered its punctuation between the voices of the guns, the terrifying explosions of grenades: the grim rattles of men clawing each other to death with steel.

At length the sound of battle ended.

Can't stay here.

The hot buzzing of flies was now the only sound. Were they all dead out there? Their would-be rescuers? The Japanese? Sally?

Must know about Sally.

Winters rose to her feet. She would leave this foetid tomb of canvas and steel that had contained her, too long and too often.

Sally was right. Salvation, if there were any, lay out there with living things, be they ever so vulpine, predatory, unspeakable. Better to risk webs and barbs and slime or even guns and honed edges of steel, than this.

Cautiously Winters looked out from the hull of the plane into the forest. She could see no one alive; only the bodies of the two Japanese soldiers who had been cut down in front of her.

She stepped over the body blocking her exit and, like an automaton, walked straight ahead into the silence of the jungle.

She would find Sally and they would get away; walk away from all this horror, find faces that would hold no terrors for them.

Winters saw something. Stopped. Somebody there, half-obscured by the undergrowth. She edged forward cautiously. It was a man, kneeling, facing her, supporting a green-clad soldier. Her heart lurched. It was the Japanese who had beaten her. Winters would have drawn back, but was riveted by what he was doing. She watched in horror. He was holding the man's hair: pulling the head back. The captive was struggling feebly. Stone-faced, the Japanese looked up and saw Winters watching. Then, with his knee in the soldier's back and the head dragged back, he cut the soldier's throat.

Winters felt a rush of vomit and covered her mouth, her eyes trying to blot out the brief waterfall of blood.

When, at length, she straightened up she was purged of her fantasy of escape.

Nagato grinned at her sardonically and wiped the blood from his knife on the hair and shirt of his victim.

Bitterly Winters looked into the face of the man who had been her tormentor. Twice now she had come face to face with him. Was she destined always to confront this beast at the end of every maze? Her face became ugly with fear and rage.

'You swine,' she said. She knelt there in the mud, overcome by a despairing anger, hearing herself spitting out the words over and over. It was as if someone else was saying it.

Suddenly the soldier's expression changed. His face distorted with rage as he responded to the hostility in her voice. In one swift movement Nagato rose to his feet and came at her with his knife in his hand. Before Winters could move he backhanded her savagely to the ground. She cried out in rage and pain. Then he was kneeling on top of her pinning her to the ground by her hair. She could feel it tearing at the roots. Somewhere behind her she heard a shout in Japanese.

Winters clutched desperately at the wrist of Nagato's knife hand, her eyes riveted on to the bloody blade, but she felt as helpless as she would have done staked to the ground. His body seemed not of flesh, but of quartz and steel. The implacable, animal power was unlike anything she had ever known. Winters knew she had no chance of resisting such force and, that if he was going to kill her, there was nothing she could do about it.

'Nagato!'

Winters heard the shout.

She was aware of the face above her losing some of its frenzy. Suddenly the crushing weight was off her. She clung on to Nagato's wrist as he stood up, but he tore his arm free effortlessly.

For Oshima it had been a close call. His rank would not have been enough. Only by cocking his weapon loudly had he stopped Nagato. The squad leader grew deadly still, then he stood up suddenly with that chilling and graceful power of his, turning to face Oshima with his bloody knife in his hand and a malevolent look on his face.

In that moment Oshima knew that, by his spontaneous act of threatening Nagato with his gun, he had triggered off a deadly change in their relationship. The fragile structure of command had been cracked. Oshima could see by the contemptuous look on his squad leader's face that he, too, was aware of it.

Winters lay for a moment holding her cheek and trembling with fear. The inside of her mouth was bleeding. She looked stupidly at the blood on her fingers then slowly sat up.

She saw her assailant and another, taller soldier, with a gun in his hand, glaring at each other a few yards apart. Suddenly Brandeis was there, running hard. Following her; a young Japanese. She knelt down beside Winters clutching her in her arms.

'Thank God ... thank God you're all right.' Winters hugged her close.

'What did they do to you?' Brandeis asked angrily. 'You're bleeding. Jesus, what did they do?'

Winters was aware of the rising tide of her own anger and controlled her voice with an effort. 'That one with the knife. He ... he cut that boy's throat.' Winters indicated the dead Australian soldier a few yards away.

'Oh, no!' Brandeis stared at the dead man, her eyes drawn to his bloody throat.

'All our men are dead,' Nagato said angrily to Oshima. He nodded towards the corpse. 'There were four of them.' He took in a deep breath and let it out slowly as though trying to control himself. 'There's only Moritoh ... who apparently can't count ... you and me ... plus, of course, these women of yours. Sir.' He fairly spat the words out, looking chillingly at Moritoh and the women.

Oshima was aware of the boy watching anxiously to one side. He seemed shaken and unsteady.

'Moritoh.'

'Sir!'

'Guard them.'

Moritoh seemed relieved to have something to do. He looked towards the women and moved a yard or two towards them.

Oshima addressed Nagato crisply. 'Take a quick look around that side, see what else you can find.' Oshima indicated the down-hill slope. 'Meet me back here in...' he looked at his watch, 'five minutes. Then we'll get out of this.'

Nagato made no acknowledgement, but walked quickly off. Oshima watched him go then, with a last look at Moritoh and the women, hurried up the slope.

Chapter 5

Moritoh stood there staring at them frankly, in turn. They looked at each other glumly. His scrutiny was too obvious, too insistent; it made them feel uncomfortable.

When Brandeis looked towards him, Moritoh dropped his gaze and looked away awkwardly.

'He's only a bloody kid,' Brandeis said, very quietly.

Winters looked at him briefly then away again, her face closed and still.

'With a grown-up's rifle,' she said.

Aware that he was being talked about Moritoh walked about nervously as although on a very short leash; a few yards one way, then the other. He looked keenly into the jungle, as though anxious to avoid their eyes.

After a time he dropped his rifle butt down

between his feet and took a tin from his pocket. From it he took tobacco and papers and slowly rolled himself a laughably clumsy cigarette. He took a lighter from his pocket and lit it. The cigarette flared like a bonfire.

Brandeis watched half in amusement, half in envy. The drift of the pungent tobacco smoke was agonising. She had given up smoking, yet again, two weeks before, but suddenly she needed a cigarette, badly.

Moritoh caught her eye. His fact twitched and he leaned forward and offered her the tin.

'Don't,' said Winters urgently. She looked at Brandeis directly. 'Don't let's take anything from them.'

'Why not? Last smoke for the condemned heroine, sort of thing.'

Winters shrugged at Brandeis' sceptical expression.

'Yes, why not?' She sounded more rueful than annoyed.

Brandeis took the tin and was shocked to find there was a packet of familiar 'Riz-la' cigarette papers. This was loot from one of the dead Australians. She bit her lip.

She glanced sideways at Winters, but she was looking the other way and had not noticed.

What the hell.

She measured out the right amount of tobacco and a paper. Handed the tin back to the young soldier. Nodded her thanks.

Moritoh watched, amazed, as she rolled a smoke one-handed with a smooth dexterity. Brandeis was showing off and could tell he was impressed. Before the war she had not smoked; in fact she had not done anything. Non-smoking, non-drinking, nice girls don't. Rolling a smoke one-handed was not the least impressive skill she had developed with the help of twenty-three men, at the last count.

Twenty-three young officers who had passed through her life and her arms since that first time, not a week after she had swapped her civilian nursing sister's uniform for that of the Army Nursing Service.

'Don't succumb to that cheap war-time morality,' her father had written in his precise, un-doctorly hand on the crested surgery writing paper.

It was just as well he did not know how totally she had thrown off his strictures. All those too-hard swearing, too-hard drinking young men with lacquered optimism in their chatter, and fear in their hearts.

Like Chuck, her first American pilot, now lying over there, under that pathetic scrape of soil, his brief memory already half-eaten away by time and worms. She had loved him no less enthusiastically and remembered him no better than any of the others. Only recency made him more tangible in her mind. Her father never would have understood.

It came to her that by now he might think of her as being dead. Would he have received the official telegram by now? She glanced at Winters sitting there nursing her bruised face in her hands. Would Mae's major think of Mae, too, as dead? Poor, foolish Mae, so bloody proper, and all the time trying to conduct a secret hole-in-the-corner affair with a married man; always so concerned with what other people thought. Why couldn't she simply do what the rest of them were doing, having a good time and trying not to get pregnant, or the clap? It was not as if no one knew. The rumour was that their affair had begun in Melbourne long before he had turned up wounded in Buna Base hospital. God knows what she saw in the wizened up little runt.

Brandeis licked the paper and smoothed the edge of it down; picked up a twig and poked in the ends of the tobacco. Automatically she patted her shirt pockets for her lighter. Left pocket, lighter; right pocket, lipstick, comb.

Before she had the button undone Moritoh snapped his lighter under her cigarette. She inhaled gratefully, again nodding her thanks. He seemed embarrassed and walked away a few yards.

She drew hard on her cigarette grateful for

the hit of the nicotine. Another good intention cast joyfully to the winds.

'Needed that,' she said to Winters, who smiled distractedly at her.

Unobtrusively Brandeis began to examine the young Japanese.

In another uniform she might have quite fancied him. He was short, about the same height as herself, well built and good looking; rather like the handsome waiter who had always winked at her in the Chinese restaurant in Melbourne where her parents took her for a regular dine-out treat.

Certainly he was a lot different from that other bastard.

Christ, what an animal!

The thought of him and his brutality to Winters sent a brief tremor of fear spasming along her back.

'I wish to God I knew what they were going to do with us.' Winters spoke, half to herself, a look of apprehension on her face.

'The other one knows what he'd like to do,' said Brandeis.

At that moment they saw Winters' attacker appear from the tangle of forest.

'Enter the Beast,' breathed Brandeis. Winters look round, scared. Nagato had a couple of looted packs in one hand and his machine-gun held loosely in the other. He came straight at them. Without breaking stride he dropped the packs and then, too quickly for Brandeis to be able to move, he struck the cigarette from her hand and slapped her face so hard she was knocked sideways off her pack.

It felt to Brandeis as if something had crushed the side of her face. She had never been struck by anyone before in her life.

'You rotten swine...'

Winters was up on her feet shouting at him: 'Why don't you hit someone your own size?'

Nagato struck her too and, although her hands were in front of her face, the force of the blow knocked her off her feet.

Brandeis lay holding her face looking up at him standing over her. She had never been so angry in her life. The words came easily.

'You bag of shit!' she said.

Looking down at her, he gave a snort of laughter almost as if he approved of her anger, and swung out of her line of sight.

He shouted.

They saw Moritoh jerk to attention like a puppet. He looked really frightened. He stood there with his head bowed while Nagato spoke angrily to him in a low voice. Suddenly he slapped the boy across the face.

'Jesus,' said Brandeis, amazed. Nagato's explosive violence was terrifying. He continued abusing the young soldier in a low, angry voice, swinging round and pointing to them, and then back to see that the point he was making had been understood.

Moritoh nodded quickly as though to avoid being struck again. Brandeis was amazed. He had done nothing. Simply taken it.

Nagato was suddenly calm. He could have been an actor playing a part, so abrupt was the change. As he turned and looked over at them, Brandeis caught the look of hatred that flickered over the face of the young soldier.

The squad leader crossed to them and squatted down suddenly. He up-ended the contents of his looted pack on to the ground: watches, wallets, lighters, cigarettes and other things. These, they saw with horror, were blood-stained gold teeth and rings. He must have severed fingers to get some of the rings off.

'My God.' Brandeis felt her legs tremble violently.

Winters her face white and pinched looking turned away, revolted.

Nagato picked up one of the teeth and held it in front of his mouth so that they would be sure to understand what it was. Then, with malicious grin, he offered it to Brandeis. She drew back in disgust.

Nagato laughed and stood up. He unslung his own pack and stowed his loot in an outside pocket.

They stared at each other in horror. Wondering if every terrible story they had heard about the Japanese was true.

Nagato suddenly whirled on them, his grin gone. He stood still for a moment looking from one to the other, his face without expression. He indicated with an impatient movement of his hand that they were to rise. They scrambled up fearfully. He unslung his weapon and checked it carefully. Very slowly and deliberately, he fitted a magazine.

'Oh, God.' Winters took Brandeis' hand, and squeezed it hard. She had never before thought about death in relation to herself. So this was it. All very matter of fact; the one thing that only happened to other people. Even when it was happening all around you, somehow it did not apply to you.

'Sorry, love. Looks like it.' She looked at her young companion, filled with pity for her.

Brandeis raised Winters' hand and, in a tender gesture, kissed it.

'I'm sorry I said those awful things, Mae,' she said. 'Forgive me. For everything.'

Nagato cocked his weapon loudly. Winters put her arm around Brandeis and they both closed their eyes.

Oshima's hurried final search for intelligence material became an agonising pilgrimage.

From each enemy corpse he took whatever documents interested him, but his mind was only half on the task. He was constantly distracted by finding the bodies of his men.

The dead were everywhere. Oshima was

70

awed by the carnage; crushed by an over-whelming feeling of despair, convinced that every one of them had died because of his mistakes.

Iwashita and Kuwanoki; dead. Lying un-resisting as he slipped their wallets and paybooks from their shirt pockets.

Iwashita's family photograph: five children and a plain wife running to fat, but smiling proudly for her handsome, soldier husband. What would he write to her? Oshima wondered. How would he console her? Would he admit that it was his fault that Iwashita had died today, lying here at his feet like a sack of skin about to be rendered in this steaming fellmongery of forest?

Young Maro's grubby collection of porno-graphic photographs Oshima removed from the paybook and dropped face down in the mud. Would Maro's parents want to see such things? The lieutenant closed the boy's dead eyes against the coming horrors of the night.

Nakadi. Oshi. The gay madman, Sato; his chest a mess of blood and flies. His wallet was coated in thick blood already turning black. Oshima wiped the worn leather as clean as possible on the dead soldier's shirt. The fastidious Sato would not mind now.

There had been a time, Oshima remem-bered, when his intense and all-exclusive power of concentration had been an advant-age. But this morning it had cost dear.

71

His private world of passion had not always carried such a high price. How many times he had watched, totally absorbed, when butterflies, coruscating gold, blue and royal purple, had fed in an orgiastic frenzy on the blossoms carpeting the sunstruck slopes of the mountains. No one had died for that.

And no one had died because he had savoured their flight and passionate rituals, staying his wide-mouthed collector's net for an extra hour, or so.

But today he had stayed his hand and his men had died: a beautiful and insidious enemy had breached his defences and he had become disconnected, confused: unmanned.

How long had it been, Oshima wondered, since he was absorbed so totally by such a private excitement? Years. And yet those old passions had sprung back to life in an instant.

And now that he possessed them, what was he going to do with them? Two days' march through dangerous country lay ahead of them. How many of the enemy were out there waiting; enemy as dangerous and treacherous as those whom he had just fought here with such fury? At every turn, blacks waiting to spear and run.

He should kill these two women now, Oshima had no doubts. But even as he forced the thought forward, he knew that he could not destroy them. He could order Nagato to do it. Oh, he would like that. The man was at

72

one with his deadly nature; this primeval wilderness, the natural haunt of the beast, which was what Nagato had become. How strange, Oshima thought, that this urban man should have found his natural habitat here.

Nagato's previous life in the city must have seemed to him like time out of joint. Or had that been another jungle? Had there always been blood to let, throats to cut, women to abuse? Had Nagato simply adapted old habits to a new environment? Who knew what creatures might have lurked in Nagato's Yokohama? Who knew what licence he might have enjoyed before this?

Moritoh? Oshima knew he could simply order the boy to take care of the matter. He did what he was told. But Oshima cared about Moritoh too much for that. Such an order would destroy him. He had not yet set aside his humanity. That took time. Moritoh had only been in this deathly country a few months and there clung to his behaviour still clear evidence that he yet remembered things like compassion and pity and all such ancient, half-forgotten and encumbered strictures. No, Oshima decided, he would not order Superior Private Moritoh Senjo to solve his problem of the women.

He knew he must escape from this place. Now. Otherwise he might never again regain the power to act. He collected two kit bags and two water bottles for the prisoners and hurried back.

'Cut that out!'

In that moment, when Oshima returned to find Nagato baiting the women, he felt his fear and dislike for this sadist crystallise. He knew then that, if this squad leader of his harmed his captives, he would kill him.

Nagato lowered his weapon with a grin.

'Shit!' said Winters. The word escaped with the breath tentatively edging from her body. She felt Brandeis' fierce handgrip loosen.

Nagato had an insolent look on his smooth face. Matter-of-factly he asked: 'Will I kill the women, or will you, sir?'

Oshima controlled his vaulting anger and said nothing. He handed the bloodied kit-bags and the water bottles to the women. From his own pack he spilled on to the ground some iron rations he had found.

'You will carry, please,' he said, in English.

'You're taking them along?' Nagato shook his head in disgust. 'You're right, of course, sir.' He winked at Moritoh. 'They're too good to waste.'

Oshima remained silent watching the two women filling their packs with rations. They knelt together looking frightened; unwilling to meet his eye. Suddenly he felt hostile towards them.

What were they doing here? What business had they entering this savage cockpit, corrupting the simple verities of killing and being killed? Damn them. And yet, how compelling they were; how familiar. Both fair-haired, blue-eyed; one a little older, a little sturdier, taller.

Now that they were no longer remote, smoky images, Oshima longed to reach out and touch them, to add that further thrilling dimension to his knowledge of them. To feel the life force in them, as so often in the past he had felt that force trembling when he had taken some rare new specimen from his collector's net.

They were staring at him. He guessed they were startled by him speaking their own language.

'What will happen to us?' the older woman asked, her eyes registering her fear and hostility.

Oshima spoke carefully. It had been a long tie since he had spoken English. 'We go now. You are war prisoner. You will be treated properly, under Geneva Convention.'

He *could* speak English! Winters suddenly felt especially angry because of this. Somehow it made their treatment less excusable.

'If that is so, why was your man going to shoot us?' She turned and pointed at Brandeis. 'He just hit her ... both of us ... for no reason.' She glared at Nagato. 'He's mad, that's what he is.'

Brandeis was scared that, if Winters lost

75

control, they both would suffer. She saw the officer's face set hard.

'You will obey orders. All times.' Oshima's voice was harsh.

'Leave it, Mae.' Brandeis put her arm around Winters as much to restrain, as to comfort. 'It doesn't matter.'

'It does matter. He talks about the Geneva Convention and then lets that swine knock us about.'

'Just take it easy, for Christ's sake! You've got us in enough trouble already.' Brandeis' anger scourged like lye.

'Enough!'

Oshima's voice made them both jump, and stopped Winters in her tracks.

'We leave now. Must hurry. You will stay close. You will not speak. Obey orders at all times. Understood?'

Winters looked at Brandeis with an expression of deep hurt on her face then back at Oshima. She nodded glumly.

Oshima's face relaxed. He spoke soberly: 'You must understand. My sergeant is angry because many men lost. Give no trouble please. This is not place for women. Now, we go. Hurry.' He gestured towards their packs indicating that they were to take them.

Brandeis was suddenly crushed by the thought that their four-hour flight, which was to have taken them from Buna to Lae, might now last for years. Prisoners of war. She hadn't thought of it in those terms before.

'We must take some of our things,' she said urgently. Winters stared back at her as if she were unable to think, or act.

'It might be years, Mae,' insisted Brandeis.

The terrible possibility that this might be the truth of the matter was reflected in Winters' shocked reaction.

'Oh God,' she said and stood there shaking her head.

Brandeis addressed Oshima directly.

'We have other things: clothes and things, there by the plane.' She pointed towards the wreck. 'Clothes and things.'

He looked puzzled for a moment as though trying to slot her unfamiliar words into his mind.

'Ah, yes.' Oshima looked impatiently at his watch. 'One clothes only. OK? Hurry please.'

Moritoh escorted them to the crumpled tail plane under which they had piled their kitbags and those useful supplies that had survived the crash.

Brandeis was overcome by a sick dread. Now they were to be wrenched from that familiar shelter, so pathetically like a child's cubby-hole, to face the unknown. She was filled with remorse about her ugly attack on Winters, but said nothing.

The act of packing their meagre belongings undammed something in Winters, loosening her iron grip on herself. She began to cry quietly, black thoughts crowding.

How quickly everything changes! The wreck had already begun to suffer a forest change; to synthesise inevitably inside this green cubicle, to change it state. Already it had settled into a shallow grave, its bottom edges melting into the mud. Already long tendrils of grass and creeper had blurred the functional edges of its shape.

Winters had come to think of it as sanctuary, something comfortingly man-made, a citadel against the press of jungle crowding in on them with a malignant energy; full of nameless terrors, sounds and unblinking eyes of night.

Collecting their kitbags from beside the familiar, broken hull brought back memories of that awful bucketing, tearing crash and her mindless panic as she struggled free of her seatbelt harness and clawed her way out of the plane, held back by the sounds of screaming and driven on by the primitive fear of fire; tumbling through the great rent in the fuselage, falling backwards on to the mud, backing away as far as possible from the explosion that never came; the feared, rolling, swirling fireball she had seen in half a dozen films in the officer's mess of one base camp or another.

Then, finding Brandeis already clear of the plane, crying and in shock; holding and comforting the girl until the sobbing and shivering had subsided.

And, after that, the slow realisation that they were probably the only survivors and alone, and God knows where, and that they would have to go back in there and risk the flames to confront the sight of the death of friends.

Those who had been their friends, who had shared their work and their hangovers and their men and their hopes and fears about love and parting, love and rejection, had proved to be broken, ripped dolls with all the stiffening gone; emptied out things with pieces missing; but all, mercifully dead.

All, except Chuck, their pilot, and Sally's latest lover who had taken up her time during the week prior to the flight.

Chuck whom they had found still at the controls, moaning piteously with all that spilling of his substance; knowing from the first glance that it was useless; yet still struggling to free him from behind the instrument panel. Lucky that there had been morphia and safety pins. Lucky that he had died as quickly as he had. If you can call two days and nights, quick.

'Bring the first aid kit.'

Brandeis' words interrupted Winters' train of thought. She looked at her companion for whom she was responsible. How young she was! She looked so alive and sounded so practical that Winters was ashamed of letting her mind run on so.

The first aid kit.

Going back inside the reeking hull to fetch dressings for the dying pilot had become, increasingly, a journey into Hell. At first they had left everything inside the plane. When, all too soon, the inside of the wreck had become a nightmare they had hauled everything out and stowed it under the comparative shelter provided by the fractured tail plane where it lay askew several yards back from the hull. They had wrenched the pathetically inadequate box of medical supplies from the bulkhead behind the pilot's cabin. Perhaps it was because of their training, but that grey box with the bold red cross on the lid had seemed especially important to their survival; a talisman; a sovereign remedy against chaos.

The box was now half-empty. They had used most of the dressings on Chuck and, after he had been pinned together and drugged into oblivion, they had dabbed mercurochrome on their cuts and scratches and on their ever-growing rash of insect bites.

Winters nodded, wiping her tear-stained face with the back of her hand.

'Let's get away from here.'

Brandeis nodded. They dragged their big personal kitbags backwards away from the stench.

As they neared the Japanese, Winters was

acutely aware of her femaleness and of their penetrating gaze.

The three men watching them had an alien presence. They were creatures of the forest. Everything about them; their strange unfamiliar uniforms, their floppy, peaked caps and the cruel power of their weapons instilled fear in Winters.

She felt naked under their gaze and, in an illogical way, she wished she and Brandeis were wearing skirts which would have, somehow, afforded the protection of formality. The trousers, gaiters and boots all the nursing sisters had revelled in since they had come to the tropics, tokens of emancipation for them, seemed now inappropriate to the formal business of becoming a female prisoner-of-war.

All their personal effects and clothes had been brought with them on the flight. The new forward area surgical unit at Lae was to have been their base for some time. As she dragged the heavy bag, Winters realised ruefully that this was the first time she had had to handle it. One advantage of being one of the few women in a man's war was that you never had to carry anything.

'Too much.'

Winters looked up and saw that the officer was shaking his head. His look was not unfriendly.

'One clothing...' Oshima groped for the

81

words. '…one clothing change only. Hurry please!' He looked around increasingly nervous. It was obvious the Japanese wanted to get away.

Winters met Brandeis' eyes.

'He's right,' Brandeis said, ruefully. 'They're not going to be perfect gentlemen and carry our bags.'

As Brandeis tried to fit the first aid box into her pack the officer came close and put his hand out. She met his eye. He snapped his fingers impatiently. Reluctantly she handed it over.

With his gun tucked under his arm, Oshima opened it and examined the contents, lifting clear the last remaining pads of dressings and packs of roller bandages. He seemed pleased. The other two soldiers looked inside the box interestedly. The women watched as the officer closed the box carefully, handed it to the young soldier, then turned his back. The box was stowed inside his pack. Brandeis felt immoderately angry about this, but there was nothing she could do. Winters burrowed into her kitbag. Change of trousers, underwear, socks, and, just for the sake of asserting her independence, two shirts. Her fingers momentarily encountered the edge of a box of sanitary towels. It stopped her in her tracks. She felt her heart start to race and she had to catch at her breath. Would she take them? she wondered. Two months gone. If she had been going to, it would have happened by now. She could feel herself begin to shake. She gritted her teeth, tried to get a grip on herself. She would take them, she decided. Maybe having them with her would, in some way, bring on her period. She felt embarrassed about transferring the tell-tale blue box to her pack under the frank male stares of the three Japanese. Blinded now with tears and with her hands hidden inside her kitbag she tore off the box top and wrapped several of the towels loosely inside a shirt. She thought wretchedly, What's the point? Taking them like some kind of good luck bringer was just superstitious nonsense. As she transferred the shirt to her pack the shaking and choking overwhelmed her. She gritted her teeth. Two months gone. There could be no doubt now, surely? But you never knew. Hope springs eternal. She felt her tears flooding. Hope? There was no hope. Not now. She would never see David again. If there was a child he would never know about it, nor see it. 'What's the use?' she wailed to Brandeis who was staring at her with startled eyes. Then she felt a terrifying sense of panic. It was as though her chest was being crushed by a boulder. It seemed she would never be able to catch her breath. The boulder swelled and forced her to her knees.

Brandeis watched in horror as Winters slumped down on all fours, beside the kit-bags. Brandeis grabbed her and found that she was shivering as though freezing cold. Her teeth were chattering loudly.

Brandeis glanced anxiously towards the Japanese. She could read nothing on their implacable faces, but the weight of their impatience pressed on her. Suddenly she felt frightened. She had seen, all too recently, what happened to the wounded in this nightmare. The slightest delay might cause their captors to change their minds about taking the two of them as prisoners. And Mae had just metamorphosed remarkably into one of the wounded. 'Mae!' she urged, shaking Winters by the shoulders. 'Get hold of yourself! For God's sake!' Again she looked at the Japanese. They were looking on grimly. She shook Winters again, firmer this time. But Winters had lost control. The terrible things she had witnessed, the deaths, the torments; the fear and pain she had suffered personally, the strain of the past few terrible days; keeping her courage up in the face of her privately held certainty that there was no hope, and never had been any hope that they might survive, had defeated her, finally. Brandeis was overcome by panic. 'Mae! Please! You've got to get up! They're not going to wait for us!' It was useless. Winters was in deep shock. Her eyes had glazed, she was having difficulty breathing and her body felt as though it might be shaking apart. She seemed as if she were screaming, yet no noise came from her twisted, chattering mouth.

To Brandeis crouching on the ground beside her companion the Japanese seemed to loom up above them like cold-eyed predators about to rip their flesh apart.

You bitch, she thought savagely. *You're going to get us both killed.*

She became aware that Nagato was speaking angrily to the officer. Suddenly the officer came close to her. His face was cold. 'We go!' said Oshima, his voice harsh.

She shook Winters angrily. 'Mae, please! You've got to get a grip on yourself.' No response. 'Mae!' she screamed into the distorted glazed face.

Never before had Brandeis felt such hatred for anyone. All the anger she had ever felt for Winters welled up. She began to shake her with a murderous savagery. She got no response. Finally, losing her control completely, she slapped Winters viciously across the face. She saw the blow bring a frightened focus to the blank eyes. Saw her fingermarks on Winters' white face.

'Mae, for God's sake get up!' She, too, was near to tears.

'Leave me alone. Leave me alone,' Winters' voice was broken by sobs. She shook her head pathetically. 'It's no use,' she said.

'Listen you weak, pathetic bitch, you're not going to get me killed. Get up!' Brandeis dragged the dead weight of her upright where she stood swaying like a punchdrunk fighter. Brandeis picked up Winters' pack, closed the flaps and pushed Winters' limp arms through the straps. It was like dressing a crippled child.

The Japanese looked on impassively.

'I'm sorry, I'm sorry, I'm sorry,' said Winters, pathetically wiping at her tear-blinded eyes.

Suddenly Brandeis' feelings were those of pity rather than of anger. She was ashamed of the force of her blow. She touched the red weal anxiously with her fingers. She hugged her close.

'Come on, love, come on,' she encouraged, pushing Winters' hair back from her eyes and wiping at her tears. 'You're going to be all right.' Winters stood there sobbing helplessly. Brandeis donned her own pack, looked directly at the Japanese officer, and nodded.

For a moment he regarded the two women as though deciding their fate, then he issued a sharp order to the young soldier. Moritoh slung his rifle over his shoulder and walked off, straight up the hill.

Oshima jerked his head at Brandeis. She gripped Winters' arm and propelled her forward. Still sobbing and shaking. Winters began to walk mechanically. After a few yards Brandeis let go her arm and fell in close behind her. Winters half-turned around and said again, 'I'm sorry.'

'Save it,' said Brandeis managing a smile. 'You'll be all right now. You've got it out of your system.'

As unobtrusively as possible, she checked her watch. Four o'clock. The sudden tropic night would not be long in coming. Where would they sleep tonight? she wondered.

In a moment the wreck was deserted and silent save for the hum of insects and the gathering voice of unseen birds. The spears of sunlight were paler now and inclined at a longer angle. A spider had begun to spin a complex and beautiful web from the distorted curve of a bent propeller blade. Two gorgeous butterflies settled briefly on the face of a dead soldier.

High above the great, still valley, the tiny spotter plane reappeared. It passed low over the sea of treetops. Its shadow briefly passed over the upreaching wing of the crashed plane. The pilot saw nothing.

Part 2

CAPTIVES

Chapter 6

Like a lit fuse; a white-hot compound of fear, sullen anger, resentment and remorse, the little group burned its silent way through the sodden and emerald reaches of the jungle.

In both of the women was a gut-churning fear of their captors. In Brandeis, anger and resentment at Winters, whose fault she felt their predicament to be. In Winters, an incapacitating remorse, since she too, felt it all to be her fault. Among the Japanese, the fearful half-guilty recriminatory thoughts of the survivors of a catastrophe.

A lethal bacillus of anger travelled with them; hanging on their breath like plague. It was a complex force of resentments; the resentment of prisoners for their captors, and that of captors for prisoners. Between the three Japanese the women sensed a murderous hostility, as though each man hated the other for surviving. As for the women themselves, the weakness that each had revealed to the other had exacerbated their natural and time-hardened hostility.

It was a barely-contained force. The women sensed instinctively that it might explode at any time and could only have been assuaged by blood. They avoided the gaze of the Japanese, aware that their eyes might betray the terror they felt, aware that any revealed weakness might trigger off, in their captors, something unspeakable.

The forced march was a nightmare for the women. The Japanese kept up a cruel pace. Hour after hour they drove on. There was always another slope, a ridge, a rocky valley gouged for a stream to rush through, an overgrown and deserted jungle garden, an abandoned empty settlement, rotting in the green heat.

Brandeis' contempt for Winters' performance just before the march had been tempered by a crushing exhaustion. She felt ashamed of the ugly question that kept on replaying in her mind, Why that bitch? Why, among all the laughing and friendly girls in her unit, had it been Senior Sister Winters who had survived to be her companion on this awful journey?

At last the officer called a halt.

The two prisoners watched Oshima numbly as he spoke in whispers to his men. Brandeis had noticed how quietly the soldiers spoke. It was some shared instinct, perhaps, for apart from her own hysterical burst of crying out the night before, neither she nor Winters had raised their voices much above a hushed whisper since they had found themselves caught in the uneasy coils of the jungle. It seemed to her as if it eavesdropped on everything that was said.

Moritoh was dispatched forward; Nagato back down the track. Oshima led the women into deep cover, where they sank exhausted on the muddy ground, too breathless to speak; trying to read one another's thoughts.

Winters looked to be at the end of her strength. She sat slumped on the ground with her eyes closed. Her head hung back slackly and her chest heaved.

Brandeis studied this stranger companion of hers. Bruises were showing vividly against Winters' ashen skin. Their swelling had distorted the right side of her jaw. Part of that painful looking bruising, Brandeis knew, she had caused. She felt a stab of guilt about her blow. There had been nothing clinical and disinterested about it – Sister Brandeis aiding a hysterical patient – she had struck Winters in a pent-up fury of anger and fear. All her dislike for her superior officer had been contained in it.

Almost as if she sensed she was being studied, Winters opened her eyes and looked directly at her. Her gaze was bleak and disconcerting. She glanced around at Oshima, pressing her fingers gingerly against her bruises, then turned back to Brandeis.

'Did it make you feel better,' she asked, bitterly, 'to hit me that hard?'

93

Brandeis felt a rush of rage. 'That's unfair,' she said, trying to keep her voice low. 'You were being hysterical. If I hadn't shut you up we'd both be dead by now.'

Winters shook her head disgustedly. 'If I *had* shut you up last night, maybe we wouldn't be here in the first place.' Brandeis stared at her helplessly. At that moment their feeling of mutual dislike was so strong that only physical violence could have assuaged it. Brandeis had never felt more alone. She avoided Winters' hostile look. Immediately she caught the eye of Oshima. From the time he had called a halt she had been intensely aware that, every now and then, he shot them a covert glance.

Several times he seemed as though about to speak, but he remained silent. He continually checked the time.

Brandeis felt uncomfortable under this surreptitious scrutiny, but she was aware that now both Winters and she were observing him in much the same way.

Something about his uniform seemed to confirm that he was an officer; perhaps it fitted better than those of the other two. It was no less mud-stained and rotted by heat and sweat, but somehow neater. Perhaps it was the authority rendered by the binoculars he wore round his neck.

He had a lean face, almost ascetic, with a fleshy, but well-shaped mouth, clipped cheekbones and a curving, beaky nose. To Brandeis he had the look of a clever Eskimo.

He seemed to be in his mid-thirties, but here, in this tropical war, Brandeis had come to realise that it was impossible to tell anyone's age. All the young soldiers she had seen in the past years had seemed old and worn; fatigued and lined beyond their years. It was as though their youth had worn out suddenly. Their real age was in their eyes; theirs were the eyes of old men who once had had a nodding acquaintance with madness. This was especially true of their captor. He looked haunted.

'What do you think he'll do with us?' Brandeis barely moved her lips, conscious that he could understand their words.

Oshima looked up sharply at the sound of her voice, but then averted his gaze again, as though he had been caught observing a woman undressing in a window.

'God knows.'

They sat in silence intimidated by the curious half hostile look on Oshima's face.

'Never heard you swear before.' With her remark Brandeis was offering an olive branch. Winters regarded her for a long moment. The gesture was recognised and her expression softened. She looked rueful and gave a half-smile. 'First time for everything. Been swearing inside my head for years.'

'They're angry about all their men.'

'Such a lot of men.' Winters was suddenly close to tears. 'God, I had no idea it was like this. How do they stand it?'

'This is our big chance to find out.'

For a time Winters remained silent, as though she had withdrawn into herself, then abruptly, she said: 'We could try running.'

'Don't be stupid. We wouldn't get five yards.' The moment the words were out of her mouth Brandeis regretted her hostile reaction.

She looked at Winters sitting there looking hurt and angry. It occurred to her then that although they had worked together – two years, marked by a continually flaring mutual antipathy – she had never really known the Senior Sister; the Dragon. As far as Brandeis was concerned Winters was a stuffy, stitched-up martinet, and a hypocrite, to boot. Here she was earnestly suggesting they simply run away, and she seemed deadly serious about it. Maybe, Brandeis allowed, there was more to Winters than she knew.

Aware of the officer watching them, Winters spoke, hardly moving her lips. 'I didn't mean right now. Later.'

'If there is a later.'

Brandeis' cynical remark brought the bleak expression back into Winters' face.

Oshima unslung the water bottle on his belt, and drank deeply. He checked his watch once more. Came towards them and offered Winters the water bottle. She turned her head away. He hesitated for a moment then offered it to Brandeis. As she reached for it she noticed the way his veins showed blue under the ivory, butter-coloured skin. His hands were narrow and well-shaped: not a workman's hands.

Brandeis nodded her thanks, holding back her automatic woman's smile. She deliberately avoided wiping the mouth of the flask, but drank, immediately bolting down mouthful after mouthful of warm, brackish water. It tasted wonderful. She had not realised how acute her thirst had been until she had seen him drinking.

She offered the water bottle to Winters, who shook her head shortly as though angry that Brandeis, by accepting the offer, had somehow betrayed them...

'I don't want any.' This, almost petulantly.

'Go on, Mae. Might as well die with a quenched thirst.'

Winters simply shook her head, withdrawing even further. Brandeis thought she was being childish, but passed the water bottle back to the officer.

A few uneasy moments later, they saw the young soldier return. After a whispered conversation between the Japanese they set off once more, at the same remorseless pace.

Two hours later.

Save for the laboured breathing of the women there was a hushed silence. The jungle had folded up its wings towards the night; the creatures of the day had vanished. Only a few minutes of light were left. The day had run out with its usual dramatic speed.

Moritoh glanced back down the slope. The girl came into sight in a moment, head down, concentrating on keeping her feet on the treacherous, muddy track. So slim and beautiful; as fair as his own Myoki was dark; both of them fragile, fine-boned as water birds.

How would he feel if it was Myoki who was threatened by Nagato?

'Would you like a wager? That I'll have both these sluts before we hand them over to the boys back in camp?'

Nagato meant it. Moritoh remembered his squad leader's smothered, wolfish laugh as he had described in graphic detail to his cronies around the wreck, exactly how he proposed to employ the women before they were killed. What chance would this girl have against that animal?

Moritoh could imagine what would happen to her and the woman, when they got back to camp. She would be treated like all the other women who had suffered there; used and cast aside like so much soiled linen. Or even killed like the two native women who had died. Nagato had been involved in that sordid incident, but nothing had been done

98

about it. The officers either had not known, or else they had chosen to turn a blind eye.

Was Lieutenant Oshima aware of what he was doing? Moritoh thought of Myoko in that bear-pit with Nagato and his like, and tasted against the brass of hatred in his mouth. How could they treat a woman so?

Moritoh wondered how he could protect the girl against the rank and power of the man. He could not outfight him. He knew that there was nothing he could do, or would do. So much for his aspirations to be a samurai – a warrior who knew no fear.

He knew the squad leader was no fool. Nagato would pick his moment.

Moritoh thought bitterly about today's humiliation in front of the girl. Nagato had deliberately dishonoured him. To have to stand there like a coolie and be slapped around by some upstart clerk who would have been lucky to get a job in one of his father's warehouses, had left Moritoh hot with shame. Moritoh comforted himself with the knowledge that no one else would have got away with it. He had proved tough enough to avoid personal attack even from those who resented his privileged background. All those hours spent in the university gymnasium – remaking himself tough enough to stand up to his father – torturing his once-frail body into the superbly muscled machine that had served him so well on the assault courses that had left other recruits retching on the ground – what good were they in the face of Nagato?

Vague half-formed fantasies involving the death of Nagato passed through Moritoh's mind, one after the other, like angry will-o'-the wisps. In their next action he would shoot Nagato ... as he lay sleeping, he would cut his throat... Now that the women prisoners had entered the equation there was no knowing which way Nagato would jump.

As Moritoh walked on silently through the rain he aimed, in his mind's eye, at the broad back of his enemy.

Moritoh was especially watchful now. The gloom under the jungle's canopy was so intense that it was almost impossible to see on the narrow track.

Fancy the girl rolling a cigarette like that! Again Moritoh saw the slender, clearly delineated muscles of Brandeis' forearms flexing, silk-smooth under her brown skin. He felt his loins stir as he pictured her sitting there concentrating on the task and, past the barrier of her arms, a disturbing curve of breast swelling under the thin fabric of her shirt.

Moritoh glanced back at Brandeis quickly. Her fair hair caught the last dappled, dying light of the day.

He speculated whether her hair would be fair all over her body, like those pin-up nudes he had seen in the wallets of dead enemy soldiers. The veterans of the Section would speak of the blonde European women they claimed to have enjoyed in Singapore; women of unquenchable lust and eroticism. Their tales triggered ribald laughter and derision, even more outrageous anecdotes and sudden, disturbing silences.

But this girl was no fantasy. Moritoh had watched the way her baggy trousers delineated her slim body; how her belt circled tightly around a waist he wanted to try to span with his hands.

He was at once chilled and disturbed by the thought of this captive girl at his disposal, 'staked out for our convenience' as Nagato had described. Moritoh's own fantasies about Brandeis: curves, shadows, skin, hair, the touch of her, the mystery, had raised in him an intense and complex curiosity.

The light was gone. It was time to make camp. Moritoh stopped.

The women were in distress, breathing heavily and struggling under their packs. As soon as they reached Moritoh they slumped down. The girl looked particularly exhausted.

Moritoh wondered what the lieutenant would say if he offered to carry her pack, but he said nothing and waited for the lieutenant to arrive.

From where Winters and Brandeis slumped

on the ground, the upward slope loomed above like a dark cliff. On this cruel journey each rest had made Winters aware of her fear, each movement, of her pain. The straps of her pack had already rubbed her shoulders raw and her bruised face was aching badly.

Winters wished she had thought of taking a pain killer from the first aid kit before she had handed it over. Would they let her have one when they stopped finally? she wondered. If they ever did stop.

Each time they had rested the mosquitoes had fallen on them in clouds, but she'd long since given up any attempt to fight them off.

She looked around the oppressive gloom of the jungle. So this was the strange, unknown country that transformed men; the once-distant crucible of war.

At Base Hospital the jungle had stood outside the limit of their experience. It had even seemed romantic; palm trees, brilliant, exotic flowers, wild, shy creatures; like something out of Somerset Maugham. But at least it was safely there, held at bay by the perimeter fence. This rain forest into which they had fallen ran off the edges of Winters' imagination. To run from this was simply to be killed, or to be swallowed up by this writhing madness of trees and tendrils.

How little they knew about survival. Two days at the wreck and she had not even worked out that there would be a river at the bottom of that great valley. The young soldiers who had come to rescue them had been wet from a river crossing when she had seen them, moments before they died. Had she had the gumption to think of that, they might have followed the river's course and come out somewhere safe.

But all such fantasies were merely exercises in futility. This was the reality, this one-way track in the forest.

Until now the jungle and the war had been only a legend of faint sounds; the soft boom of gunfire and the crackling reports of bombs gouging at far and misty slopes.

For her and her nursing sisters, the war had begun at the airport when the tiny Austers had brought in the badly wounded from some battleground up there in the looming mountains.

Some they could help, but others were too far gone. These broken strangers came into their lives, the tags and serial numbers on their wrists the only evidence of the men they had been before they had set out on their journey; complete.

Some of them, with shattered bones, or pain that no man should be asked to bear, had been without the grace of morphia for too long. Afterwards their eyes told of a never-to-be-eradicated suffering that would haunt them while they lived; if they lived. Others came back with no mark on them, but broken all the same.

And now here, high in the rain forest, Winters could feel the inexorable force of the furnace exerting its changes upon her.

How would this place, and this terrible ordeal that was happening to them, transmute Sally and her? Would it turn them from flesh and blood women to memories, statistics of 'missing believed killed'; fading images in a group photograph of some Nursing Service's album: Sisters Winters and Brandeis, Buna Base Hospital, August 1943; two of a group of grinning girls all saying 'cheese' for the camera?

Brandeis' eyes looked enormous in her white face. Winters was too breathless to speak but she tried an encouraging smile. It would not gel.

Lieutenant Oshima halted opposite the women and looked at Moritoh, oddly. His eyes did not seem to relate to the rest of his face. There was a hunted look about him.

'Why are you stopping?' he asked.

'Sir, it's getting too dark to see.'

Oshima looked around uncertainly almost as though he had not noticed.

Moritoh was shaken by his officer's disturbing appearance. It was almost as if the man were possessed.

Yet, he thought, it was little wonder. Moritoh counted back and could only think of five casualties lost in skirmishes in the six months he had served under Lieutenant Oshima, and two of those had been wounds, although bad enough for the men to be sent back to the coast.

Today, the lieutenant's whole Section had died, bar the three of them scurrying through this dangerous no-man's land like fugitives.

The thought that the disaster might be his fault nagged at Moritoh like a blister in a boot. Had he really failed to see some enemy soldiers crossing the river? He pushed the thought away. They could have come from another direction. In this nightmare country the enemy were neither in front, nor behind; they were everywhere.

Or was the lieutenant distracted by the women? They had never before taken prisoners, let alone women prisoners. Prisoners here were as deadly as an unexploded bomb. The orders were explicit: prisoners were killed.

Moritoh, to whom it had never occurred to ill-treat a woman, could understand why Lieutenant Oshima had failed to carry out such an order. Had they died during the ambush that would have been one thing, but to kill them in cold blood was another. Oshima, Moritoh was certain of it, was incapable of such a thing.

But here inaction was likely to be, in itself, a fatal act.

Moritoh's natural optimism was gone. He felt as though the fates were conspiring to finish off his life before it had properly began. Instead of enjoying his inheritance of wealth and happiness, here he was clinging like a survivor in a shipwreck, all because he'd been fated to live in this ludicrous moment of history.

And ahead of him lay two more days and nights before they reached even the fragile safety of the camp.

Oshima gathered himself with an effort and peered at his watch. 'No, go on! Up to near the top. Then we'll stop.'

Moritoh thought of arguing. He saw the look of desperation on the women's faces as they forced themselves back on to their feet.

'How much further?' Winters asked.

Oshima looked at her strangely as though he had not seen her before then shook his head curtly.

His sense of danger sharpened by his despair, Moritoh pushed on upwards into the blackness towards the unseen ridge.

'Shit.'

Winters heard Brandeis' breathed protest. There was always a droll quality about Brandeis and her attitude to orders. The familiar oath caused a tired grin to light up the space between them.

On and on. How much further? Winters felt as if she might die if they did not stop soon.

She was aware of her own harsh breathing.

She concentrated on fixing her eye on the back of Brandeis' sweat-soaked shirt. As they stumbled up the track she pressed her hand flat against her belly.

The irony of it! Winters' thought was as much rueful as bitter.

A few days ago, the child within her, David's child, had had no future. Suddenly it had one, of sorts, although it was likely to be brief.

Having missed her second period, Winters had been steeling herself for her visit to the good doctor who saw her girls all right when they found themselves in trouble. He did the deed for them all with dispatch and without censure. Then the news of their transfer had come through.

She had not told David of her plight, of course. He had more than enough on his mind getting himself back into shape after his wound, and in making his outfit ready for the big push they all knew was coming. Winters had made the decision to abort without remorse.

But now this present nightmare meant hat she would not be visiting the doctor after all. Was this His Divine retribution for her sin of David?

Winters felt disgusted with herself that she could not permanently lock out this ancient corrosive nonsense of guilt. Here it was again. Whenever things went wrong for her the inevitable crippling guilt started twisting away like an interrogator in the sweating prison cell of her mind.

God might not forgive, but Ian would have done so. He might have been sad, even angry about David, but he would have understood. 'Life is short,' he had said on the night before he had left, by which time she knew she felt nothing for him. 'Don't wait around for me. If anything happens that's good, you grab it. We only get one turn in the barrel.'

Winters remembered shaking her head and protesting; meaning it.

When Ian had been posted overseas she had busied herself with her work and waited dutifully for his letters. And they had come; all too frequently, with bits and pieces cut out by the censor, and each friendly, chatty, optimistic letter was a recrimination.

'Dear Mary Jane,' they began; even his use of her given names was a shared privacy as out of date as their love. She preferred Mae. All the sisters called her that now, kidding her about Mae West and her buxom bosom.

After a few token protests about being married and past that kind of thing, she started going out with the girls on their off-duty nights, to dance and drink gin-and-it's. She never got involved, although there were plenty of offers.

For the other girls in the service it was all

so casual and easy. They had all said 'it's war time, so what the hell' and they swore and smoked and made love to handsome strangers and got pregnant and fixed abortions and got treated for the clap, while she stayed pure with a purity which soon began to curdle at the edges.

When she had heard that Ian had got out of Tobruk, Winters had hardened her resolve to keep herself for him. But, behind the proffered barrier of her wedding ring, there had been many times when she'd wished she had not made that commitment and was free.

Then she had met David. The child within her was his, not the acceptable issue of Mr and Mrs Ian Winters who are happy to announce the birth, etcetera, but another source of guilt and self-recrimination.

Winters wondered what'd happen to them all, before this present nightmare was all over. Herself, Sally and this uncertain, and, as yet, unformed creature she carried in her belly.

Chapter 7

Nagato appeared silently. He ignored his officer; his eyes were on the prisoners.

This man had made tangible all Brandeis' previous fears about the Japanese, fears that had until then merely lurked at the very borders of her mind.

Each time they stopped on the march Nagato had reappeared from behind. To Brandeis he seemed like a black spider scuttling in from its lair to check if the victim were still caught in the sticky toils of its net.

Aware of her panicky fears of the man Brandeis wondered if her own face was betraying her. She tried, by composing herself, to convey to Winters a calm she did not feel.

She forced herself to look at the man, a disturbing shadowy figure in the faint firelight. It was no ordinary fear she felt for Nagato. It was not only that he had knocked them about and done such barbarous things to the Australian soldiers. There was more to it than that. Even if she had not experienced his brutality she would have been frightened of him. Neither was it simply that he was Japanese. Oshima, sitting beside him, was no less foreign, no less their foe, but this man she would have feared and hated had he been on her own side. This one was the Enemy.

Brandeis' men were usually young and strong and straight to the point; easy to talk to, easy to deal with, willing to take no for an answer; fun sometimes and occasionally exciting enough to be worth her passion. It was not that she was indiscriminate. She had disliked some men. There had been plenty of those with whom she had dealt directly and

110

without fear of retribution; the ones who wanted her body and offered nothing in return save for the drink, the 'leg openers' that were supposed to facilitate the seduction.

But Nagato was another kind. Brandeis had met his like only once: a young pilot who had been all right until he had become drunk. He had turned into something frightening, had tried to rape her in a hotel room in Melbourne and when she had begun to scream had slapped her around. Full of contrition next day of course.

After that, Brandeis had been careful to be certain of her man before she got herself into such a position with anyone else. That was the first and only time she had met the Enemy. In this Japanese NCO she recognised him again.

This jungle was no hotel room with thin walls. No amount of screaming would save her here, she knew it, and anyway, who would hear her cries? There would be no curbs, nor checks on his behaviour in this wilderness.

What a big gun you have, Enemy. All the better to terrify you with. Who would be her woodsman in this dark forest? Brandeis wondered. The officer with his shifty preoccupied eyes? The handsome young soldier? Would his axe cleave the Beast? Some hope. Despair took Brandeis in an iron grip.

Bitter thoughts. They had been let down. No one had really spelled out the risks to them. Even when they had come to New Guinea, several thousands of miles nearer the action, the war had been kept at a careful distance from them as though by some unspoken conspiracy.

In the safety of their camp, with a great army all around them, the sisters had lived their calm adventure with regular letters, three meals a day, dances, camp concerts and occasional stolen hours in the swift arms of men, some of them on a one-way ticket to oblivion.

It was as if the war were some myth to which they all paid lip-service. No one ever talked about what might happen if it were lost and they were captured. Even when they had volunteered to go to Lae to establish the surgical theatre of the forward base, no one had mentioned the possibility of engine failures, of storms, or of crashes.

If only someone had said something, perhaps she might not be here in the middle of this nightmare.

Nagato was on his feet now. His neck looked immensely thick and sloped down smoothly to massive shoulders; the belted waist was absurdly small, almost girlish. He had the intimidating bulk of a weightlifter. Brandeis guessed he was in his late twenties.

Brandeis had seen men as powerful as he; even been attracted to them. She liked strong men; the feel of beautiful, thick, delineated muscles excited her; but this man's brute power was, in some way, malign.

He picked up his gun and looked over towards her suddenly; catching her staring. She jerked her eyes clear of his gaze and clutched hard at Winters' hand. The answering squeeze was meant to comfort, but did not. Brandeis knew then what it was that frightened her. His eyes: crystal black, cheerless, cold as any reptile's; but, worst of all, excited.

From time to time the boy would look directly at Oshima as though about to speak. Then he would look away to concentrate on his food.

Oshima's own meal went untouched. Enthralled, he watched the faint light of the fire make a shadow play upon the face opposite him; a young, pale face with troubled eyes. A familiar face. It seemed to Oshima that it was that of Kurosumo, once his prize student and first and only close friend.

They had shared a passion for their subject, Kurosumo and he, and went together on field expeditions and camping trips. Just the two of them in perfect rapport, sometimes hardly needing to speak for days on end. They had agreed about everything except one. Kurosumo had found Oshima's acquired passion to possess absurd, and constantly ragged him about it in his good-natured fashion.

'You've been corrupted, you maniac!' He joked once when Oshima proudly showed him his latest capture. 'The West has corrupted you. What a dreadful metamorphosis. You go to America a Japanese, and you come back a Collector! Where's the gain in your dusty mausoleum of dead creatures with their wings fraying? What's the use of your tattered collection of corpses?'

For Kurosumo, in the Japanese tradition, observation was enough.

Kurosumo; who dragged Oshima out of his monk's cell of learning into the light of the real world, introduced him to theatre and music, drinking and whoring; who taught his teacher more than he learned from him.

Kurosumo; son of a Court doctor, dazzling honours student in the natural sciences, a big, laughing young man who seemed to have been born with total knowledge; total recall.

Kurosumo. Loving friend.

'What will happen to them?'

It was if a dead man had spoken. The words triggered off a spasm of shock in Oshima's mind, but then the face of Kurosumo dissolved and became that of Moritoh, his dark eyes probing for an answer to his question.

How alike they were! The same youth and beauty, the same handsome, arrogant features. Again and again, over the past six months Oshima had seen the face of his friend on that of his new recruit.

114

Ah! Kurosumo. The old sorrow stirred within him yet.

Kurosumo: whose loss had marked the end for Oshima.

Long after Oshima's other students had gone, Kurosumo had worked on, cheerful and scathing, consistently supporting Oshima as his university career was torn out from under him. But finally he, too, was obliged to leave Oshima's sinking ship. The pressure from his powerful father made it imperative.

The day he had resigned his course he had sent a gift to Oshima by messenger. It was typically ironic: a precious matched pair of birdwing butterflies from Bougainville, *O. Allotei* – absurdly beautiful with their black and green wings and golden body: the pair resplendent in a glass case. With it was a Haiku, 'by way of apology'.

'The butterfly
can scarcely light on the lily
swaying in the wind.'

Kurosumo did not change departments, as Oshima had urged him to do, but joined the Army as a private soldier. He died on the first day of action during the invasion of Malaya.

Again Moritoh spoke, his voice insistent now.

'The women ... what will happen to them?'

Moritoh's question dragged Oshima back to the present on a cruel hook. With a physical effort Oshima turned his gaze from Moritoh to his prisoners.

They sat pressed close to one another as though for comfort. Their faces were mostly obscured by their hair spilling untidily over their closed and shadowed faces, but every now and then a tiny flicker of flame would catch their pale hair and eyes.

Both of them carefully focused on their food, ignoring their captors' glances as though to meet them might be seen as some kind of a provocation.

Oshima knew he could fall back on his rank and say nothing; always an officer's option when he would not, or could not, answer a question. But, with Moritoh, Oshima was reluctant to do this. There were already too many things he held back from the boy; feeling he had not, could not, express.

All the things he might say were simply evasions: it's none of your concern, the fortunes of war, someone else's problem, and so on. There was no honour in such answers. There was only one response.

'I do not know.'

The women were watching now, aware that they were being talked about. Moritoh ate in silence for a time, then:

'May I speak, sir?'

Oshima thought of forbidding it. He did

116

not want to hear this inevitable, sentimental concern for the women.

He nodded, aware of the anger rising in him.

'Sergeant Nagato...' Moritoh began. 'What I mean is ... will you be staying near the women on the march...?'

Moritoh stopped awkwardly.

'The squad leader has his orders. They will be treated as prisoners of war. When we return to camp they will only be questioned...' Oshima heard himself falter, 'I will see that ... I can only assume that they will be treated correctly.'

Moritoh flushed, his face set rigidly.

'Of course, sir.'

'Nagato will relieve you in two hours.'

'Sir.'

Moritoh stood up and buckled his belt. Taking his rifle he vanished into the darkness.

Oshima watched Nagato throw off his equipment, put down his weapon and squat by the fire. Confident, truculent.

'All clear?'

A grunted reply.

There was a primordial ferocity about the squad leader perfectly suited to this barbarous land, where everything, everyone, even the children, seemed innocent of pity.

Oshima remembered the children in the hill village he had entered on his first patrol with Section Seven. The captive butterflies. But what was the point of recalling such ugliness now?

'Moritoh?'

'Up the track. About thirty yards.' Contempt showing. 'What now?'

Children shrieking with laughter. The butterflies clawing frantically upwards, their huge, kaleidoscopic birdwings beating in a panic. Living kites.

'A guard tonight,' said Oshima, concentrating on the flames. 'Change two hourly, you and Moritoh. I'll stay with the prisoners.'

'A guard? Think they might get away?' Nagato insolently. 'Tie them up. Make them easier to enjoy.' The wolfish grin.

Tie them up?

What stamina! Flying upwards trailing fetters heavier than themselves.

'That's enough.'

'But what are women for, if not to enjoy?'

'I said, enough!'

The women. It had been agonising to watch the two of them struggle to keep up, but in the end, they had amazed him with their stamina.

Were they instinctively aware, Oshima wondered, that, had they been unable to continue, it would have been impossible for him to justify their existence? He would have been obliged to shoot them.

Exhausted from flight, the great butterflies clung on to flowers or twigs high above the ground. But their laughing captors, bored with such inaction, would twitch them loose.

The girl was watching now, half risen up on her elbow. Beside her on the ground the huddled shape that was her companion lying, still as a corpse, utterly spent.

How little of the march he had noticed, Oshima reflected; neither the terrain they had passed through, nor the events. His focus, his heady, all-consuming concentration had been on this matched pair.

Oshima's learned skill for survival, honed to an exquisite edge by the brutal realities of jungle conflict, had gone into suspension. It had been as if he had covered the journey in a palanquin carried by the others, sealed off from reality.

For the whole journey he had been entirely dependent on Moritoh's sharp, reflexive skills gliding there in front and the terrible, silent power of Nagato trailing behind.

A long atrophied passion had been re-kindled within him this morning: the ancient, god-like power of the unseen observer.

All along the trail, almost sick with excitement, he had watched the prisoners at close quarters as they struggled up the long quarter-slope of the mountain; slipping and sliding, steadying themselves with trees, branches and creepers where the going was especially steep. Picking themselves up when they fell, wiping sweat with muddy hands.

Flying upwards, trailing fetters heavier than themselves.

Instinctively Oshima had noticed their matched characteristics: the set of shoulders, the configuration of the body, the carriage of head, the rhythmic pattern of movements: the curve and fusion of flesh and bone.

The vivid, too-delicate kites fall exhausted and lie trembling on the ground, their great lobes pulsing too fast.

When they had rested on the hour, close enough to touch, he had observed the faces: hairline, sweep of eyebrows, the placement of features: eyes blue, hair fair. And noted the differences: one slightly older, taller, heavier, thicker of waist, more lined of face, darker of skin, broader of feet and hand.

'Seems a pity to waste them.'

'I said, leave it. They are prisoners of war. We will treat them accordingly.'

'Then you mean kill them,' Nagato said, triumphantly, a debater scoring a palpable hit. 'We are under orders not to take prisoners, sir.'

The 'Sir' was spoken with insolent contempt. The squad leader was pushing his authority to the limit.

Nagato had an instinct for the jugular. He pin-pointed weakness with a brutal directness. The frightening combination of primitive savagery and shrewd cunning was what made him such an effective soldier. And such a deadly enemy.

'It would be a pity, sir, if we were hampered by these prisoners of yours and failed to make our report in time.'

Of course what he said about the women was right, Oshima knew it. The prisoners *were* endangering them and the mission they had been sent out to perform.

The haul of intelligence Oshima had gained on this patrol was especially rich. Two successive ambushes, on the third and fourth days, had provided evidence of an unusual amount of activity by the enemy. He had identified infantry from new regiments not seen in this area before. Later on he had encountered an unusually large number of enemy patrols it had not suited him to engage. Then there was the wreck itself: a gold-mine of information. Nagato well knew the significance of such material.

Oshima concentrated on the food, absently stirring the rice with a twig and waiting for the water to boil.

The girl was watching still. Each time Oshima glanced up under his brows he found that she was staring over at them. Set in the gaunt oval of her face, her eyes caught the light from the guttering blue flame.

What was she thinking, this beautiful aberration? Was she aware of the destruction she and her companion were causing; two rare, previously undiscovered creatures blundering about in the laboratory, upsetting the experiments, wrecking display case, spilling preserving fluids, knocking over microscopes and scattering his papers, his life – so carefully arranged in order.

Nagato bored in.

'You're making a mistake. It's better for everyone if they don't make it back to the camp. Apart from anything else, your reasons would be misunderstood.'

'That's not a consideration for you, Sergeant. They are prisoners and I am taking them back.'

A cynical grin.

'You'll be welcomed with open arms.' Nagato grinned. 'Or, at least, they will be. A hundred and fifty men who haven't seen a decent woman for the best part of two years, except for a bit of stray black stuff. Open arms.' Nagato looked over at the girl and clicked his tongue against his teeth lewdly. 'Open legs.'

Oshima felt a terrible surge of rage, but held check.

Beautiful creatures are prisoners of their beauty. The children fly butterflies for kites because, for a thrilling moment, they are the possessors of beauty of an extraordinary kind.

Normally alien interlopers in the laboratory were simply disposed of. But he could not dispose of these two. He possessed them. Or, perhaps, they possessed him. Already they had created havoc and Oshima knew that they would go on doing so, but, no matter how much destruction they wreaked, he could do them no harm. They were his chains; fetters of beaten gold, and beautiful.

When a butterfly wears out the children tear the string loose, severing the already crushed thorax. Then they rush off to seek new and ever more beautiful victims to fly. The forest rings with their excited cries.

Was he any better than the children who had horrified him with their unfeeling callousness?

Any better than Nagato who desired to possess them in his own way?

He was aware now that a new set of rules applied. Normally the Section had operated with an easy and untypical informality that stemmed from men sharing a special kind of danger. They had learned to respect and depend upon one another. This had enabled each soldier, and especially Nagato as squad leader, to disagree with him, or at least, put forward contrary suggestions. The unwritten rules of this relationship were understood by everyone. Each knew that he, Oshima, would make the final decision. Each knew when to speak and when to remain silent. No disagreement had ever moved so close to a confrontation. Nagato was playing a deadly new game.

'They'll make good sport for the boys

back in camp.' He looked over towards the women with a lewd wink. 'But I think, since you're making me share the risks, you ought to let me have first turn with them.' He grinned at Oshima like a salesman who had made an irrefutable point, then, with mock deference said: 'After you, of course, sir.'

There was no backing down now. Oshima turned his gaze on the insolent face across the campfire.

'Nagato, I'm giving you a direct order. You will not molest the women in any way. You will treat them as prisoners of war. And you will not bring the subject up again. Is that understood?'

Nagato got to his feet.

'Clearly, sir.'

He picked up his weapon and Oshima felt a chill of fear. For a moment he thought the man was going to shoot him.

'I'll relieve Moritoh. Sir.'

Nagato turned and stared over towards the women. Both of whom were watching wide-eyed. He swung around contemptuously and disappeared into the darkness.

The long night ground on.

Afraid to sleep the women watched the guard change two hourly; either Moritoh or Nagato coming and going in turns. Oshima never moved. Sitting alone by the tiny fire he seemed to have withdrawn into himself.

'I reckon he doesn't know what to do with us,' breathed Brandeis. 'And that, I don't like.'

Winters was looking at her, her face a pattern of dark shadows, eyes withdrawn and troubled. She did not seem to hear. Since they had left the plane wreck she seemed to have gone into a trance. Brandeis wondered if she might be suffering concussion from the beating she had taken from the squad leader.

Brandeis' hostility towards Winters was very close to the surface. It had guttered and flamed every step of the brutal march they had been forced to take.

'Mae!' Brandeis spoke urgently.

Winters' eyes came into focus. 'We'll take turns at sleeping,' she said firmly as though she had not heard Brandeis speak. 'You sleep first, then I'll have a go.'

Senior Sister Bloody Winters organising the ward rounds. The bitch fell into her bossy role effortlessly. Brandeis felt like shaking her.

At that moment she felt Winters' grip on her arm. Nagato had reappeared beside them. Their fingers linked nervously, inadequate chain mail against the fear the man engendered in them.

He stood there staring hotly at them, provoking a response. Brandeis felt the probing force of his will, almost a tangible thing.

They watched him cross, to squat down wordlessly beside the officer.

'Don't let him get to you, love,' Winters said quietly. 'Just let's stick together and we'll be all right.'

Brandeis nodded but, at that moment, neither of them believed it.

'I know it's an awkward time, Ma'am,' she said, 'But I'd like to put in for a transfer.'

Twice in the past month, faced with Winters' disciplinary action for especially outrageous escapades, Brandeis had put in for a transfer. Twice permission had been refused. It was feeble enough, but the irony was not lost, Winters rewarded her with a nervous smile. Brandeis was glad she had made the effort.

For a couple of hours now she had been ignoring her body's signals, but now there was nothing else for it.

'I need to pee,' she said vexedly. 'What happens now?'

'We'll both go.'

They stood up slowly, trying not to alarm the soldiers.

Oshima looked up sharply, but then, seeing Winters pointing into the blackness of the forest, he nodded.

'A few yards only, please. It is dangerous.' That strange guttural English with the pronounced American accent.

Brandeis caught the ugly grin of the squad

126

leader. Saw him say something to the officer. His comment was ignored.

They felt their way blindly into the pitch dark, hands in front of their faces, recoiling from nameless things that seemed to clutch at them. Within a moment they were entirely disoriented, clinging to each other.

'They can't see us. Here'll do.'

As much embarrassed as frightened they squatted together in the dark, then, almost thankfully, went back into the company of their captors.

Once more on the groundsheet with their backs against a tree, facing the fire.

'They're not worth the money.'

'What?'

'Cheap Japanese bladders.'

Winters' smile got as far as her eyes this time.

'Get some sleep. I'll wake you in two hours.'

Brandeis curled herself into Winters' lap. For a moment or two she felt as though she were back in her mother's arms, safe and protected from the dark. Her hostility vanished and she felt safe.

The feeling did not last. A few minutes later she saw the officer rise and disappear into the jungle.

Immediately Nagato got to his feet and came towards them, almost casually. Fear entered. Winters' arms now seemed too fragile a barrier against his menace.

Standing a yard in front of them Nagato made a sudden violent and frighteningly obscene gesture, ramming at them with his fist. Then, with a dead face, slowly and deliberately, he began to unfasten the fly of his trousers.

Brandeis' nerves had locked solid. She felt sick. Was this to be the moment? she wondered. She felt Winters' arms tense around her.

She had just decided to scream out as loudly and unnervingly as possible, when she saw Oshima return.

The squad leader with his back to his officer, grinned at them, lecherously and simply walked straight past them into the jungle.

'Jesus.' Brandeis felt no sense of relief, only an acute awareness that there was going to be no end to this fear she felt.

'I'm sorry I got you into this,' Winters mumbled, bitterly. 'It's all my fault.'

'Don't. Don't. It's not.'

'It is!' Winters was close to tears. 'You don't know, but it is. If I'd done what you wanted all this wouldn't have happened.'

'Don't. Don't. It doesn't matter.'

Brandeis clung hard to Winters. Much later she slept, but sleep provided no escape. She left one nightmare only to enter another; an unspeakable universe of fear.

Part 3

ESCAPE

Chapter 8

Moritoh felt the brush of wings. He swivelled his eyes uneasily, using his night vision to try and make sense of the anthracite patterns of the forest.

He was puzzled. Why was he here on guard? Normally, when they were off the track in deep cover, they never posted a guard. Nobody moved in the jungle night; not even the blacks.

Leaving the cooking fire burning so long, like a comforting candle in a child's room; then setting a guard. It was something to do with the prisoners and not simply because they might try to escape. In some obscure way the lieutenant was trying to reassure the women by separating them from the malign presence of Nagato.

And well he might. They would need protection before this march was over. If anything happened to Lieutenant Oshima, Nagato would have them before an hour was out. He had said so.

'Your turn to eat with our personal whores.' The squad leader's voice hissing in the darkness. 'You know what they say about these blonde European women, Rich

Boy? Can't get enough? Well, before we're through with this little jaunt, I'll test out that theory with both of them. And that pansy lieutenant of yours had better not try to stop me.'

Moritoh had said nothing, amazed that the squad leader would think he would be party to his plans for the women.

Nagato had misinterpreted Moritoh's silence.

'But then I forgot. You don't like girls either.'

In fact, Nagato's instincts had not been much different from Moritoh's own. During his long night watches he had been plagued by sexual fantasies about the girl. Endless erotic permutations had disturbed him, stirring his loins, leaving him trembling in the dark.

A sense of possessiveness about the girl persisted. What might have happened between him and this alien girl, had they met under different circumstances? Moritoh knew it to be a futile thought. He pushed it away.

'One thing,' Nagato had warned, catching Moritoh by his shirt front, 'the girl is mine. Got that?'

From the beginning of the march Moritoh had wondered what he might be able to do to save her from Nagato. He knew that if he tried to interfere his throat would be slit in a minute. To save her from that rabble back

132

at camp would be even more hopeless.

Even Lieutenant Oshima had as much as admitted that he did knot know what would happen to them there. He had implied they would only be questioned then treated as prisoners of war, whatever that might mean. Moritoh knew their fate would be terrible. Oshima, he was certain, knew it too. He was avoiding the issue. Perhaps he simply did not care.

Moritoh felt a sense of foreboding. The lieutenant, that quiet, but steely effective warrior on whom Moritoh had modelled himself, seemed to be faltering badly. He had become most strange since these two prisoners had come into their lives. Unconsciously Moritoh ran his fingers along the edge of the charm belt he wore under his shirt. Myoko's parting gift: a fragile defence against death.

Moritoh had thought of death often enough, but usually in a romantic way. You died bravely, your weapon spitting retribution, taking several of the enemy with you; your warrior's life like a camellia in the fullness of its beauty, falling in one piece to the ground. In your imagination, you saw the held-back tears in your father's eyes – he, who had so misjudged you – as he received from the hands of some high ranking officer the little urn containing your ashes. *'I have used my influence to have you transferred to a combat unit,*' his father had written, *'to give you an opportunity to learn not only the meaning of discipline and sacrifice, but also the ways of the samurai.*' Of course, with the front of your mind you knew that, serving in this war, you would rot where you fell and your ashes would never be recovered. But you pushed that verity away.

Serving in Lieutenant Oshima's Section, you more often thought of death as something you inflicted. You thought of great and swift victories, successful ambushes, brilliant intelligence coups; of the kudos you shared after each successful patrol; the warmth and congratulations in the camp, the awe in the eyes of the new recruits.

Until now these fantasies had slotted readily into the pattern of observed realities; the known rhythms of march and observe; ambush and counter-attack; probe, harass and withdraw. Until now, Moritoh's soldier's life had been a sweet equation of symmetry, and victory.

But everything about the present equation jarred: women prisoners; the girl and her disturbing beauty; Lieutenant Oshima's strange, irresolute behaviour and, worst of all, Nagato's frightening, erratic violence. Moritoh had a terrible premonition that it would be Nagato who would resolve the situation with gun, knife and terror: war's primal answers.

He stared again into the blackness of the

134

forest's deeper night. The first one-thousandth part of daylight had changed the nature of the sky.

Around him he heard the stirring of creatures moving unseen and mysterious into their battle order for survival.

Luminous figures glowed green in the dark. Mathematical fireflies. Moritoh compared the dials of the five watches on his wrists: his own and four other new trophies, his richest haul ever. Four-fifteen.

The new recruits always liked captured watches. That would mean more tobacco and perhaps even some liquor when he returned to camp.

He adjusted two of them that were running marginally slow, feeling the smooth, warm metal beneath his fingertips.

It felt like skin. Myoko's? The fair girl's, perhaps? What would her skin feel like, this Myoko/prisoner of his? Pressed against him thigh to thigh, beaded with desire? He felt his blood stir once more at the thought of her.

One more night over, another to survive and then, if he was lucky, he would make camp.

A night flyer whirred overhead, fleeing the coming light. Moritoh shivered.

At first the sky changed imperceptibly, then, gathering speed, the sun slipped upwards towards the horizon behind a thunderous and

135

lovely anvil of Eastern cloud. Birds stirred nervously. Leaves unclenched their tenacious grip on the night and cat's eyes of dew, strung along spider's webs like fairy lights, refracted the subtle changes of the light.

Lieutenant Oshima sat motionless with his back against a tree. An insect scuttled crabwise by his hand, but went unnoticed. Over to his left, the thick bulk of the sleeping Nagato; to the right, the women, entwined in each other's arms like waifs, made another shapeless bundle of limbs and flesh.

He stared straight ahead, unseeing. In his mind he was in another place, another time; seeing the play of light on wings; feeling the warmth of a soft Northern sun upon his bare head; the feel of gorse underfoot.

The air on Mimoro mountain that day was cold, even there on the lower slopes, but the sun was predicating summer and already the gorgeous wings of the season's first butterflies were spread eagerly to drink in its warmth.

Oshima felt as though he had not breathed, not ever. They were never so close as now; the rare and desired creatures that had drawn him to this heady place. All morning he had stalked them up from the valley floor where, with a start of excitement, he had first spotted them, caught in the margin of the wind. Oshima had moved slowly, content to observe their pas de deux, *their partings and couplings, their brief, soaring joyous flights from blossom to blossom. How he*

136

*would have liked to have shared this moment
with Kurosumo, whose absence was now a
frozen space in his life.*

*He trailed them patiently, a lone figure moving
up and across the face of the mountain slope still
wet from the Bai-u rains and already painted
with a blazonry of the first flowers of the season.*

*Oshima's rucksack sat lightly on his back,
with his books, collecting box and food and
drink for the day. The long, wide-mouthed net
balanced sweetly in his hand and Oshima was
content to leave it there until later when,
regretfully, if the fates would so have it, he would
bring to an end the amorous merry-go-round of
his coveted prey.*

*What was it Kurosumo had said? 'Your
tattered collection?' The jibe hung accusingly in
the sweet air.*

*Each time the butterflies settled he would move
as close as he dared, then refocus his field glasses
until they came into sharp and thrilling detail.
The startling power of his lenses let him look at
the very texture of their wings, the delicate
shadings of colour; powder gold burnished by
subtle shades of bronze and brown.*

*Then without warning, almost as though they
had received some signal that his was a fatal
presence, they would sweep up in unison, their
refractive, iridescent colours bright as lanterns,
and soar sideways, up and across to another
honeyplace in the sun.*

All morning long the sight of them drew him

137

on. Time was forgotten: there was no such thing as hunger or thirst. Closer. Closer. There was a moment when the urge to possess them tightened his grip on his net. He would add them to his collection. Tattered collection... Tattered collection...

The insect bumped against his hand, butting blindly, breaking his reverie. For a long regretful moment Oshima stared at the little black, hard-backed beetle with its swaying antennae. He moved his hand away gently. Quietly he rose to his feet.

He was about to wake Nagato, but then changed his mind and crossed to the prisoners and stood staring down at them. The woman had her arms around the girl. The two were breathing as quietly and slowly as patients on a death bed. The familiar feeling of regret overcame him. How quickly the bloom begins to fade after the netting!

Gently Oshima touched Winters' foot with the toe of his boot, then stepped back so as not to frighten her. But she woke with panic in her eyes and sat up abruptly.

Oshima felt a sense of disappointment, and even some hostility, that she had made him feel so clumsy.

During the night: nameless images of torment, flesh ripped with hooks, unspeakable acts with fire, the cleave of steel. The turmoil of fears coalesced into one sharp realisation; they must escape, or die.

138

In Winters' dream there formed a brilliant, diamond-cut escape plan, complete in all its parts. She was running lost through a forest of night, then she was falling, endlessly slewing and bucketing through the cloud cover, down and down to be dashed to a bloody pulp against the instrument panel of a plane. The impact was a sickening, tangible force that jerked her awake, sweating.

The escape plan fragmented into pieces. The tag end of it slithered down a hole in her mind like a jewel down a drain. She grabbed at it desperately, but it was gone.

The Japanese face looming above her in the pre-dawn darkness was her only reality.

She sat up, stiff and scared. One part of the dream was true. Somehow they would have to escape from this.

War was simpler for men. There were no complications in the death of one man at the hands of another. But, with Sally and her, it would be different. Her attacker had made that obvious. In the power of him and his kind there would be no simple transaction with death; only pain and humiliation. A camp full of Japanese, perhaps dozens of them in a ravaging pack; the prospect was appalling and Winters was shaken.

The numb exhaustion of last night, powerful as a general anaesthetic, was now replaced by the tormenting sharpness of despair.

'Sergeant.'

Nagato reached instinctively for the weapon by his side and woke in one piece like a wild creature. He looked around with a baleful glare as though expecting to see the prisoners gone.

He stood up sourly, stared over at the women then hawked and spat, tasting the sourness of his mouth with apparent relish.

Oshima looked at Winters who was clutching her knees to her chest and easing the stiffness from her neck. The girl was now awake and she, too, sat up silently.

Oshima lit a can of fuel with his lighter, poured water out of his canteen into a Dixie and stood it on top of the flame.

'Bring Moritoh down. As soon as we eat, we go.'

Nagato stretched and shook the stiffness off. He stared over at the women then back at Oshima.

'We're taking them along, are we?' He shook his head in exaggerated disbelief and sucked his breath through his teeth.

Oshima looked at him directly, fighting down the anger erupting within him. His instinct at that moment was to gun Nagato down.

Content to have made his point, the squad leader walked slowly off, swivelling round to stare at the women as he passed them. He made an obscene sound with his mouth. The women shrunk under his looming presence. The man's goading, his hot eyes, seemed to drop the temperature around him as though someone had opened the door of a crypt.

'The evil, dirty bastard.' Brandeis' voice was teetering on the knife-edge of panic. 'We've got to get away. We've got to, Mae!'

The tag end of Winters' dream snagged again in her mind. The answer to their survival lay in the forest's capacity to swallow them totally.

It would be fatal to try to escape and to fail. What they had experienced the day before; the astonishing savagery of combat, the sounds and vivid images of death, told her that they could expect no mercy if they were recaptured.

She no longer had any illusions. Feelings did not count here. The squad leader's grisly collection of trophies; bloody rings and gouged teeth, showed the cost of the forfeits in this brutal game of truths and dares.

But those very horrors were reminders that equally terrible things, even worse things, might await them at the end of this journey. It was unthinkable simply to allow themselves to be led to the slaughter.

'We're going to have to run for it, first chance we get.' Winters kept her eye on the officer as she spoke, barely breathing the words, aware he might understand them.

'You think we can?'

'There'll be a lot more like him, wherever it is they are taking us.'

'Say when.'

Brandeis looked at Winters with an eager expression. A surge of affection for the girl swept over Winters. In spite of the dirt, the swell of insect bites and the ravages of bruises and broken sleep, how pretty Sally was! No wonder young men swarmed after her. She belonged to them, to their arms and their laughter, not to this. In that moment all Winters' hostility towards this spoiled, wilful charge of hers, disappeared. How grateful she was to have Brandeis' spirited presence on this awful journey.

They were both aware that the officer was staring over at them, almost as if he were eavesdropping. When the young soldier reappeared they saw Oshima give him some biscuits and incline his head towards them. Moritoh's face was neutral and there was a suspicion of a formal bow when he handed them the food.

They waited until he returned to the cooking fire and squatted down.

'When?' Brandeis spoke quietly, through a mouthful of biscuit. 'At night?'

'We wouldn't get five yards, and anyway they might have torches. No, too risky. Daylight'd be better.'

'We'd need a bigger start.'

'I'll choose the moment. OK? Game?'

'You say "go" and we go.'

Later Moritoh came over with a tin bowl of tea. Once more the odd, formal courtesy and unthreatening face. Brandeis nodded her thanks.

'Surprising, isn't it?'

Winters felt the bitterness rise. If a man didn't actually beat her, Sally wagged her tail like a terrier.

'Don't fall for it, love,' Winters warned, tiredly. 'I wouldn't trust any of them as far as I could kick them.'

'They can't all be as bad as Beast-features.'

'Don't bet on it.'

Before long Nagato returned and reported 'all clear' but, when he began to eat a yard to one side of Oshima, his malign presence was enough to regenerate a feeling of sick rage in his officer.

Hurriedly, Oshima got to his feet and buckled on his harness. He was overcome by a feeling of panic. He had to get away.

'I want the prisoners ready to move as soon as I get back.' His voice sounded unsteady.

Nagato looked up at him enquiringly and went on sipping his tea in silence.

Oshima checked the magazine of his weapon and moved towards the women, carrying it loosely in his hand. As he approached they scrambled awkwardly to

143

their feet, looking scared.

Oshima shook his head irritably to indicate he meant them no harm. They had an annoying way of making him feel clumsy and menacing.

'Soon I return. We go then.'

Their eyes showed their relief.

'Please understand. If you try...' He groped in his mind for the elusive word. 'Escape, yes? Escape. My men will shoot you.'

He watched their faces close and go still. They nodded in unison.

'Where are we going?'

Oshima looked hard at the hostile face of the girl, waiting for her blurted words to form some meaning. Then he understood her question. Oshima again felt the anger building up explosively inside him. Did they not understand their position? They were prisoners with no rights to know anything. He had to be free of the women; from all of them. Oshima moved blindly past the prisoners. Then stopped uncertainly.

'Moritoh.'

The boy joined him quickly. Nagato looked towards them sharply, his attention caught.

Oshima spoke so that Nagato could not hear.

'If the prisoners are harmed I'll hold you personally responsible. Is that understood?'

Moritoh looked at Oshima in astonishment, his eyes widening.

'Sir.' This in the dismayed tone of a man who had just been handed a scorpion.

Oshima was already on his way, escaping upwards, towards the top of the ridge.

The officer's going left Winters in a formless panic, like that of a child suddenly left by its father in an empty house. For a few moments they heard the soft swish of undergrowth, then silence. Although Oshima had stood there cold and hostile, with his gun a chilling, lethal grey in the morning light and had made no bones about what would happen to them if they should try to escape, his presence had been some kind of comfort.

The young soldier pointed to their packs and groundsheets and tapped his shoulders. The march was to continue.

Winters felt relieved. Each such decision: an order to pack, or to march, meant a going on; another chance to survive. But, as she began to roll up her groundsheet she was shocked by an ugly sound. The squad leader had laughed.

Nagato rose and stretched elaborately, his eyes upon them. Then he sauntered near with a sardonic, half grin on his face.

He was not carrying his gun. Somehow this made his approach more mischievous, more deadly.

'Oh, Christ,' breathed Brandeis, 'here's a go.' She looked around as though looking for somewhere to bolt.

'Just ignore him.' But her own words sounded absurd to Winters even as she spoke them.

A yard from them Nagato stopped, staring down at them coldly. They were still on their knees beside their half-rolled groundsheet, conscious of the soup-thick menace he exuded. They stared straight ahead, determined not to catch his eye.

He moved closer. He was no more than a foot directly in front of Brandeis. Winters stared at the ragged and dirty fabric of his uniform and the tattered condition of his gaiters and boots, trying not to think.

His hands were moving oddly. Winters' breath caught as she realised what he was doing. With the studied slowness of a stripper, Nagato was unfastening his trousers. She forced her gaze past him to where she could see the young soldier who was standing looking towards them anxiously.

For a long moment everything seemed to freeze; an image when the film is caught in the frame of the projector, the instant before it blackens and bursts into flames: Sally's white, taut face; Nagato's naked flesh, half erect and half in his hand like some obscene blunt instrument.

Then a thick coil of yellow urine steamed and splashed on the ground between their feet. An overwhelming sense of disgust rose

146

in Winters' craw. From very far away she heard a voice.

'You're a filthy swine.' It was Brandeis. She was talking in a steady, conversational tone, looking up directly at him. Her face was a mask of contempt.

Teeth gleamed. Again the sound of laughter.

Nagato held his two hands in front of him as though holding a woman's hips and then thrust at Brandeis obscenely. He drove a finger towards her face indicating very clearly what he had in mind.

'A suppurating bag of pus,' Brandeis said, evenly looking him straight in the eye.

He went dangerously still for a moment as though absorbing the meaning of her words through the tone of her voice. A convulsion of anger crossed his smooth face. Then Nagato had Brandeis by the hair; was dragging her face hard against his flesh.

Brandeis writhed and struggled desperately to escape his grip, but now he had her hair in two hands locking her against his sex. She clawed frantically at his hands and arms, all the while making muffled, animal-like sounds of panic and disgust.

Screaming, Winters threw herself at him, smashing and raking at his grinning face.

'Leave her alone!'

Nagato clubbed her down. As Brandeis twisted free she, too, was struck and fell on her back crying out in pain.

She lay there, her face contorted with rage and fear. Over and over again she ground out: 'Bastard! Bastard! Bastard!'

From somewhere close behind Nagato. Winters heard the boy say something.

The squad leader whirled and silenced him with a glare, then turned back to face the women. He drew himself upright and stared down at Brandeis. Once more, the obscene thrusting, then, with an oddly self-righteous look, he slowly fastened his trousers.

Passing the young soldier he grabbed him by the shirt front, backhanded him once, twice, across the face, released him, then sat down by the cooking fire and poured himself some tea.

Moritoh stood at attention, looking broken and humiliated, his head bowed.

The oppressive silence was broken, at last, by a raucous bird screeching somewhere overhead.

'My God.' Winters felt befouled.

'I'm going to kill that one,' Brandeis looked sick. Her voice was trembling. 'Just give me half a chance. I swear to God, I'll kill him.'

Slowly Moritoh began to stow away the cooking things.

Chapter 9

From the top of the ridge that morning Oshima surveyed the country through which they had to pass; a long valley sloping north and east with a re-entrant at the far end, a mile or so away. Beyond that, a seemingly endless range of switchback ridges.

He noticed the massive flanks of the mountains, the precipitous slopes, a drift of smoke rising straight up above a hidden village.

From somewhere over there he half-registered the faint crackle of small arms, weak as firecrackers in the dawn's misty air; evidence of the death and destruction of some surprise attack that meant nothing to him. Something happening in another country.

Oshima was well aware that there had been no need for this reconnaissance, and his mind was not on it. He had not left the others to spy out the land, but to escape from them and from himself. He needed time to get a grip; to think. He needed, even for a brief time, to be free of command, free from his disgust, anger and fear of Nagato; free, above all, from the crushing burden of the prisoners.

There had been a time once – Oshima

remembered ruefully – was it just a day ago? – when, in spite of all the random hazards of jungle warfare, he had felt himself to be in charge of his life.

However mindless and destructive war might be, it was played out within an identifiable framework. The rules were rules of a kind, to play by them was to be comparatively safe.

But these women had changed all that. They were an irresistible force of nature; beautiful tendrils of doubt that were insidiously pulling down the walls of his private citadel.

How had all this come about?

It occurred to Oshima sharply that he had no clear idea of why the women were her, how they had come to be in a plane wrecked in the jungle; why he was taking them back to camp with him and, worst of all, no idea of what might happen to them once he got them there. That their fate might be terrible was a thought he had pushed away each time it had crept its way from out of the darkest part of his mind.

He did not even know what he felt towards them. As a scientist having discovered a rare new species? Certainly those first hours observing them had filled him with an excitement so great that he had felt as though he were weightless; god-like.

He was aware of their femaleness; aware of

the effect they were having on Nagato and Moritoh. Yet, although he could not stop being enthralled by them – the way they were formed, moved, interacted – he did not lust after them. But he did have the covetous feelings of the possessor.

At length, feeling calmer, Oshima returned to the bivouac. His brief respite had taken him away for only twenty minutes, but it proved to be enough to start the day badly. Yet another mistake.

He arrived back to find Nagato truculent, Moritoh sullen, and the women angry and afraid. In spite of his private instructions, perhaps even because of them, Oshima realised that something ugly had happened. He did not bother to find out what had transpired, but vowed not to leave them at Nagato's mercy again.

They left at once. For hour after hour they trudged on. And every step of the way Nagato's menace affected them all. The day formed around them as they drove on, like silent fugitive ghosts. The jungle passed in a kind of exhausted blur; nineteen kinds of green on green. They saw no one. They passed through deserted villages, and overgrown jungle gardens, climbed steep tracks, forded rivers and streams. Always Nagato was there somewhere behind them. Brandeis had found herself compulsively looking round, sometimes glimpsing him, sometimes not. His malevolent force made her think of hyenas.

The pace was relentless. The officer called a halt only twice, and then briefly. Each time they saw the young soldier dispatched forward to reconnoitre, to return some time later and converse in low whispers with the officer.

Once, when they stopped, and Winters was sitting on the ground with her head flung back and her breath coming harshly, Brandeis asked her if she were all right. The officer's face darkened and he shut her up with an angry look. After that she said nothing, too frightened to speak, acutely aware of the uneasy fragility of their collective hold on life.

The Japanese officer and the boy had a hunted look. Brandeis was aware that some obscure power struggle was taking place between them and their squad leader. She was certain that Nagato had deliberately humiliated Moritoh in front of her and wondered why the boy had not fought back. Why just stand there and take it? He had a gun. What was this man's power that he could demean another who was armed with a gun? If only she had one: a gun, a knife, anything.

Brandeis was angered by her vulnerability. Why had they not been trained to fight as the men were? Oh, they had been given a few lessons on the firing range with rifles, she and Mae and the sisters. But it had been tokenism, a desultory part of their basic training turned into a social occasion by the young officers eager for any excuse to put their manly arms around them and surreptitiously fondle their tits. She had even been promised a turn with an Owen automatic, but no one had ever got around to showing her how.

Cathedral shafts of light shot with steam slanted down, turning their clothes black with sweat. The sun moved to the vertical and, at last, they stopped at a barrier of river. It was little more than a narrow canal between solid walls of trees; a few yards of space and light.

The Japanese soldiers led them upriver a few yards, in off the narrow track. Winters and Brandeis sank down gratefully. Moritoh filled their water bottles for them when he filled his own. Oshima gave them each a tin of meat, and two bananas he had picked from a jungle garden, and the inevitable biscuits.

They ate in silence; five shadowy figures in the zebra-striped light-and-shade of the jungle floor.

After a time Oshima ordered Nagato to cross over to reconnoitre the other side and wait for them at the top of the next ridge. That way, he reasoned, the man would be in front of him. Nagato frightened Oshima, this he now acknowledged. To have that baleful presence trailing always at his back was

153

unsettling and deeply disturbing. As he issued the order, normal enough in ordinary circumstances, Oshima was aware of how distorted their relationship had become. He was careful to keep his voice neutral. For some instinctive reason he did not want Nagato to know how deeply felt was his anger. Until now, within the functioning framework of his Section, Oshima had been free to express his true feelings; whether anger, concern or triumph. The need to worry about his tone was new.

Nagato listened carefully to Oshima as though feeling for nuances, assessing whatever real significance might lie behind the expression, but then he obeyed.

He got to his feet, slid down the bank and forded the river, cleaving shoulder-deep through the blackish green water like a juggernaut. He reached the dense tangle crowding the opposite bank and, a moment later, was gone.

It was astonishing to Brandeis how fast the jungle swallowed a man. One moment Nagato was there, the next it was as though he had been erased. The tension that had hung palpably over the group vanished with the squad leader. Only then did the disgust and anger Brandeis felt finally subside. All that morning she had seethed with a black rage against him and her own helplessness in the face of Nagato's raw and brutal power. Again and again she had relayed the image of his disgusting flesh thrusting at her. Again and again she had smelt the sweat of him; the foul reek of the Beast.

On every step of that relentless journey Brandeis had fantasised retaliations; with words, bullets, knives. If only she could have struck out. Cut. Slashed. Hacked. In her mind's pitiless eye she watched Nagato writhing and bleeding from her knifestroke; at her rake of bullets. She saw herself clawing at his obsidian eyes with her nails; kicking; biting, gouging. Saw him brought to swift military justice; hanged, shot by a firing squad...

If only they could be ambushed! she mused. How she would enjoy seeing him die!

Brandeis stared hard at where she had seen him last. There was nothing to see. He had been swallowed by the rioting palisades of leaves and layer upon layer of creepers and plants clawing upwards towards the light that deckled the ceiling of the jungle high above. Her eyes probed deeper into the gloom, but there was nothing to see save formless shadows.

Insects roared and whirred with hesitant boldness. Butterflies, big as birds, staggered drunkenly from one blossom to another. Things scuttled unseen. The jungle seemed as expectant as a baited trap. Brandeis shivered and was glad she was not alone.

Oshima felt an overpowering urge to talk to the women.

All that morning, as they had marched, the sounds and shapes of long-forgotten words of spoken English, locked for years in the deep cellars of his mind, had synapsed their way up into the light: words of politeness, greeting, hail and farewell; colloquial expressions, scientific phrases, swearwords and obscenities, the use of which he had been carefully coached in by roguish colleagues.

What a year that had been! Struggling with his language problems, working alongside men whose names he had known from the classic texts of his discipline; men who, to his surprise, knew of his own work, had read his papers, wanted to work with him when he established his departments. A marvellous year spent wrestling joyfully with his thesis, breaking new ground, learning the latest methods of collection, classification and preservation.

That brief period of happiness had been cut bitterly short.

'You should have stayed in America,' his father told him over and over again when he made his visit home at the end of the year. 'This country is going to hell with these madmen running it. It's a police State.'

Drinking sake with an untypical abandon Professor Oshima had questioned his son closely about his life and work in America. 'Could you extend your studies there? Live and work there?' he had asked. The implications of his questions became apparent only when Oshima's own career was later destroyed in the wake of his father's.

He was back at UCLA in early 1937 and just beginning the final draft of his thesis when his father wrote regretfully to say he could no longer afford to support his son in America. He had been dismissed from his post as Professor of Political Philosophy at Tokyo Imperial University.

Oshima returned home on the first boat, to a Japan that was profoundly different from the one he had left. His father was suddenly an old, tired man, embittered by his dismissal – a professor no longer allowed to profess – and by the disgust he felt about the way things were going in his beloved Japan.

Eighteen months later, he and his wife were dead. A pathetic ritual suicide.

Only then had Oshima understood that his father had, in fact, been reaching out for help from his son. He had received none. Oshima was ashamed that he had been so preoccupied with his own narrow world that he had failed to hear his father's cry.

Ah, but that was all so long ago, thought Oshima ruefully. That part of his life he had once thought was real.

Oshima looked at his women prisoners

eating, delicate as foxmoths. What would be the point in talking? Except perhaps to Kurosumo, he had never talked much anyway. There was only pain in talk. No words he could speak to these women would enable him to control the forces they had unleashed.

And what did it matter? There was no past; no future. Oshima felt as though the whole fabric of his being was unstranding like old silk.

Already his complex of feelings about the women had compromised him hopelessly. To speak to them would only complicate matters beyond the possibility of action. He decided that he would say nothing.

Brandeis studied Oshima curiously. He was sitting opposite her, in profile, looking across the river. His face was gaunt and tired. At length he turned back and concentrated on his food. His eyes gleamed in the dark ivory face. For a moment he glanced up and briefly caught her eye, but immediately looked away.

Brandeis noticed that he seldom looked at them directly, but often, when she looked at him, she found him regarding them in an intense manner. She felt as if she and Winters were being studied under a microscope; being observed objectively, unthreateningly, without passion.

Who was he?' she wondered. What was he

thinking? What did he intend to do with them? Brandeis wanted to shout out the questions to him; shake him until he answered but, even as the questions crowded in, he rose to his feet.

She glanced concernedly at Winters, who was slumped, white-faced, against her tree. Surprisingly, as soon as Oshima moved she gave a rueful moue and got to her feet quickly, as though she were becoming stronger through this ordeal, rather than weaker.

They were about to don their packs when the officer shook his head and indicated by signs they should carry them loose in their hands.

Moritoh went over first.

Oshima looked at her and inclined his head. She was to go next.

The water looked mysterious, forbidding. Water frightened Brandeis, but she determined not to panic.

Fearfully she made her way down the steep bank and into the stream. She moved forward blindly; chest deep, then on the next step, chin deep. The force of the current exerted a subtle and insistent drag on her.

She gasped as the water partly covered her face, jerking her head up. Suddenly she lost her footing. She was out of her depth, off-centre: everything was on a curious sideways plane. Her pack, held high above her head, was driving her under as a hammer does a nail. Brandeis knew she was going to drown. She would have cried out, but the water covered her face. The trees and sky above her whirled in a panic of blackness and shafting light.

Suddenly there was an arm around her shoulders. The ground was under her feet once more. The officer was beside her in the stream, bracing her; steadying her. Brandeis clung to him feeling stupid and weak.

The panic subsided quickly as she caught her breath. She found herself looking directly into Oshima's face. He was regarding her with a curiously vexed gaze as though she were a house guest who, by clumsiness, had broken a precious vase.

He took her pack from her and, still gripping her right shoulder, pushed her towards the far bank. She felt Oshima pushing her and scrambled gratefully on to dry land. He handed up her pack and she climbed further up, relieved to be safe.

Brandeis turned back to watch him returning to the other side.

But something was wrong. She saw that Oshima was not moving. He stood there, chest deep, his black hair plastered flat on his head. Except for the slow, greenish surge of water moving past his bulk, causing a slight, sunstruck wake, everything was still. He seemed transfixed.

Brandeis saw that he was looking towards Winters. Brandeis followed his gaze. Winters too, was motionless, standing on the bank above him looking down, into Oshima's face.

Brandeis saw the two of them as caught between forces; like a ball at the peak of its parabola, at the instant before gravity exerts its force.

The jungle seemed as silent as a sound-proof vault; she could feel her heart thumping.

Winters was holding his pack in one hand. In the other, she held his gun. She was pointing it towards Oshima and the barrel was aimed directly at his heart.

Winters did not remember picking up the officer's pack, or his gun from where he had dropped them, but she had them in her hands; the heavy pack in her left hand and the gun in her right. It sat there held sweetly by the trigger grip, feeling balanced and natural.

Oshima was most of the way back, just below where she stood before he looked up. He stopped, silhouetted against a sparkling patch of water. His face was in shadow, featureless against the blinding light, but his eyes gleamed as though they were lit from within.

Winters found herself locked on to his gaze like a plane flying along a powerful radio signal.

It was only then that she became aware the gun was pointing at him. She was shocked by the circumstance of this sudden and unplanned acquisition of life and death power: incapable of the slightest movement.

On the periphery of this timeless tableau she was aware of Brandeis, a still, watchful figure; a reminder of their prisoner's talk of escape only hours before.

They were joined, Winters and Oshima, by a potential and lethal trajectory of steel, yet there was no fear in his eyes. His look expressed rather, regret.

Moritoh had his sights trained on the centre of Winters' chest. The tip of his foresight moved slightly with his breathing, up and slowly down. At the moment of decision, you steadied, breath held. The sights go rock solid and you are taken over by that curious and sweet sense of elation that comes with knowing that you are about to perform the ultimate act; take another man's life.

But now Moritoh felt only a sense of panic. A woman in his sights made him feel like an assassin.

She stood there; a clear target, haloed in light against the dark green of the forest, with the lieutenant's gun in her hand, threatening him.

He could shoot her. Perhaps he should

shoot her. Prisoners who pointed guns at their captors are shot down like dogs.

The foresight continued to move rhythmically, tracking the line of buttons on her shirt.

Moritoh felt as though he were conducting frozen music over a sequence from a silent film. In the scene, the lieutenant was a black granite fish that had been hooked by the woman; the two of them locked in a motionless death struggle. At any moment she would strike and Oshima would be dragged by an invisible thread of steel and landed, gasping for air, on the bank at her feet.

Moritoh made up his mind. There was nothing else for it. He steadied the foresight centred on her chest. He held his breath. His finger curled around the trigger.

Perhaps it was the sharp contrast of the sunlight striking the dark water which made it difficult to see, or perhaps it was simply that Oshima's thoughts were on the girl, but it was not until he was directly under the bank that he realised his deadly mistake. The woman was standing high above him, with his own gun in her hand, aiming it at him.

Oshima's system locked like a machine that seizes in mid-stroke.

His first reaction was puzzlement. She did not shoot; did not move. She seemed paralysed. He could read nothing in her face;

neither hate, nor fear, nor the corruption of power; nothing.

Although the gun was pointing straight at him, it was not so much aimed at his heart as angled at him merely by some geometric coincidence.

He did not feel afraid, but empty; the same sickening emptiness he had felt after those other deadly mistakes of the ambush and after he had exposed the women to Nagato's frenzy. Those mistakes! It was as if there were some death wish on him.

There came over him a feeling of disappointment. Was it all going to end here before he had unlocked all the words he wanted to speak to these women? Before he solved their mystery? Before he found out why the fates had caught him up in this affair?

He saw Winters thrust the foresight at him. He felt the nerves of his face and stomach flutter wretchedly; yet still he was unable to move.

He could have acted; dived to one side, spoiled her aim, but to move was impossible for him. To move was to disturb the creature and therefore to lose privilege of the observation.

The woman was looking straight into his eyes. With a feeling of disbelief he realised what she was going to do.

She handed him the gun.

Oshima gripped the barrel gently. She let

go at once. He stood there unable to move a muscle until Winters handed him his pack. Then, holding her own pack, and watching carefully where she put her feet, she came down into the water beside him as gracefully as a woman stepping into a bath.

There was an expression on her face Oshima could not bear. He turned away.

Already the woman was wading strongly through the water heading for the opposite bank. He swivelled round to watch her go and became aware of the girl staring incredulously at her companion.

Winters reached the far side and held her pack up to Brandeis. It was obvious to Oshima that the girl was angry. She took the pack and dropped it at her feet, then pulled her companion roughly from the water.

Oshima felt shaken and lost. He stared back at the bank from where they had come as though checking to see if the incident had actually happened, or had been some fantasy.

As Oshima climbed up the bank, Morotoh came out of the bush with his rifle held at the port. He said nothing, but Oshima was aware of the reproach on the boy's face. He saw Moritoh slip his safety catch back into place, evidence that he had seen Oshima's mistake.

Why had she not fired? he puzzled. Had she been aware that she would have died with Moritoh's bullet in her? Had she weighed up their chances of survival and decided pragmatically, cold-bloodedly, that this was not the time to shoot? Had she spared his life out of fear? Out of logic?

Oshima knew that these were not the reasons. The decision had been a woman's decision but, in a way, he wished it had been that of a soldier. He would have been able to accept that. Had she taken his life it would have solved everything. So many mistakes! And the march not yet half over.

Oshima felt a sense of dread, as though the fates were grooming him for some destiny worse than death.

Chapter 10

'Why?' Puzzled and angry, Brandeis gritted out the question as she pulled Mae up the river bank. 'Why, for Christ's sake, didn't you let him have it?'

Mae simply shook her head.

'Jesus, you make me puke,' Brandeis' voice was contemptuous. 'Can't you get anything right?'

They sat side by side, in bitter silence – Winters with her face buried in her hands, as though not willing to face the younger woman's anger.

The stupid bitch, Brandeis thought. Twice now Mae had had the chance to do something to free them from this nightmare. And twice, she had done nothing. Brandeis heard again Mae's stupid order to stay close to the wreck. Where had that got them? And now she had thrown away a perfect chance to act again.

But perhaps Mae had been right, Brandeis thought. The young soldier had probably been covering them. Even if Mae had killed the officer, what chance would the two of them have had against the other Japanese? Brandeis was no fool. She knew that behind it all lay the real question: without the officer what would be their fate at the hands of Nagato? Was that why Mae had not acted? Did Mae see, in the officer, their one chance of survival?

In that long moment when Winters had had the Japanese officer at her mercy, Brandeis' mind had crowded with fantasies: had seen herself with the gun, her captor in her sights, felt the squeeze of the trigger, the bucking of the weapon, live and lethal in her hand. She had seen the face of the enemy erased like chalk from a slate under the impact of her bullets.

Brandeis knew now that the face she had obliterated in her mind had been that of Nagato their attacker; the Enemy: not that of Oshima. And she knew, too, that had she been the one with the gun, she would have acted without thought and both she and Winters might have died for it.

Brandeis regretted once again having spoken rashly, and was ashamed of her feelings. She wanted to reach out and touch Winters to show that she understood her decision, but the moment was not right. Later, when her anger had subsided, she would make the gesture; but not now.

Despair crushed down on her. If, with a gun in their hands, they could not act, how were they going to escape; survive?

'If your name's on the bullet' was the phrase with which one of Brandeis' soldier lovers had once expressed his fatalism. She wondered if Winters' name and her own were on some bullet yet to be fired.

Escape was in Winters' mind, but the green, walled-in native track they travelled would have been as impossible to break out of as an iron steam pipe. At last it gave way to a government road – no wider than the width of a cart and heavily overgrown. It ran between high, overleaning towers of jungle and curved around a huge ridge that fell away steeply to their right. From time to time they picked their way along the edge of great washaways carved by the rains, the fresh scars on the slope made it look as if a giant had clawed furiously at the earth.

Even when there was a clearer view beyond the green tunnel they followed, Winters glimpsed, on the other side of the valley, a landscape exactly interchangeable with their own.

The cloud seemed to press down upon them, obscuring the tops of the ridges. The air was steamy. Warm rain coursed down their faces, blackening their clothes and boots. It felt as though they had never been dry, and never would be dry again.

Winters felt as though she was suspended between the rot and genesis of the jungle. When the sun shone the smell of decaying vegetation was all around; their clothes stank of it.

How could you learn to find your way out of this maze? she wondered. What subtle indicators would you learn to read; a tree here, a meeting of paths there?

Once, far below, Winters caught sight of a river whose valley, half a mile and perhaps a day's march away, turned some meaningless corner, going nowhere. Apart from brief intervals there was no sun to act as a guide. It was mostly hidden behind the swirling rain mist that rolled in from somewhere; north, south, who could tell?

Winters wondered how men could live like this; spying out the track furtively; moving forward cautious as hunted beasts; stopping to listen as though for the baying pack;

scouting, moving, stalking, hour after hour, day after day: living dead preserved in the formaldehyde of the jungle's putrefaction.

Not even looking at her watch, which for some reason her captors had not taken from her, could convince Winters that the time it showed was the real time in this unreal world.

Two o'clock. To her aching body it seemed much later. She needed to sleep, to stop walking just for a moment, to cease the piston-like pattern of her own sodden boots coming into view: left, right; left, right.

From time to time Brandeis would glance back attempting an encouraging look, but her eyes betrayed her own fear and exhaustion.

How could fear belong in the world of such a beautiful child? Winters had complex feelings about the girl. Laughter and love were the conditions that should prevail for someone so young. Oh, she was spoiled. Headstrong. Without an idea of self-discipline. And she had proved to have a cutting tongue. But there was no real malice in her. Their quarrel had been the result of Winters' authority opposed to Brandeis' natural rebelliousness; plus the kind of terrible strains that provoke hurtful truths. Sally, who had never done any real harm to anyone in her life.

Winters speculated with a real sense of pity about her companion. As far as she knew Brandeis had only known those quick exchanges of service-life passion that were but the counterfeits of love. Never to have loved! What a waste, if Sally were to die here, in some fickle way, without having known someone the way she, Winters, had known David.

Winters was never more grateful than now for having experienced that all-consuming passion for her lover.

That attic room in Balmain, all soft places and angled light, by the edge of the Harbour, with the dawn colouring the Bridge in gold and green. And the smell of him and the taste of him and the imprint of his kisses on her flesh.

That marvellous coincidence that had brought them together again in Buna: nursing him after his wound; slipping once more into the silken mesh of one another's being.

The sound of the gramophone playing dance music somewhere back there in the darkness; the rough texture of an army blanket under them; his soft scar tissue healing on his too-thin chest. The sense of wonder that it was just as good as it had been before.

As she trudged on, Winters swore to herself that never again would she allow guilt to sully those memories. She thought of the nickname the sisters apparently had for David – the one that Sally had blurted out when the two of them were quarrelling. She couldn't bring herself to say it, but a ghostly affectionate laugh sounded within Winters. David would be flattered by that.

Her boots were sinking now in ankle-deep black mud. Her breath heaved as they struggled up a greasy incline in the track. Yet, in spite of all the hardship, Winters suddenly felt released. All this was an expiation. Her hard-dying habit of guilt had never been less of a burden than now.

'Take what you want and pay the price,' David's Arab proverb.

At the time she had met David she had badly needed to take. The guilt price had seemed too high, then. Unable to tell Ian, she had paid a terrible toll.

David had pressed the right buttons. They conducted their affair on the run whenever they could arrange leave passes; in hotel rooms, parks, anywhere. It was reckless, wonderful.

At first she ignored the guilt. Her only regret was that they were obliged to be furtive and secretive, when all she wanted to do was to shout it from the rooftops.

Yet perhaps that furtive, hole-in-the-corner behaviour had had its value. At least Ian had never known. Why would you tell a man such a truth? Afterwards, when he was dead, she had been grateful for her lie of omission. Ian had died, as far as she could know, thinking that nothing had changed; thinking they had been in love. And perhaps briefly, they had been.

Now she was here; being hustled along a hidden trail in a frightening, eerie jungle the prisoner of men she did not know, going someplace she did not dare think about.

At least Winters sought comfort from the thought that she had loved. There was that to compensate, whatever else might await her.

Someone coming! Moritoh was suddenly right in front of them signalling urgently as he came.

Something lurched in Brandeis' breast, but she was given no time to consider the implications. They were both grabbed firmly and bundled off the track into the bush. Within a moment they were five yards into the tangle. The trail, that narrow evidence of man in this primeval place, might never have existed.

The squad leader moved behind them silently, his gun pointing directly at them. The three Japanese moved carefully.

Another couple of yards, then Oshima signalled them to get down. The soldiers squatted down immediately in front of them.

There might have been something in Brandeis' face as she looked over in the direction of the track straining to hear the intruders. Nagato made an eloquent, throat-cutting gesture.

Oshima leaned forward close enough for her to feel his breath on her ear.

173

'My squad leader will kill you if you make the slightest sound. Understand?'

As though he had heard the words Nagato moved the tip of his weapon in a short arc so that it pointed directly at her.

'Now, please, flat on the ground.'

Brandeis rolled over and lay face down. Winters followed suit and they lay, side by side, looking in anguish at one another.

Nagato lay half on his side, close enough for her to be conscious of his rank smell and see the weave of the rotting fabric of his uniform. His knife was a few inches from her throat.

The blade looked black in the rainy gloom of their hiding place. Brandeis caught his eye. Sudden death dwelt there. She jerked round, seeking Winters' comforting gaze. Almost imperceptibly Winters shook her head. This was not the time to try anything.

They lay on the rotting green floor of the jungle and held their breath listening for the sound of the unseen intruders. A thick silence. Even the jungle seemed to be listening.

Close to Brandeis' face; a tangled, muddy microcosm of the formless world they inhabited. She felt like some god, looking down at a jungle landscape where anonymous creatures played out their rituals of survival.

Was some enormous presence similarly looking down at them, engaged in this game of life and death that seemed to have no apparent logic, no rules?

Brandeis felt herself overtaken by an overpowering urge to stand up and shout out that the game was over. She wanted to go home. She was tired of this charade.

The compulsion to bolt began to act on her muscles. She began to tremble violently and had to gag herself with her fist jammed into her mouth.

Winters' hand moved on to her arm anchoring her to life. The trembling subsided, then stopped. Relief flooded through Brandeis as she got a grip on herself.

A sound; almost at the limits of her perception; more a pressure on her ears. A creak of fabric perhaps, no more. She saw the officer stiffen. She looked back at the squad leader. Nagato was looking at her with the same deadly expression on his face, but now there was a goading part to it that dared her to try something. Brandeis forced her head away and stared back in the direction of the track.

Something registered on Brandeis' retina; no more than a momentary shadow. After a long time another, then another; fragmented images of the legs of men in green uniforms passing them within a few yards. Not men with faces; there was no substance to them in the variegated gloom; only the impression of olive cloth and steel passing her low line of vision.

For ten aching minutes afterwards they lay perfectly still in the sepulchral silence of the forest. Brandeis had a frightening image of herself grown over by creeping vines, pinned to the ground by the living fingers of the jungle, forever unable to cry out.

Now the raucous and irrational sounds of birds signalled that the intruders had passed.

She felt like weeping. The patrol had been of their own kind: warm, friendly men who would have comforted them and healed them and taken them home again.

During that uneasy, silent wait Brandeis became acutely aware of how helpless and nakedly vulnerable they were; she and Winters. Until now their captors had given them no time to think. Her mind crowded with fears. Once more they would be driven forwards into the unknown, moving further from hope with every step they took.

Brandeis turned to Winters whose sorrow showed in her eyes. Winters' hand moved a few inches until it covered Brandeis' hand comfortingly. All the sulphurous anger that had burned between them for so long ended with Winters' gesture. Brandeis saw Winters' encouraging smile refract through a prism of tears.

Oshima dispatched Moritoh to reconnoitre the trail. When the boy had gone he allowed the women to sit up.

Uneasy silence. Nagato staring goadingly at the women, Oshima unable to move, preoccupied with his own anguished thoughts. Cling as he might to his own dogged, methodical, personal discipline, he had been aware for a long time of his own descent into chaos. From the women Oshima derived some stability – they were a pair. They represented symmetry, logic and order. He had only ever been able to grasp things when he could see a pattern: they were a reminder that there had been, once, a framework to his life; not the eternal disorder of an arbitrary and random nature, not the jungle's anarchy of death and violence that he had come to know and detest.

The prisoners sat opposite him with their backs against the bole of a huge tree as though pinned to one of his display boards with bayonets. They looked infinitely sad. Already, Oshima noted, regretfully, they had begun to lose their lustre; already they were sad travesties of the unique specimens which had set his heart trembling with excitement. Their colours were fading; a fine coating of dust had begun to settle on them; their gossamer wings had begun to fray at the edges.

...*your tattered collection.*

Kurosumo'd been right. The sharp-edged remembrance of his loving friend, long dead, almost made Oshima cry out with grief.

Many times before Oshima had lain as the enemy passed within a few feet of a hiding place. He had felt only the thrilling tension that comes from a proximity to danger. But, minutes before, when the enemy patrol had slipped past, Oshima had recognised them as silent harbingers of his own coming death. He felt that his fate was slipping relentlessly from his own careful grasp.

He was a prisoner of his prisoners. He knew it, Nagato knew it and it occurred to Oshima that the women knew it too.

'We ought to kill them right now.' Nagato spoke the words matter of factly.

His brutal statement snapped Oshima out of his reverie. He stared at his squad leader with revulsion, as though seeing him for the first time. Something that had come from under a stone. But in truth, Nagato had struck a nerve. He was right. There was no room here for complications.

Until now it had all been so simple. When his career had finally crumbled and he had followed Kurosumo's example and joined the Army, the shock of service life had immobilised him, the first few months had been miserable. But then, as though he had been a clockwork soldier set down facing in another direction, Oshima had moved directly forward, proving to be as single-minded and brilliant at soldiering as he had been with everything else.

His grip of English had been sound enough to take him into intelligence work. In the Malayan campaign and again in the drive south to New Guinea he had served with distinction. He was given his own Section to operate in hostile country, probing the enemy defences to gather information about their movements, size and strength.

Oshima found a scientist's fascination in the work. His effortless energy, his absorption with the task in hand, his training in the business of unlocking secrets and patterns, of being able to see the truth and structure underlying the surface of observable fact, and above all, his insights, made him an outstanding intelligence officer.

The jungle was his laboratory; only the specimens were different. Everything else was the same. It made no difference that his knowledge now came from dead men, from bloodied map cases and wallets, photographs and unposted love letters. It was simply information which with careful analysis, would yield results. You went about your job armoured against feeling by logic. You had no more lust for killing than a soldier art impregnable to the doubt of dream.

But now doubt had entered. These captives were a deadly new factor. A failed ambush and nine of his charges rotting around a wreck were proof of that.

'Your women are going to get us killed,'

Nagato gouged away. 'Sir.'

Again Oshima remained silent. He looked at the women.

It was clear they had been disturbed greatly by the proximity of their own kind; soldiers whose appearance had implied their own death as much as his.

Once more Oshima was struck by their complementary beauty; like two halves of the same exquisite creature. As the dirt, mud and decay of the forest blurred their outlines, they had begun to fuse in his mind. They were becoming creatures of the forest taking on the protective resemblance to their surroundings. Oshima had the odd impression that they would finally coalesce into one unity that would, in turn, fuse with this wild and disordered nature.

Who were they? What did they think? What did they feel? From where had they come? It occurred to him that he did not even know their names.

Like all the specimens he had ever studied he knew only the most superficial things about them. He could classify them: homo sapiens, female, Caucasian race. Describe them – their plumage, shape, coloration, size, weight, skin texture. But still he did not know them any better than his thousands of other matched pairs. No matter how much he observed these women, these gorgeous exotics, he would never understand anything about them.

But then all women had been equally mysterious to Oshima. His mother had been one mystery: fussing endlessly over his father, always anxious, always talking, never saying anything. She had taught him nothing about her sex.

Neither had he learned anything of them in those days and nights when Kurosumo had decided he needed to be introduced to Life and had dragged him reluctant, into the real world of flesh; faceless, nameless girls, bought and paid for. Their expert hands, their soft bodies, had told him nothing of what they thought, or felt. They had assuaged drives, had performed their function like robots, had been forgotten the moment he had returned to his laboratory.

'There's no need to take them along,' Nagato drew his knife. 'If it's information you want, I'll get it for you in two minutes.'

Nagato's knife blade drew all their eyes.

The women stared fearfully at Nagato.

Oshima felt nothing but contempt for Nagato and for himself.

Yet another matched pair.

His study had been lined with them; hundreds upon hundreds of specimens that were the admiration of his peers. What was it Kurosumo had called them, 'your ragged collection of corpses'?

It was only after Kurosumo had resigned

that the futility of it all had become apparent. In the year that followed, butting like a blind worm against the political realities, paralysed by despair and bewilderment, Oshima had worked on alone in his laboratory department.

Then, that day on Mimoro's sacred mountain, he had faced the truth about himself. The following day he had returned to Tokyo, destroyed his collection, burned his notes and left the campus forever.

Truth had entered and destroyed him then, as surely as it was destroying him now.

'If you ask me you're making a…' Nagato pretended to grope for the right word, 'fatal mistake.' Nagato had a cynical smile on his face.

With a parodied look of regret he clicked his knife back into its sheath.

Oshima ignored him, continuing to look in the direction from which Moritoh would return.

About Nagato and himself, Oshima cared not at all, but it troubled him deeply that his action in taking the women prisoner, might spell mortal danger to Moritoh, for whom Oshima had deep and complex feelings.

More than anything else he hated Nagato for the truth he spoke.

The rain stopped and the late afternoon sun was blazing again when they came to the

182

broken sandbanks of a shallow river at the bottom of a wide valley.

The jungle stopped abruptly as thought it had been violently cleft by the steel-blue water.

They spent a long time under the last cover afforded by the forest while Oshima studied the banks on both sides, upstream and down, through his field glasses. The river: forty yards of dazzling water on which they would stand out like diamonds on black cloth. He felt apprehensive at the prospect of crossing that space that yawned before them beguilingly. How he hated open spaces, thought Oshima. How much more bearable it was in this familiar claustrophobia of rioting vegetation: this reach-out-and-touch security of the jungle.

He sent the squad leader over first. Nagato waded away though the shallow water. The four of them watched him take a seeming age to gain the cover of the far side. He did not look back once.

Moritoh went next with the girl. Oshima and Winters stood side by side and watched the two make their slow crossing. They moved easily through the meandering water, at most waist deep.

Watching them Oshima could feel his stomach churn. He had felt nothing when Nagato had crossed, but with Moritoh and the girl, it was different. Both of them seemed to move in deliberate slow motion. Oshima was shaken by their vulnerability; their harsh light-and-shadow silhouettes etched sharp as figure targets against the shining mirror of river. He forced them along their silent way with an unvoiced stream of curses.

Winters, too, had felt anxious about Brandeis making her way over to where their tormentor stood watching, no doubt, from the mysterious and foreboding shadows of the far bank.

She looked anxiously at Oshima and made as if to follow. He shook his head.

'No. Please wait.' Again the sound of her own language surprised and slightly shocked her. The words sounded strange coning from that alien face.

Oshima said something to her in a low, clear voice.

For a moment Winters did not register the meaning of the words. She turned and looked at him in astonishment, but already Oshima was looking towards the far bank, his face closed and still, as though he regretted having let something slip.

'I am sorry,' he had said.

She stared at him wondering if she had only imagined the words, or misheard. At length, he turned to her, the planes on his face softer. He looked unhappy.

'About this.' He made a slight gesture that encompassed the place and the situation.

Winters acknowledged his words with a rueful moue, not really sure how to respond.

He made as if to speak once more, but checked himself and turned his gaze back towards the others already approaching the sandbank on the far side.

They watched Brandeis and Moritoh wade clear of the water, the sun glinting on the tiny waves they carried on to the bank with them, to disappear out of sight into the dark sanctuary of the jungle.

'We go now.' Oshima began to move, but Winters did not follow.

'What will happen to us?' She heard herself ask in a clear, but unsteady voice.

Oshima stopped and stood staring at her for a long time, as if he were in a trance. Then, without seeming to have understood her question, he turned abruptly and headed across the sandbank towards the river.

Winters followed him, feeling naked and vulnerable as she entered the spotlight glare of the sun.

When, at last, Moritoh and Brandeis had made the safety of the jungle beyond the river, Nagato had been waiting for them, his face expressionless.

Behind them, the lieutenant and Winters had begun their crossing. Moritoh was concentrating on watching the opposite bank for signs of trouble when he became aware of a muffled sound behind him.

He turned to see Nagato, with one arm around Brandeis' neck, his hand covering her mouth His other hand was down the front of her shirt.

The girl struggled wildly in his grasp but was helpless to cry out.

'Leave her!' Moritoh's angry words ground out spontaneously from some terrible anger inside him.

Nagato, grinning sardonically, ignored him. Continued to fondle the girl's breasts grotesquely while she fought unavailingly.

Perhaps it was a soldier's response, or perhaps there was something more personal in it, but instinctively Moritoh pointed his rifle at Nagato, aiming from the hip.

The squad leader lost his grin, but went on regardless. Moritoh brought his weapon to his shoulder, slipped off his safety catch and aimed deliberately at Nagato's forehead. For a moment Nagato went completely still. Moritoh felt a surge of panic when he saw the expression of cold hatred in Nagato's eyes.

Suddenly the tension was broken. Nagato laughed derisively and flung the girl away from him. Brandeis barely recovered her balance without falling. She stood looking at her attacker, frightened and shocked, her breath coming in harsh, broken gasps.

She pressed her bruised flesh and her face betrayed her pain.

'That's the last time you'll point your gun at me, Rich Boy,' Nagato said, evenly.

Moritoh kept his rifle aimed.

Nagato bent down slowly and, with his eyes on Moritoh, picked up his weapon.

'From now on,' he said, 'you'd better not turn your back.'

Moritoh risked a fleeting glance towards the river. Lieutenant Oshima and the woman were practically across the river. The girl stood watching them come, near to tears. Her hands were clutched protectively across her breasts.

Shaking slightly, Moritoh lowered his rifle. He was overcome by a feeling of despair. To have threatened Nagato was suicidal.

Oshima and Winters joined them, their clothes streaming with water. They saw, at once, that something had happened.

Winters rushed to Brandeis and put her arms around her.

'What did they do to you?'

Moritoh saw that the girl did not reply; simply shook her head as though not wanting to talk about the incident. He felt curiously detached from the scene. His pre-occupation was inward. He knew that he had just made the deadliest of enemies. Moritoh was frightened in a new and very particular way. Nagato represented, in Moritoh's mind, fear itself.

'What happened?' Oshima's anger showed

187

in a pinched look about his mouth.

Nagato said nothing. Oshima repeated the question to Moritoh. Conscious of Nagato's eyes upon him, he simply shook his head.

At that moment, Brandeis broke free of Winters' arms and, to Moritoh's astonishment, walked a few paces to stand in front of Nagato. Very deliberately she spat on the ground at his feet.

Nagato's weapon was up and pointing straight at the girl.

'Nagato!'

Oshima's harsh cry had just enough authority to prevent Nagato pulling the trigger.

A murderous, crackling silence. The pent-up force of Nagato's rage seemed to charge the air all round them.

'Go on ahead,' ordered Oshima.

Nagato seemed to jerk out of a trance. His eyes swung on to Oshima. He stared at his officer wildly for a long moment then, very slowly, he lowered his weapon.

'Go on ahead,' repeated Oshima, his voice oddly placatory as though he were talking to someone sleep-walking on the edge of a cliff. Nagato walked off into the jungle like an automaton.

His going left them shaken. They stood like actors waiting for a principal character to remember forgotten lines. At last Oshima harshly ordered them to move. Numbly they stumbled on into the maw of the jungle.

Part 4

THE BEAST

Chapter 11

Once more, very slowly and carefully, Moritoh swept the field glasses over the ragged village. He still felt shaken by the events of the past few hours. First the lieutenant's carelessness in allowing his gun to be taken by the woman; then his own terrible mistake in confronting Nagato.

At the very instant he had been about to shoot the woman, she had handed over Oshima's gun as casually as if it were a parcel, then she and the lieutenant were wading together towards him for all the world like bathers by the edge of the sea.

Shooting the woman would have been one thing; threatening Nagato was entirely another. How could he have been so stupid? He scarified himself, and cursed the girl for having been the catalyst of all his present fears.

The native huts lay on the other side of an overgrown garden carved out of the jungle on the side of a steep hill.

Some old women with pendulous, sexless breasts were hoeing the soil in desultory fashion, clearly unaware that he was only a few yards from them.

Some banana palms grew down one side of

the garden and he could see the dark green leaves of sweet potato; the russet of sago.

Three ragged huts and a bigger communal house huddled together in a space of light; a beleaguered fort barring the inexorable, forward-creeping voraciousness of the forest.

Moritoh always felt a sense of wonder when he saw these primitive villages hacked out of this wilderness he hated so much. Even the fragile sense of order afforded by the crude dwellings gave him pleasure. He feasted his eyes on it as a desert traveller might, seeing an oasis.

How often he longed for the clamour of Tokyo's raucous streets, instead of this unnerving ticking silence. How often he had wondered, why, if his father and his like were so keen on conquering territory, they coveted this stinking country? Everything about the jungle made his flesh creep, with its unexplained sounds, its mud, the enemy, the hostile blacks; its stinging, biting, whining, crawling, slithering insects.

In the doorway of the bigger hut Moritoh could pick out some old men sprawling on the ground. The lieutenant could find out from them if there were any enemy patrols in the area. There were no children, and no animals save for a few scraggy hens anxiously pecking at the ground between the huts. Smoke drifted up, wavering uncertainly towards the clearing, mid-afternoon sky.

Moritoh was suspicious about the deserted state of the village; either it had been raided recently, or the intruders had been spotted on the way in, or else it was a trap.

Most of the villages they passed through were like this; near-deserted. Unless they were taken by surprise only the old, lame and halt were ever left behind. And that happened less and less. The locals had good reason to be frightened of the soldiers. They knew it was best to take no chances with their young men, or especially with their women.

Most likely that they had been spotted, Moritoh reasoned. The jungle was full of eyes. The inhabitants, likely enough, would be deep in the forest by now and would return only when the intruders were long gone.

Moritoh had left the track and approached the village through the bush, moving laterally, careful to keep himself orientated by the sun. It was all too easy to get hopelessly lost in the space of a few yards. He had felt particularly vulnerable on his way to this vantage point. He had seen nothing tangible, but twice an inexplicable flicker of movement, like a shadow, had caught the very outer edge of his vision. The hair on the back of his neck had risen and the skin on his back had anticipated one of the wicked barbed spears the blacks used with such silent and deadly effect on the rearguards of patrols.

But now it was not so much the blacks

that bothered him; Squad Leader Nagato was his main concern.

Moritoh was not only afraid of Nagato. He was jealous of him. The squad leader, that upjumped clerk, now knew something he, Moritoh, was deeply curious about; how the girl felt to the touch.

Several times, when they were making their brief private river crossing together, Moritoh had been tempted to reach out and touch Brandeis, perhaps on the pretext of steadying her. He had not done so. To Moritoh there was a purity about her. Brandeis' compelling combination of fair hair, brown skin and those ice-blue eyes awed him.

That had not stopped Nagato, and the taste he had stolen would cost her pain. Of that Moritoh was certain.

He tried to rein in his fear and anger. If he were to survive this journey he would need to keep his head. It had been bad enough when the squad leader had only had the authority conferred upon him by his rank. Now, with all restraint apparently gone, he was terrifying.

Moritoh was in no doubt that Nagato would kill him the first chance he had. It occurred to Moritoh, with a helpless sense of being able to do absolutely nothing to prevent it, he would be a dead man the next time they were in action together.

He panned the field glasses slowly over the

village yet again. Satisfied that there was nothing there that could endanger them, he snaked backwards through the bush to report to his lieutenant.

Winters was saddened by the sight of the village. It had a neglected, spiritless appearance; as though it had given up the unequal fight against the jungle. There were a few sagging huts and some ancient men sitting in the doorway of one of them in a haze of smoke.

As they made their careful approach, Nagato leading the way, she became conscious of some old women moving up from the garden, chattering in high voices. They carried with them their pointed digging sticks.

The old men watched sleepily. They seemed to be sharing some kind of pipe. Winters guessed it was probably a drug. But when Oshima began talking in rapid pidgin, one of them scrambled hastily to his feet. He kept shaking his head sullenly in answer to Oshima's questions.

The village women came close; seven of them with thin, emaciated bodies and shrivelled, dry dugs. Their faces registered astonishment and their jay voices shrilled with excitement, their eyes on the two white women. They ignored the soldiers who were looking around carefully, obviously uneasy about being in the open.

The women approached nearer and nearer

until they were crowded around Winters and Sally, chattering, giggling and reaching to touch them. Their hair was matted with dirt. There was ash and mud all over their bodies. They smelled of pigs.

The commotion they were making obviously upset the soldiers. Nagato glowered at them menacingly, but this only seemed to slow their interest temporarily.

Winters smiled at the women. She saw that Sally was grinning too and miming having her hands tied like a captive, trying to explain that they were not with the Japanese by choice.

This produced a gale of laughter and much shouting.

Winters felt hands touching her hair and she swung around to smile at the women behind her.

She heard the squad leader say something sharply to the village women, but they ignored him.

Suddenly Nagato was driving them away, pushing at them and slapping. The women fell back. One of them laughed at him. He lashed out at her, striking her on the face. She fell with a cry of fear, her forehead bleeding.

'Leave them alone, you bloody swine,' Brandeis shouted, enraged. She bent over the women to pick her up. Nagato grabbed her by the shoulder and propelled her past the women. Angrily, Brandeis shook off the squad leader's hand, glaring at him, her face distorted by rage.

'Bastard!'

He ignored this and crowded them both twenty yards away from the villagers, pushing at them two-handed with his gun. They heard Oshima say something sharply. Nagato answered back, annoyed. In a moment the two men were shouting at each other.

Moritoh was some yards off looking around nervously. 'The first chance we get, I'm off. The bastard's insane.' Brandeis spoke in a low, scared voice.

The hostility between the Japanese was beginning to surface in an alarming way. Winters could see that only Sally and she would be the losers. It was becoming increasingly obvious to her that Lieutenant Oshima was unable to keep Nagato under control.

They saw the argument finish abruptly. Nagato went off behind one of the huts, pulling his knife. One of the women began to wail. Oshima shouted at them. There was a tense and angry silence.

After a brief time Winters saw the squad leader return with three dead hens in his hand. There was a brief murmur of anger from the villagers, instantly silenced when Nagato threatened them with his weapon.

The soldiers then went in and out of the huts as though foraging, but they returned empty-handed.

Ten minutes after they had arrived, they left the village under the glowering gaze of its inhabitants.

Winters looked back at the villagers and, on an impulse, waved. There was no response, which left her feeling dejected.

The track turned a bend; the village disappeared as if a curtain had been pulled.

Chapter 12

Twenty minutes out of the village, moving fast. Nagato was about ten yards ahead when, suddenly, he vanished.

Moritoh cried out and, at that exact moment a spear nicked Oshima's shoulder.

The sound of a shot, from in front.

Oshima hit the ground. Another spear drove into the soft mud a few inches in front of his face. He swivelled round and round and fired a burst into one side of the track; then the other.

There was a scream and some shouting. He caught a fleeting impression of Moritoh with a spear sticking out of the middle of his back; the women frozen in the centre of the track, then he was scrambling desperately deep into cover.

He fired again; again there was a scream. How many of them? Oshima wondered. He crawled forward rapidly, firing blind, burrowing as deep into cover as he could. He paused long enough to change the magazine, then went on again. There was a thrashing in the dense bush in front of him and to his right. Oshima fired once more; the movement stopped.

Far over to his right; another burst of firing. Oshima guessed it came from Nagato. That lunatic. Oshima was angered. If Nagato had kept his hands to himself in the village, they might not have had this trouble. Oshima had no doubt now that their attackers were the young men of the village. They must have hidden when he arrived there, seen the vulnerability of his little group, and planned this ambush.

The thrashing had been made by a black. He was nearly dead. Oshima made sure with a single shot.

Silence; then over to his left the crackling of undergrowth as someone got away. He wondered if Moritoh had died by spear.

'Moritoh?' he shouted, anxiously.

There was a cry in reply. Oshima felt a flood of relief. The boy was alive. Getting to his feet cautiously Oshima made his way in a low crouch towards the sound. Was Moritoh wounded? He had seen him speared, of that Oshima was sure.

'Nagato?' This time, no reply. Had he, too, been hit? Oshima wondered. He glanced at his own shoulder. Only a slight graze. Again he heard Moritoh cry out.

Oshima moved with extreme caution. He saw something and stopped, his heart pounding. It was another black. The man was sitting on the ground with blood spouting slowly from a bullet wound in his thigh. He looked up, his face calm. Oshima shot him with a short burst. The black fell back, his chest a wreck, and in a few moments was still.

A few yards further on Moritoh was kneeling wide-eyed on the ground, beside the body of another dead black, his rifle trained on Oshima's chest. He lowered it with relief.

Out of the centre of his pack, a long spear stuck up like the raked mast of a ship. Oshima walked over to him and, without a word, pulled the spear. It's wicked barbs caught in the fabric of Moritoh's pack and it was difficult to tear it free.

'You were lucky.' He gave a brief smile, running his fingers along the deadly serrations.

'I got one of them,' Moritoh was breathing hard, his eyes gleaming.

'That's three at least.' Oshima dropped the spear. 'A couple of others back there. See many?'

'Didn't see any.' Moritoh spoke ruefully. 'Not even him.' He nodded at the dead man by his feet.

'The rest have gone, I think.'

'Nagato?' Moritoh asked.

'He was firing a while ago – from over there. Let's go.'

They went back to the track.

The women were gone.

Dead? Oshima felt sick. He went rapidly along the track. Stopped. Listened.

Moritoh was about to speak, but Oshima caught his eye and held up his hand for silence.

From far below the track, on the downhill slope to their right, came the faint sounds of movement through the jungle; a swish of leaves, the distant crackle of twigs snapping.

Moritoh raised his eyebrows quizzically.

'The prisoners?'

Oshima felt oddly light-headed. He listened again. The sounds had ceased.

'Shall I get them?' Moritoh made to move off.

'No!'

The boy was puzzled, surprised.

'But, sir…'

Was this the answer to his dilemma, Oshima wondered, simply let them go?

'First we'll find Nagato,' he said. 'He might have been hit.' Then, for Moritoh's benefit: 'They won't get far.'

Moritoh seemed about to protest again, but then his expression changed. He remained silent. Oshima had the feeling that he understood.

Suddenly they were alone. In the silence after the firing and screaming Brandeis knew that this was the moment she had been waiting for single-mindedly since Nagato had pawed her by the river. This time she decided she would not discuss it with Mae. The prison door had swung open; in front of them was the haven of freedom.

'Let's go.' Brandeis was aware of the sound of her own voice; harsh with tension.

'No!' Winters shook her head and looked anxiously in the direction of the fighting. There had been silence for a few minutes now. 'They'll be back.'

'Yes!' Brandeis moved off the track feeling angry with Winters. Christ! It was staring them in the face. This *was* the moment. There was no time to stand around and debate.

'Sally! No! This isn't it.'

'Bugger you! You said we'd go the first chance we got.'

'It just doesn't feel right...'

'Well, I'm going.' She began moving determinedly. 'You can stay if you bloody like.'

Winters went with her, hesitantly.

For a few yards they moved slowly, furtively, as though creeping from a room in which a gaoler was sleeping. Then the firing and shouting began again, propelling them with great force, faster and faster until they were moving down the steep slope in a shambling, blind run.

Winters was ahead of her and to the left. Brandeis stayed as close as she could. *Mustn't get separated.* She wanted to shout: 'Slow down, slow down!' but she dared not cry out. Down, down through the gauntlet of claws and blades: thorns, razor grass, snares of creeper; hands in front of her face to protect her eyes.

Winters was further ahead. Too far. Thick foliage separated them. She was out of sight now.

Suddenly Brandeis pitched headlong over a fallen branch. She scrambled to her feet, winded. Although she could hear Winters crashing through the jungle somewhere below her, she could no longer see her. She began to run after her companion then stopped uncertainly.

'Mae?' It was no more than an anguished whisper.

She heard only the diminishing sounds of Winters' progress.

'Mae!' Louder this time, although she dared not cry out. Her voice seemed to travel nowhere, absorbed by the trees. She heard only the diminishing sound of Winters' progress.

An eerie silence.

She was alone.

'Oh, God!'

Brandeis looked around in awe. The trees reared up over her balefully.

Seized with panic, she began to stumble down through the menacing green maze.

Winters stopped suddenly, realising to her horror that she was alone.

She looked back up the steep slope. Brandeis had gone; vanished. She would reappear soon, Winters reassured herself.

Minutes passed, but there was no sound save for the humming stillness of the jungle, dozing indifferently in the afternoon sun. Nothing moved.

Had Sally fallen? Been caught? Vexed, worried now and annoyed Winters began to make her way slowly and carefully back up the slope.

Winters was angry with herself for not having put her foot down.

Damn Sally! Wilful little bitch. Where the hell did she imagine they would run to?

Winters' mind crowded with anxious thoughts. They might never find one another in this featureless maze. If she went all the way back to the track she was bound to run into the Japanese. *Oh God, would this nightmare never end?*

She wondered how far had she come since

she had last been aware of Sally crashing along beside her, no more than a yard or so away? How stupid not to have kept together. But that mindless terrified flight had emptied her mind of rational thought.

As she moved upwards, Winters' mouth grew dry with a growing fear that Brandeis had been caught and killed. *Oh, no. They wouldn't kill her in cold blood, surely?*

Winters knew very well they might do worse. She thought of the squad leader's knife and a chill suffused her insides. There was something especially terrible about knives. (In her mind, Nagato crouched behind a young soldier: a knife: a line of scarlet at his throat.) *Oh no no no.*

Upwards: slowly, cautiously.

Something moving there?

Nothing. On again.

Damn Sally. If she had fallen she could have cried out. But, maybe she did.

Winters practically tripped over the dead man. He was looking straight at her, but his eyes saw nothing. She barely managed to suppress the scream that rose in her.

She stood hypnotised by the sight of the dead warrior, his long, fragile bow still clutched in his free hand. It seemed such a pathetic thing to pit against the guns of the Japanese.

He lay flat on his back wedged against a fallen tree. His left hand was pressed against his stomach, but it could not cover the gaping tear in his flesh through which his guts had oozed, spectacularly red, pink and white against the grey-black of his skin.

In spite of Winters' long and close acquaintance with death, it took her a long time to squat down beside him. She could see he was dead, but an ingrained habit caused her to feel for the pulse at his neck. Nothing, of course. His flesh was already growing cold. She closed his eyes.

A magnificent, muscular body, his skin marred by some disease that also pocked his face. He would have been about sixteen; the face bony and strong, the curly hair a thick, beehive thatch. His sex was revealed under the faded lap lap he wore. Somehow that made the young man's death seem all the more pathetic.

Winters stood up.

Again the thought that Sally was dead forced its way into her reluctant brain. Was she, too, lying here in this wilderness; perhaps even hurt and dying, with this pitiless jungle waiting to claim her?

How in God's name am I going to find Sally?

She blamed herself for leaving the girl behind. The all-too-familiar wave of self-revulsion swept over her. She had persuaded Sally to stay by the plane when they would have been better off getting away from it; she had failed to shoot the officer when she had had his gun in her hand. And now this. Running blindly; thinking only of herself, not knowing until it was too late that Sally was no longer with her.

What was she going to do? Winters felt helpless. Sally could be half a mile back, or fifty yards. In this horrible, lunatic tangle she might never find her; but she must look. She might be hurt and simply lie there until she rotted, literally rotted, where she had fallen.

Logic began to slither away from Winters like the string of a freed kite. Desperately she clutched after it; steadied. She knew what she must do.

As she began to move on up, something familiar took her eye. A fleur de lys design.

The dead warrior was wearing a leather belt around the top of his faded lap lap. It was clasped by a boy scout buckle like the one her young brother had worn when they were children. Attached to the belt was a sheath with knife in it.

Winters stared at it for a time then, furtively, and with the delicacy of a pickpocket, she removed the knife.

On an afterthought, she twisted the catch on the belt and slipped off the sheath. She pulled the leg of her trousers out of her gaiters and tucked the knife in its sheath into the top of her boot, then rebuckled her gaiter.

The knife had no more relevance to survival than the dead man's fragile bow, but it gave Winters a feeling, for the first time, that her destiny was not absolutely in everyone's hands but her own.

There was nothing else for it now. She began to walk up the slope as nervously as though she were approaching an unexploded bomb.

Above her the chaos of forest. Sally must be back up there somewhere.

It was as if the women had never existed; had never dislocated the simple patterns of his life.

Once, in another place, another time, Oshima had known this identical feeling of release.

The memory of it had been triggered by the dying sounds of the prisoners' escape.

Now, he was alone in the forest casting about desultorily for the body of Nagato, wondering, if, indeed, the squad leader was dead, or if he had simply gone in avenging pursuit of the blacks who had ambushed them.

As Oshima picked his slow, preoccupied way through the undergrowth he was momentarily startled by a crashing nearby. He dropped into an instinctive crouch, his heart racing, his hand by his trigger.

Another ambush? His heart pounded, then he realised, feeling slightly foolish, what it had been. Wild pigs.

208

In a few yards he came upon the body of a dead black. The wild pigs had started on him already, hard on the heels of the flies and ants.

He stood staring down at the dead man, no more than muscular boy; thinking how transient flesh was here in this jungle. No doubt, as soon as he passed, the pigs would return to the feast.

Blood had stained the white cockatoo feathers with which the warrior had adorned his hair.

Once, in a hill village, during his first week in the Islands, Oshima had seen a black no less handsome than this one, with two huge, blue birdwing butterflies like slabs of sky, tethered to his pride of hair. When the black passed a girl, he would pinch the living decorations into frenzied, eye-catching flight. The great wings soon thrashed themselves to tatters.

Had this bushy crown once been decorated with doomed butterflies, to catch the eyes of the village girls? Oshima thought of his own living decorations – was that all they had been? – somewhere in the forest.

Even now, yard by yard, they were distancing themselves from him, soaring free of him. The thought of that both exhilarated and saddened.

He felt confused. He wanted to be free of the women, yet he had sent Moritoh after them. He could easily have held him back until Nagato had been found. Was it simply that he could not bear to lose possession of them?

Oshima's mind would not function. His brain felt ravished by the heat of the sun beating on the treetops far above. The towering foliage seemed to crush him with its green weight. Fatigue claimed him. He slumped down, leaned back against a tree and closed his eyes.

Once, long ago, on the slopes of Mimoro's sacred mountain he had felt this same sad exhilaration, this same confusion of feelings.

In his mind's eye Oshima saw again his golden prey. Ten times that day they had been in his grasp; his to possess, to triumph over; his to boast about, to display.

They had fluttered together, two lovers on the bed of a single flower, or had soared, bright gold against the dark green gorse, competing with the spectrum colours of the nasturtiums, butterwort and poppies, the garish warp and weave of the mountain's fabric.

They had been aware only of themselves; involved totally in their own, brief, beautiful lives; flirtatiously indifferent to his god-like powers over them; his prisoning net and his fell designs.

Yard by yard he had fallen behind them, drawn on by their sublime mystery, yet unable, finally, to let go.

Their images had diminished on his lenses. At twenty yards they had soared suddenly as though revelling in their complete freedom from his stalking shadow. They had hung weightless, settled momentarily once more then they were gone, slipping over the shoulder of the slope, out of his life.

He had stood there perfectly still, sensing the first cooling afternoon breeze. A cloud, slipping across the face of the sun, eased the pressure on his reeling brain.

Oshima had discovered a truth about himself. His beloved Kurosumo had been right. All that had gone before: his collection, that sum of beauty and death; pride and obsession, had simply been a habit learned without understanding, a passion without love.

He had ravished beauty for the last time.

Oh, there would be a gap in his collection; Oshima had known it then; that pair had been the rarest species of them all. But he had known, too, that the gap they would leave would be the one thing in the collection that had real value.

All the rest of it was behind him now; all those matched pairs, all that decaying perfection; all those degenerating reds and yellows, all that dust-gathering evidence of an impersonal passion which demonstrated no more than the futility and emptiness of his life.

Oshima had looked at the deadly weapon in his hand; the slim, flexible shaft of yellow bamboo, the voracious mouth of the catching net, and he had broken it over his knee. In the late afternoon sun the jungle around Lieutenant Oshima Eeji hummed and ticked. Half dreaming, he remembered that moment; thought about that favourite catching net of his. The pieces of it may lie yet on the windy slopes of Mimoro mountain. The thought was oddly comforting.

He slept.

Mae must be down there somewhere.

Below her, a river.

Brandeis decided that at least the banks of it would give some shape to her search.

She looked up at the sheer slope. Somewhere back there the Japanese would be searching for them. In her memory of her flight, there was gunfire and the sound of the soldiers' cries. She was sure they had not all died in the ambush.

Damn Mae! She must have heard me fall. Must have realised I wasn't with her. Why the hell didn't she stop? Didn't she care?

Brandeis' anger and resentment mushroomed.

It wasn't fair, she felt, that she should be lumbered with someone so stupid, so incapable of taking action, so slow to make her mind up. So old. First Mae hadn't recognised their chance when it was staring her in the face and now she had wrecked things. *Silly old cow.*

Anger was replaced by a sudden fear. The officer had said clearly enough that if they tried to escape they would be shot.

Brandeis began to move down the hill fast, but tried to keep as quiet as possible. A twig snapped under her foot loud as a firecracker. She slowed, fearfully.

She dared not cry out again. Even if Mae heard, so might the Japanese. She looked back again, but there was nothing to see in the shadowed tangle above her.

The river down there, that's where Mae will be, probably waiting for me.

Doubt entered at once. But what if Mae had got worried and had come back up the hill and gone straight on past her? Straight into the arms of that animal? And what if he killed her? *Oh God, oh Mae I'm sorry. Sorry.*

Anguished at her own stupidity for falling over, for bolting away from the Japanese without thought, for her unkind thoughts about Winters, Brandeis hurried on down, making more noise than she intended; panic rising.

What if Mae had waited by the river then given up, crossed over, leaving her here on this side alone in the forest, and those men coming to kill her?

She wouldn't do that, the bitch, would she?

Down through the walls of trees and creepers and ferns and bamboo, down to the magnet of light and space that was the river, the place where Mae would be, must be.

From where the jungle ended abruptly at a sandbank on the edge of the wide river, Brandeis looked out.

No one; only the river whispering past, deep and impassable. The sandbanks on both bank were featureless and empty.

Cautiously she peered up and down on her side of the river. Not a sign of Winters.

Brandeis tried to get her bearings by thinking of her position relative to Winters just before she had tripped over. Winters had been on her left, so logically, she would be upstream, if she were here at all.

Keeping under the cover afforded by the jungle, Brandeis began to make her way upstream, parallel to the river.

She thought of going out on to the sandbank where Winters, if she were anywhere around, might see her. She decided not to risk it: she would be in full view of anyone else.

Brandeis stuck close to the edge and kept looking to her left, back into the forest where they would come in search of her. If she spotted any of the Japanese she determined not to make for the river. They would cut her down the moment she was in the open. No, the jungle would be safer. It might hide her from the soldiers for long enough to evade them. If she could not find Mae, she reasoned, maybe the Japanese would not be able to find her.

Damn you. Damn you. Where the hell have you gone you miserable, selfish bitch? Probably over the river by now and clean away while Muggins, here, is searching for you.

Brandeis looked across the river to the other side. Beyond the barrier of green water the jungle beckoned oddly peaceful; unthreatening in the late afternoon sun. It came to her that she should forget about looking for Winters and cross over on her own to safety.

Mae would survive. Anyway she would have to take her chance on that. Why should they both be at risk? After all, it was Mae's fault. She was the one who had wanted to stay by that damned wreck. Mae was the one who had run off and left her.

To hell with her...

Brandeis pushed her ugly thoughts away.

No. *Mae would never do that. She's too decent, damn her. More likely she's back up the slope there looking for me.*

Brandeis stopped. It was hopeless. She turned back uncertainly. *Have to go back up there and look for Mae. Up there. Where the Japanese were. Oh God. Oh bugger you, Mae.*

Something came at Brandeis from the side. Before she could cry out, a hand had

215

clamped over her mouth. The edge of a knife was glinting four inches in front of her eyes.

'You'd better go after the prisoners,' the lieutenant had said, at last. 'There's a river down there. That'll stop them. Bear downstream.' Oshima pointed at an angle to the right, then looked at his watch. 'I'll go on looking. We'll meet back here in half an hour, whether you find them or not.'

There had been an odd inflection in Oshima's voice. It was obvious to Moritoh that he hoped the women would not be found.

Moritoh crossed the narrow track and headed down into the river valley. Halfway down the slope he stopped and listened. Nothing save the murmur of the river somewhere below. He stood for a moment, staring hard, trying to pierce the gloom for signs of them. Set off again, moving faster, hurrying down the slope, slipping and sliding in the mud.

Would the lieutenant find Nagato dead? It was a pleasing thought, but it seemed inconceivable that the squad leader could be killed by an arrow, or a spear. It would take more than that to put the madman down.

Although they had searched over a wide area of the thick bush around the ambush point, the only sign they had found of Nagato had been another dead black with a bullet-riddled body and a cut throat.

Lieutenant Oshima had agreed that Nagato must have gone after their attackers.

Suddenly a terrible thought came to Moritoh, bringing him skidding to a halt.

He knew where Nagato had gone.

Moritoh drew in an anguished breath and plunged headlong down to the river.

There was murder in his heart.

He sat above her; across her thighs, his stone weight pinning her to the ground. Foreshortened, the wicked tip of his knife. Beyond that his hot, stone eyes.

At first, Brandeis had struggled desperately against Nagato's awesome power, her mind racing. If only she could cry out; break free.

But this was no hotel room with a stupid drunken young man, readily unnerved by thin walls and the sounds of people passing in the corridor. Here, screaming would not bring help at the cost of a little embarrassment. Here, Brandeis knew, screaming would bring death. She shook her head, pleading with her eyes. But there was no hope of pity in that smooth, cold face.

When, at last, Nagato had removed his hand from her mouth he had first made it obvious from his gestures that her alternative was the knife.

He began to undo her shirt buttons. She grabbed at his hand. Instantly, the knife threatened. She released her grip. As Nagato

217

unbuttoned her shirt she felt the gorge rise, and lay there shaking her head unavailingly. Brandeis felt the colour rise in her face. The beginnings of a triumphant smile was on his face.

'Please,' she begged, her voice a whisper.

Suddenly Nagato changed the grip on the shaft of his knife. For a moment she thought he was going to drive it into her belly, but then she realised what he had done; cut her brassiere so that her breasts were bared.

Brandeis began to shake helplessly. Now he unthreaded the cloth belt from around her waist, jerking against her weight savagely until it was clear. Once more she clutched at him. This time the squad leader snarled at her and roughly jerked his arm free.

He pressed the point of his knife under the tip of her chin, and grinned down at her wolfishly, shaking his head in admonition.

Then she felt the knife point trace down her breast and at her nipple.

'No. No. Please, no.' Quiet as a prayer, over and over.

Her skin quailed before the touch of steel. There was a blank moment then. Perhaps she fainted but, whatever the reason, there were a few moments of time lost as though they had been erased. When Brandeis became aware again the knife had stopped its chilling course. Nagato took the knife in his teeth and he began to undo the front of her trousers. One button proved stiff. He jerked at it. The fabric ripped like flesh and she cried out.

Brandeis knew her belly was bare now.

His tongue moved in his mouth like an animal in a cage. Once more the knife point tracing at her flesh. She sensed rather than felt the silk fabric part.

'Oh, please.'

Nagato made a tiny threatening gesture with the knife again, almost tenderly this time, then began to undo his trousers.

She closed her eyes. She would not watch. If she didn't make him angry, maybe he would not do anything really horrible; kill her.

Nagato stared to drag at Brandeis' trousers. Instinctively, she grabbed at them. He had her then by the hair, his face contorted with rage. She could feel the breath of him; see the pores of his sweating skin.

Aware of his flesh now, of her own nakedness. She lay looking up at the sky, feeling his weight shifting, trying to re-enter that blank, know nothing, feel nothing, erasure of time; hoping that it would not be unbearable, for there was nothing to stop him now.

Brandeis heard Nagato speak, but determined not to open her eyes. She could feel the dead weight of him crushing her. Again Brandeis felt Nagato drag at her clothes. A seam ripped, sickeningly. She gave a sob of fear as another barrier fell before his remorseless power. Again his voice. It sounded harsh and angry.

Oh Jesus, what's he going to do to me? Fragments of sickening scenarios crowded her mind.

There was a loud crack; the whine of a bullet. Suddenly his weight was gone.

Brandeis opened her eyes. Sky.

Fearfully she sat up.

Nagato was kneeling on the ground beside her looking angrily at someone behind her. He was speaking in a cold flat voice. His face working with rage.

Brandeis craned around.

She saw Moritoh five yards away, his rifle at his shoulder. The boy's face was white with anger as he confronted her assailant.

For Moritoh it was the moment of truth. He knew then that he was hopelessly out of his depth.

'You clown,' said Nagato. 'Didn't it occur to you that an escaping prisoner is fair game?' Slowly on to his feet, one eye on his weapon. Moritoh was relieved that it was a yard too far out of reach.

Nagato shrugged himself back into his trousers, fastening up.

'You should have killed me while you had the chance,' he said, arrogant now. 'Bad mistake that. Now, Rich Boy, you are a dead man.'

Brandeis found herself unable to see through her helpless tears. She fumbled at her buttons, fastening them clumsily, one by one. She wiped her face with the back of her hand and stood up, straightening her clothes and trying to compose herself.

She moved behind Moritoh, as though he were a barrier that might diffuse the lightning-bolt power of the squad leader's rage. Moritoh flicked his eye momentarily at her and gave a brief nod. The menace Nagato exuded was remarkable. It was like being in an open field with a maddened bull. Even with Moritoh and his rifle and five yards of space between her and Nagato, still Brandeis felt threatened.

'Think you're going to be her guardian angel, Rich Boy, do you?' Nagato snorted with derision. 'No chance. You're finished, Moritoh.'

Suddenly the squad leader laughed shortly and jerked his head. 'Here he comes. The fairy princess.'

Moritoh risked a quick glance round. Lieutenant Oshima and the woman were coming towards them. They were a yard clear of the jungle's edge, not more than fifty yards away. He felt a rush of relief.

'I told you I'm going to have her, and the woman...' said Nagato. 'And I will.' Staring directly at Moritoh he picked up his weapon. 'And you, Rich Boy, are not going

221

to stop me, and neither is your boyfriend.'
Moritoh lowered his rifle uneasily.

As Winters came running towards her
Brandeis began to feel angry.

'Oh Sally, what did they do to you?'
Winters put her arms around her, attempting to give comfort.

Not even the real concern apparent in
Winters' voice could assuage Brandeis'
anger. She drew away from Winters, twisting
herself clear abruptly.

'Where the hell were you?'

Even as she spoke, Brandeis knew that she
was being irrational and unfair.

Winters was shocked at the icy tone.

'You just bloody well ran off and left me,'
said Brandeis. 'You don't give a shit for
anyone, do you?'

Winters' arm dropped to her side. Her
face showed how deeply the words had cut.
When she replied, at last, Winters' voice was
low. 'I went all the way back to the track
looking for you.'

'You couldn't have looked too bloody
hard.'

'That's a rotten, spiteful thing to say.'

They stood glaring at one another.

Winters bent down and picked up Brandeis' pack, which Nagato had ripped off.
'You'd better put on another shirt,' she said,
tersely. She handed the pack to Brandeis.

'It's your own fault. You're a stupid,

thoughtless, spoilt little fool. You don't think about the consequences of anything. Just charge off and everyone else has to pick up the pieces.'

'Shut up!' Brandeis rummaged in her pack for her shirt, blinded by sudden tears. 'Shut up!'

They became aware that, a few yards away, the tense and angry exchange that had been taking place between the Japanese had ended. The soldiers had turned to them.

Brandeis found the shirt. She turned her back on the Japanese and quickly put it on.

'I'm sorry,' she said stiffly, not looking at Winters.

'So am I,' said Winters, tiredly. 'But for God's sake, Sally, let's get it right next time … if there is a next time.'

Brandeis' rage surged afresh. 'Jesus, Mae, I said I was sorry! Don't you understand? That bastard tried to rape me.'

In a moment Brandeis had moved in front of Oshima, her torn shirt in her hand. She held it up angrily in front of him and pointed at Nagato.

'He tried to rape me. Rape! D'you understand?' Her voice cracked with fury.

'Sally!' Winters' voice was sharp with concern. 'Take it easy.'

Oshima took Brandeis' shirt from her, so much shredded fabric. He looked at it, his expressionless face chilling.

'You said we'd be properly treated.' Brandeis was shouting now, out of control. 'You said...'

'Silence!' Oshima's harsh tone brought Brandeis' diatribe to an abrupt end. 'You are prisoner.'

Winters came close and gripped Brandeis' arm, her fingers digging in.

'Sally, for God's sake. Shut up.'

'Not to escape!'

For a moment Brandeis thought Oshima might hit her. But then his enraged expression passed.

'Cannot be responsible,' Oshima said, looking strangely distracted.

Brandeis felt her own anger evaporate. She kept forgetting this was not real life, but some deadly game, the rules of which she was only just beginning to comprehend.

Winters took her hand.

'All right?'

Brandeis nodded sullenly, still half furious with Winters for her lack of sympathy.

Oshima jerked his head at his two men who had been watching the confrontation impassively. They walked off, straight up the slope from the river bank and into the jungle.

Once more Oshima turned his attention to them. He stood in front of them, straight and stiff as though he were on a parade ground dressing down some recalcitrant recruits. His angry gaze moved from one to the other.

'Apologise for Sergeant. I give order. He will not touch you again. Sorry.' Oshima bowed slightly to Brandeis. She met his eye. For a moment he looked directly at her, then turned his sad, troubled face away and stared out across the river. A muscle twitched in his jaw.

They stood side by side with their eyes lowered. In some curious way Oshima had made them feel that they had disappointed him; betrayed his trust.

'I give second order to my men.' Oshima spoke clearly. 'You run away again. Shoot. Finish. Understand?'

He looked at them keenly, probing for a response. They nodded in unison.

'Now. Go on,' he ordered. He turned his back.

They followed on after the two Japanese soldiers up the slope from the river.

When Winters looked back she saw him, a still figure silhouetted against the dark green plane of the river.

He stood there watching them out of sight, Brandeis' shirt dangling from his hand.

Chapter 13

'You're a dead man, Rich Boy.'

Again Moritoh heard Nagato's matter-of-fact voice threatening death. He wondered why he had aimed off. He knew he would live to regret that. Nagato would extract a terrible price for Moritoh's weakness; from him, and from the girl.

He glanced over at Brandeis. She sat a yard or so away, like her companion, silent and subdued, her eyes downcast.

Had she struggled? Or had she been willing? *The light and play of the sun on her shoulders as she sat up rearranging her clothes. The paleness of her lovely skin.*

She had avoided his eye since, as though ashamed.

The food was nearly ready. Moritoh could feel the fierce heat of the blue-edged flames, nearly invisible in the gloom of approaching night.

Staring off into the shadows of the forest; Lieutenant Oshima. On that grim two-hour march up from the river he had not spoken a single word.

To Moritoh he seemed strangely shrunken. Had Oshima's famous luck spilled out on the mud all around that planewreck, like so much blood?'

He had been worn by Moritoh – by all his men – like a talisman, for he had been that most precious of all creatures; a lucky officer.

No matter how stiff and awkward a man he seemed, the men of Section Seven had come to believe that, with him heading them, they were invincible.

But now they were worm meat. And Oshima who, like the seed in the fruit, had been protected by his men and by his rank, now had no barrier between him and Nagato.

'Food's ready, sir.'

The lieutenant jerked out of his private world, said something to the women. They all came nearer the fire.

Cross-legged, Moritoh scooped food on to some broad leaves he had stripped from a bush to serve as plates for the prisoners. As Brandeis leaned forward to accept her rations, down the front of her shirt he saw the shadowy swell of her breasts.

He served the woman. She nodded her thanks for the food, then said something to the lieutenant. Moritoh was aware that she was talking about him. He felt himself flushing with embarrassment. There was a warmth in the girl's expression too, that he had not seen before.

Lieutenant Oshima looked at him with an

odd expression; almost of regret.

'She says her friend owes you thanks.'

How ironical, thought Moritoh. If only the girl knew the anger he had felt about her since the incident; sentencing him to death by her very existence.

Oshima refused food. Stared off into the shadows.

'Mind yourself, Moritoh.' Oshima looked directly at him now, across the flames, his eyes expressing concern.

'There are no rules out here. Only survivors.'

Moritoh ate slowly, not knowing what to say. Never before had the lieutenant seemed so close.

For a time he watched the women. They ate as though famished.

'What will happen to them, sir?'

Oshima was silent for a long time, then began to help himself to some food.

'You'd better relieve Nagato.'

Moritoh flushed, knowing he had overstepped the mark. He bolted the last of his food, put his bowl in the outside pocket of his pack, grabbed his rifle and walked up the slope towards the track. The girl did not look up.

The track: a dim tunnel in a darker forest.

Ten yards. Twenty. His eyes probed anxiously for the shape that will be Nagato.

'*You're a dead man, Rich Boy.*' Nagato had

meant that. Some time it will happen, and Moritoh wondered if this was to be the moment. He must be close to the guard position now.

The hair on the back of his neck began to stand up.

Where the hell is Nagato?

Moritoh released the safety catch on his rifle, all the while realising how useless a precaution it was. He knew it would take more than a cocked rifle to survive a fight with the squad leader.

An arm like an iron bar suddenly crushed his neck; a hand clamped over his nose and mouth. Moritoh couldn't breathe. Everything was seizing.

Nagato's voice rasped against his ear.

'I told you, Rich Boy. You're a dead man.'

Everything stopped for Moritoh; heart, breath, mind. He anticipated the agony of Nagato's steel.

Then everything started again. Heart pounding, chest sucking air, mind racing. A rustle of foliage. Nagato was gone.

Moritoh stood holding his bruised throat in the darkness, his heart a crazed animal in a too-small cage.

Night sounds; mysterious stirrings, inexplicable clicks and squeaks and rustlings.

Winters listened, wide-eyed, hearing Brandeis' soft breathing and her faint sighs and moans as her mind smoothed off the raged edges of the day's ugly memories.

There would be no quarter next time, Winters knew that now. They would either get away, or they would be dead.

Winters felt worn out; consumed by her own anger. Yet unable to sleep. Her mind felt as though it were careering off the rails.

It's all very well for Sally, lying there. Escaped from it all by a young girl's resort to distancing sleep. She doesn't have to be responsible. Winters bitterly thought of all the irresponsible and stupid things Brandeis had done; the escapades, and the excesses that had made them each other's natural enemies. How she wished she could be like Brandeis who seemed to feel no guilt about anything, neither about sleeping with anything in trousers, nor about breaking any rule that got in her way. How typical. The spoilt daughter of a doctor, playing at nurses, and believing that she had a divine right to ignore the rules that applied to lesser mortals. Winters thought of the ugly things Brandeis had said.

'You give me the shits. Always so bloody tight-arsed about the rest of us.'

'Sister bloody Prim and Proper. Jesus! What a hypocrite! Don't you realise everyone knows you're on with that Major? You're the greatest scandal on the base.'

Sally had apologised, of course, but it was

so typical of her lack of self-control. And perhaps it was true, Winters reflected ruefully. But what did all that matter? Now, because of their botched escape attempt, everything was ten times worse.

Lucky for Sally that boy had saved her for some extraordinary reason. Now the soldiers were quarrelling amongst themselves and that strange officer – there was a kind of glancing madness about his eyes – was losing control. Without his protection from the madman, God knows what would happen.

Winters had no doubt he would try again. But what to do? When the Australian patrol had passed them within a few yards this afternoon she could have cried out, but they both would have died for it, and where would have been the advantage in that?

Winters knew one thing: more than ever before in her life she wanted to live. They must escape.

But, what if they did not? What awaited them?

A camp full of trained killers like their captors; men who, perhaps, had not seen a woman for years; officers who might simply throw women prisoners to their men like so much meat to a pack of savage dogs; trophies to improve their morale?

Brandeis moaned softly in her sleep and stirred restlessly in Winters' arms, her body pressing close. She'd to admit to herself that she felt different about Brandeis now. Spitting at that madman! She'd guts all right. The undisciplined, selfish, don't-give-a-damn attitude that had so often infuriated her could also express itself in a raw, if crazy courage. Winters hugged the sleeping girl close.

Poor kid. What must it have been like to feel herself in the power of that man with his knife?

Winters caught her breath.

The knife!

Cautiously she reached down to feel its slim and strangely reassuring shape against her ankle.

Was this the key to their escape? But how does a knife represent the key to anything, when her captors had guns? She wouldn't stand a chance.

Winters stretched out, trying not to wake Brandeis, but the girl whimpered, thrashed around feebly for a moment and gave a cry.

Winters tried to quieten her, but there was a change of breathing. Sally was awake.

'What's the matter?' Brandeis spoke loudly, an edge of panic to her voice.

'Nothing. Nothing. Go to sleep. It's all right. I'm here.'

Brandeis began sobbing quietly. Winters comforted her.

'I'm sorry … sorry,' but she cried on. Winters felt a great surge of compassion for her; this girl whose free ways with men had made her feel contemptuous – even jealous. Sally was suddenly like her child; real flesh and blood, not like David's phantom child that was, perhaps, growing within her.

At length the sobbing ended.

'You all right?'

Winters pressed her mouth close against Brandeis' ear and felt the sweet texture of her skin and hair against her lips. Felt her nod.

'I was having a bad dream.'

A shape loomed up, black on the velvet blackness of the night. Whoever it was was peering down at them for a long, terrifying time; then he was gone.

'It wasn't him.' She soothed Brandeis' shaking. 'It was either the officer, or the boy.'

'I hate him. I hate that filthy swine.' Brandeis' body tense and rigid as though she were about to burst. 'I mean it, Mae. If I get one chance I'm going to kill that bastard.'

Winters heard the steel in her voice.

One of the soldiers was stirring. A brief swish of foliage; the heavy sound of someone peeing; the return. Silence again. They lay listening.

Winters felt impelled to tell Brandeis.

'A knife!' Brandeis breathing the words, excitement in her voice. 'Where did you get it?'

'Off one of the natives they shot. He was dead and I took it.'

'Where?'

'In the bush ... just after I lost you.'

'No. Where is it now?'

'In my gaiter. Sssh.' Out in the blackness there was unease. The soldiers must have heard their whispering. After an age; a slow easing of tension as the soldiers settled once more.

'Let's try to sleep.'

After another half an hour, Winters knew that unless she got up, she would not sleep. She began to ease herself clear of Brandeis' close grip. Gently, gently.

'Where?'

'Pee.'

'Me, too.'

As quietly as possible they got to their feet and, feeling with their hands, began to edge into the bush to one side.

An odd scratching sound then, suddenly, they were bathed in the incredibly bright light of a single match. It caught the angular planes of the officer's face. He was sitting up.

Frantically Winters shook her head hoping he would understand that they were not trying to escape.

The match went out. They stood in the darkness breathing hard.

'Stay close, please.' The voice was calm. They heard him settle back somewhere over there in the blackness.

They moved another couple of yards then squatted down, side by side, and pee'd with an embarrassing loudness. Brandeis leaned close to Winters in the dark.

'Will you give me the knife?'

Instinctively Winters shook her head and felt for the weapon. It was there; solid, reassuring, the only tangible evidence of hope she had.

'No. Better if I keep it.'

'Please!' This, urgently.

Winters did not reply. The girl's request annoyed her. Winters began fastening the buttons on her trousers.

'It's me he's after!' There was petulance in the voice.

Unfair! Thought Winters, not to mention a lack of tact. Did Sally think she was the only one in sexual jeopardy? Is one a crone, and past it because one is over thirty?

Winters unbuttoned angrily and withdrew the knife and its sheath from inside her gaiter. Felt for Brandeis' hand. The weapon was snatched away.

Winters stood there buttoning up, feeling furious with herself, but then Brandeis' arm was around her and she was kissed on the cheek.

'Thanks, love.' The voice was grateful and Winters' anger began to melt.

They had no sooner sat down than there was the briefest flaring of another match, this time instantly extinguished. The after-image of the officer like a Hallowe'en mask;

beyond him the sleeping shape of the squad leader and starkly beyond that, the writhing shadows of the forest.

Winters lay in the darkness with Brandeis' hand gripping hers tightly. Without the knife she felt more vulnerable than ever.

Moritoh was uneasy. Something was wrong; out of joint.

The enemy? The blacks? Nagato?

How he hated the night watches.

Nagato! Was the squad leader stalking him this very minute under cover of the fag end of night?

He got to his feet cautiously. His night vision was working and he could see shapes. There was a first light that was not yet light; the last flare of stars; a subtle change that only hinted at the coming of the day.

Moritoh was not due to wake Lieutenant Oshima for at least half an hour, but he eased himself back towards the bivouac, slowly, carefully, trying not to make the slightest sound.

He came to the place. At first glance everything was normal. Black lumps on the ground. The sound of breathing.

But something was wrong. Instead of two groupings: the lieutenant and Nagato; the two women, there was a false look to the equation.

Moritoh turned his head from side to side

236

using the rods and cones of his night vision, trying to make sense of the new configuration.

There was a third black lump. Looking directly at it made it disappear. Moritoh swivelled his head frantically endeavouring to pick up details with his peripheral vision.

On the ground, close to his comrades, one of the women was crouched.

The light was changing by the second.

There was no doubt about it. It was her; the girl.

He watched, not breathing and instinctively his rifle came up. His thumb sought and found the safety catch. It slipped off, smooth with oil.

Brandeis was on all fours no more than two yards from the thick bulk of Nagato, lying flat on his back on the ground like a piece of black granite growing out of the earth.

Moritoh saw her inch forward and moved with her. Now he was no more than two yards behind her.

Something in her hand caught the light. He knew at once what it was. A curious mixed feeling of disbelief, admiration and excitement flickered through his mind.

In the stopped motion of the moment, a film still from a murder sequence, it felt to Moritoh as though he were examining the scene of a crime through a magnifying glass with all the time in the world to examine the

237

faces and positions of the people involved: the murderer and the victim; to draw circles around the details that were of special significance; the weapon, the exact position of the body.

Nagato looked vulnerable, even innocent, lying there. But his murder had not happened yet. The girl knelt there, a would-be assassin; knife in her hand, a yard short of her victim's throat.

Moritoh regretted that he had come.

His mind was racing. Would he have to shoot her, locked in the middle of an unresolved act? In that moment Moritoh knew that even if she tried to complete her attempt, he would not be able to gun her down.

The squad leader stirred slightly in his sleep. She turned away from Nagato, as though doing so would shut him out and therefore end the threat of discovery.

At that moment Brandeis became aware of Moritoh. She became perfectly still, her head frozen as if she were afraid to look.

Nagato settled with a soft grunt. The girl's eyes were on Moritoh; a soft gleam in the darker space that was her face.

Was she frightened, Moritoh wondered: believing that she was about to die? Strangely, although she knelt on the ground like a supplicant, it did not seem so. There was something defiant about her.

How familiar her face was in this light that

was still not yet light; the planes and curves of it; the shape of her head, the way her hair fell.

Moritoh knew that he had to get her away from Nagato and take the knife from her. After that he could decide what to do.

They were both aware of his rifle, she and he. Moritoh held it low on his hip and pointing straight at her. He swung it away and slowly shook his head from side to side.

Brandeis lowered her gaze in a regretful, defeated gesture. Her hand came up slowly, palm up. The blade of the knife caught the quickening light. Moritoh reached forward and took it, feeling momentarily the warmth of her skin in shocking contrast to the cold of the steel.

Nagato's face was still. There was time.

He tapped her shoulder sideways with the barrel of his rifle. She glanced up at him quickly, a scared look in her eyes. Moritoh inclined his head in the direction of her sleeping place. There was a long moment as though she was steeling herself to face execution, then she took his meaning.

With her eye on Nagato, she rose smoothly. Her reprieved victim did not move.

Brandeis' face was more visible now. She looked directly at Moritoh. There was a bleak, shocked expression on her face. He shook his head in admonition and disbelief. He had no way of conveying to her the admiration he felt for her nerve and spirit.

She traversed the space silently and sat down beside her sleeping companion; not looking at him now. Put her head down between her hands, as though in shame.

Back at his guard position by the track Moritoh squatted on his heels and looked at the knife.

It was old and blunt, with a pearl inlay in the grip and a piece of frayed cord wound around the hilt where the shaft joined the blade.

He shoved it deep into the mud down to the hilt, then stood up. With his boot heel he drove the evidence into the ground, blade, haft and all.

Chapter 14

Oshima was shaken. If it had not been for Moritoh's sharp eyes they might have died three times this morning. This part of the country was normally free of the enemy, except for their occasional reconnaissance forays. In the first hour of the morning he had run into three enemy columns, one after the other: big sections of men and blacks laden with supplies, heading up towards the Japanese stronghold in the hills. He had expected to make the camp this afternoon, but it was going to be more difficult now.

The last section had passed just five minutes before, but already the jungle hummed and ticked as normal. The fierce heat of the sun beat down through the trees. The air seemed thick and steamy. He found it hard to breathe.

They were all watching him: the women, lying side by side face down, anguish in their eyes; Nagato, alert with that open-mouthed, almost sensual look he wore when in expectation of combat; Moritoh, regarding him quizzically, a yard beyond the women.

Oshima judged that they had lain low long enough. He nodded assent. The boy crept away to reconnoitre.

Oshima spread out his sketch map. Unless they could cut across the trackless bush it was going to be hard to stay alive. He orientated the map to the track, which lay out of sight some ten yards in front of them; traced his finger in the direction of base camp. There could no longer be any doubt. A really dangerous situation was building up threatening the Japanese positions beyond the ridge. This heavy movement of troops verified his original evaluation. The enemy must be backed by strong reserves to move with such careless confidence.

He felt trapped. It was vital now that he should make it back. The feeling of despair about the loss of his men was sharper now than at any time before.

What would those men of his, now dead, have done to the clumsy, laden-down enemy soldiers who had just passed? The thought saddened him. More than ever before Oshima regretted stumbling upon that plane-wreck.

Three pairs of eyes weighed on him. Oshima busied himself with his map. He rifled through old memories of rivers and re-entrants, ridges and native pads, and thought out a route. It would be desperately hard going: work for their bush knives. What if the women could not keep up?

Had they been men they would have been dead already. But he knew now that he was incapable of killing these captives; snuffing out their lives in the vacuum flask of expediency. So, what would happen? And, when he got them back, and had finished questioning them; what then?

He pushed away these futile speculations and put his map back in his pocket. Nagato inclined his head questioningly. Oshima nodded and the squad leader disappeared in the opposite direction from Moritoh.

Oshima jerked his head at the women. They sat up stiffly, clearly glad to be freed from the face-down position he had made them adopt while the enemy soldiers passed.

The woman seemed about to say something to the girl. Oshima frowned and shook his head angrily. Had they no idea how voices carried here?

These two women had put faces to all this madness, and by doing so, they had made a mockery of all that he was and all that he did. It occurred to Oshima that he still did not know their names. Did Army nurses carry paybooks? He had not asked.

It did not pay to be so familiar with one's enemies. No, he would not ask their names. It would be like giving pet names to laboratory animals. Everything was changed by that act.

But who were they? How had they come here to interact with the rhythms and directions of his life. Why, out of all the places on earth where they might have found themselves, had they appeared, like alien creatures from the spirit world, softly, insubstantially on the lenses of his field glasses?

From the first moment when they had taken shape and form, personality and individuality before his eyes, they had denied Oshima the power to act. It had shaken him profoundly. He had known at once, with a sickening awareness, that he would not be abler to order his men to fire.

And the more he had watched them that first morning, the more he had known that something terrible would happen.

Women could only corrupt men in this

terrible place.

Oshima hated them for it now; hated the circumstances that yoked them violently to him and put him in their thrall.

Here they were; he and his two women, still locked together, nameless strangers in every sense of the word, yet, to Oshima, deadly familiars.

Looking at them through his binoculars had been one thing, but proximity had increased his power of magnification a thousandfold. Now they were as fascinating as creatures seen through the most powerful microscope, and as menacing.

In theory, Oshima thought bitterly, it was all so simple. Prisoners were shot. It was just that no one in this anonymous jungle war had thought of women as possible prisoners. No doubt the order would have been the same. It is easy to give such orders when you are sitting at a desk somewhere in high command. But those faceless men with their dispassionate orders had not been bewitched by their captives as he had. Oshima knew it now.

He remembered something. Patted his shirt pocket. They were still there; the things he had found in the pockets of the girl's shirt after Nagato had attacked her. He fished around and pulled out her lighter; held it towards Brandeis.

She hesitated for a moment, unsure of his intention, then took it.

'Thank you,' soberly. Reflexively, she flicked open the cover and thumbed the wheel. The flame failed to ignite. She put the lighter in her pocket.

'Did you find anything else?' she asked tentatively.

Oshima seemed about to speak, but then looked away quickly and shook his head.

Winters raised her eyebrows at Brandeis.

'Wasn't anything valuable. Just make-up. Lipstick and stuff. A comb. Doubt if I'll be needing it.' Brandeis' sense of irony was still there. 'They seem to find us attractive enough without it.' The last part was as much aimed at Oshima as at Winters. He seemed not to hear.

Nagato and Moritoh returned within a minute of one another. All clear.

Oshima checked his watch. Nine o'clock. He gave the signal.

Nagato, after a long, provocative look at the women, led off towards the track.

All that grim morning there was a sense of desperation about the Japanese as they hurried towards their camp.

The few tracks they risked were mostly overgrown. The soldiers often had to hack their way through the tangle with their knives and bayonets.

A series of switchback ridges took them up-wards; deserted native gardens, stony streams and agonising slopes. For the women it all became an exhausting, featureless blur.

They rested on the hour, but briefly. Not a word was spoken. Then they would drive on again, staying close together, seeking the clearest spaces beneath the towering, dripping trees.

Even the superbly fit Moritoh found it hard going. To him it was astonishing that the two women had kept up. In front of him he could see the sweat black on the girl's shirt. Watching her, Moritoh felt the elation of a conspirator, powerful as any aphrodisiac.

Only he and she knew of the strange events of the morning, a secret shared in the darkness of the pre-dawn; the fusion of their lives at that moment, with Nagato lying there helpless under her knife and both the assassin and victim in Moritoh's control.

To Moritoh it was incredible that the girl had been willing to risk that, so stupid an act. How did she imagine she could have got away with it? Even if she had killed Nagato, or had tried and failed, she would have died immediately. There could have been no saving her. For all his anger at Nagato, Lieutenant Oshima would have killed her; killed them both. Why had she not seen that she was risking not only her own life, but that of her companion?

And yet Moritoh was deeply impressed by the courage Brandeis had shown. To avenge herself for her dishonour, to conquer her great fear by destroying the very thing that caused it he recognised as the very spirit of the samurai, whose valour he coveted.

Had he been the prisoner, he might have done the same thing. They were alike, he and she, Moritoh decided, in their shared fear and hatred of Nagato and his malign power over them all. He could picture himself, knife in hand, within striking distance of that bare, hated throat.

In front of Brandeis' slim figure Nagato, wide as a tank, forged through the forest.

Moritoh wondered what was going on in the squad leader's mind. It occurred to him that he had never known anything about what the man thought, or how he felt. Had anyone? The squad leader was a cipher: a primitive force with a gluttony for survival. Each excess added power. Nagato was thriving on all this death, Moritoh thought bitterly, like a maggot on a dung heap.

Each time Nagato had loomed up on Moritoh's life – a dressing down for incompetence, a punishment issued, a blow for something – he had felt fear. He had felt it as he watched Nagato in action, or especially, his gorge rising in horrified disgust, when he had witnessed Nagato tormenting a wounded enemy soldier before dispatching him with a knife, or gun. Now the fear was very personal and overwhelming.

Since their last clash, by the river, Moritoh had kept his safety catch off. Whenever possible he tried to stay facing Nagato. It was like facing one's own executioner hour after hour.

Some time in the future, Moritoh knew it, Nagato would come for him. Maybe not on this patrol, if they did get out of it alive, but some time.

Why had he not shot Nagato instead of aiming off? That weakness would cost him his life, of that he was sure. Why had he not given the girl time to complete that act of assassination? Moritoh cursed himself for not having allowed that sequence to run on.

In his mind's eye Moritoh aimed at that great wedge of shoulder and back, but he did nothing. Shooting Nagato in the back was the one action that could save him. He wondered what it was that prevented him.

He wanted to look into Brandeis' face directly to convey to her that he would do her no harm, that she was under his protection against Nagato – for all the good that might do – but she avoided his eyes. Even when they had lain facing one another waiting for the enemy patrols to pass, she had looked away; as though she and he were party to a deadly and embarrassing secret.

For Moritoh, the normal, almost casual routines of patrol and ambush, death and violence, had gone crazily out of rhythm.

For the first time he felt more like the hunted than the hunter.

Even the forest seemed to have changed sides; had become personally vindictive towards them. It clutched at them with octopus tendrils. Knife blades of grass slashed their faces, vines tripped them. Ankle-deep mud sucked at their legs and tree branches coated with beards of rotting moss exuded foul smells that seemed to corrupt the very air they breathed.

Moritoh felt vulnerable in a way he never had in the comforting structure of Section Seven, now destroyed forever.

At last they reached the top of the ridge. Below them, deep in a massive valley, the first glimpse of the river they had crossed nearly a week before.

He looked in awe at the height of the climb on the other side of the great jungled amphitheatre, the last climb they would have to make before they reached the sanctuary of their camp.

A surge of excitement gripped him. Maybe he was going to make it after all.

Stupid. Stupid.

The word had dinned away at Brandeis all the way here to the top of this ridge, where they sprawled on the ground gazing down at the river booming uneasily far below.

Brandeis drank from her water bottle with

her eyes closed. She felt infinitely weary; sick of her own stupidity and selfishness.

How could she have been so self-indulgent in her hatred of that man? She looked at her companion.

Winters' eyes were closed. She appeared exhausted, fatigue betraying her age in an amalgam of purple shadows and a web of worry lines around her forehead and eyes.

Mae. Senior Sister Winters; 'The Dragon'. Mae, for whom she had never felt anything except dislike. Mae, whom she had put in deadly jeopardy by her weakness and lack of restraint.

Brandeis remembered The Dragon saying to her, after one especially wild escapade: 'You'll be a fine nurse the day you learn one ounce of self-discipline.' Christ! Maybe Mae was right. Maybe it was time she learned.

She thought of herself kneeling upon the ground waiting for Moritoh's bullet, only then thinking about what they might do to poor Mae. She had put Mae at risk just because she wanted her own primitive revenge on a vicious lout.

What annoyed Brandeis was a that she had simply not thought it out. A yard short of her act, the hatred had evaporated. Not only was she incapable of going through with it, but she had realised she had no plan, no way of getting herself and Mae away afterwards. Had she succeeded in killing him, the other two would simply have shot them down without a second's thought. It was easy for Brandeis to see that now.

And the thought of what might have happened to her, to both of them, if Nagato had wakened and caught her, was something she could only push away. Again she saw those bloody teeth and that pathetic pile of watches and rings.

She remembered once more how Moritoh had looked her straight in the eye and taken the knife, and had said nothing. For God's sake, why? Now she was in his debt again; twice he had saved her from the Beast and once from her own stupidity.

It had been the longest moment of Brandeis' life yet, oddly enough, she had not been frightened. Relieved in a way that it was over; that she had not gone through with an act which expressed something ugly in herself.

When she had handed over the knife she had felt certain Moritoh would wake the others and tell them. But simply to let her go! It was incredible. They must hate each other, those two, after what happened by the river. She had seen the rage on the face of one, the fear on the other.

The worst part, thought Brandeis, was that she had not told Mae about it. She could not. How could she admit that she had been so uncaring about the outcome of her mindless little murder plot?

The idea had come to her the moment she had heard about Winters' knife. Brandeis had wanted that weapon, not so much to defend herself, as to kill, cut, tear, slash at that evil face above her there against the sky with those hot eyes and that filthy mouth and those hands of steel toying with her as though she were a whore bought and paid for.

Brandeis agonised; how could she admit that to Mae, who had comforted her and soothed her and looked after her? How could she admit that she had woken up halfway across the tightrope not even having worked out how she was going to get off?

The water was warm, but it slaked her thirst. She wondered idly how many different kinds of killing bugs she was drinking in with every drop, here, in this disease-ridden, hellish place.

Why had he let her off? Something had told Brandeis that she was being watched; and there he was, a shadow rebuking her in a curiously gentle way, and she with murder in her heart and nothing in her head.

Since then Moritoh had kept looking at her, but Brandeis had avoided his eye. She did not want to share any secrets with this young man with his frank eyes and his graceful body. His alien uniform which marked him as different from her and her kind in every single way.

How long would they keep up this urgent,

killing pace? The three Japanese never seemed to tire. They were silent now, preoccupied with their thoughts, sitting in a row facing her and Winters, concentrating on spearing food from tins with their knives.

With their weapons by their hands they looked deadly and implacable. How she resented that each of them was entirely able to decide upon her life and death. They knew where they were going and what they could expect when they arrived. Above all, Brandeis hated all three of them for dragging her towards some unknown, unspeakable fate.

The sight of their captors eating made Brandeis think they should, too, although she really felt too exhausted to feel hungry.

She pulled some biscuits out of her pack. The bloodstains of the already forgotten soldier who had once owned it had turned dark brown.

The Japanese were watching now.

'We'd best eat something.'

Winters opened her eyes tiredly, gave a brief smile and took a few biscuits. Brandeis felt deeply protective towards her and put a hand on her arm.

'We'll be all right Mae,' Brandeis said, trying to encourage.

Winters ate in silence for a time with her eyes on the Japanese then:

'What happened this morning?' She was looking at Brandeis now. 'I heard you go and saw you come back.'

'I'm afraid I lost your knife. The young one took it.' Brandeis felt better now that it was out. Winters said nothing, absorbing the information.

'I was angry...' To Brandeis, her rationale sounded lame, pathetic.

'Don't blame you.'

Mae did not reply; went on eating. Brandeis knew she would tell the rest of the story at another time. It would come easily then. She took Mae's hand.

'Angry *and* stupid. Sorry about your knife.'

Winters shrugged.

'We'll be OK,' Brandeis urged. 'If we just stick together, we'll be OK..' She handed Winters her water bottle.

'Have a drop of typhoid, beri-beri and yaws.'

Brandeis watched Winters drink, her throat working as the water coursed down.

Winters handed the bottle back with a rueful smile.

'It hardly matters,' she sounded resigned. 'You see ... the problem is, love ... I've had it. I don't think I'd have the strength to run now, even if we got the chance.'

They sat together in silence. From the valley far below, the leaden roar of the river came up at them like a warning. Once across the other side of that barrier and they would have too far to run anyway.

Chapter 15

The promise of the river tugged at Oshima, dragging him down the steep, matted slopes of the valley.

On the outward journey the same great river had been relatively benign. Below him now, where they must cross, it was squeezed between the great walls of the valley. Already he could hear its hectoring voice.

On the far side, up that precipitous green slope, was sanctuary. Once over that towering ridge they would be within an hour of their camp. There, he knew, all these confusions and all this unstructured, uncontrollable situation would resolve in some way equally beyond his control.

Oshima was resigned to that, and aware of a profound sense of regret about the fragmentation of his hold over himself and the events of his life.

He felt himself to be in the grip of an irresistible force. His will was no longer strong enough to resist the pull of events.

Once his iron self-discipline had been his counter to the chaos of nature all around him in the jungle. Now he felt helplessly caught up by the disordered and random

255

anarchy of it all.

It was a familiar feeling. Once before the wild nature of political events had been the destroyer. When the political sins of his father had been visited upon him, not even Oshima's blinkered concentration had saved him. He had watched helplessly then as his career was wrecked by forces he was unable to control.

And now, once again, his solid and protective armour of discipline and order had cracked open, this time to reveal a presentiment of death.

Oshima watched Nagato and Moritoh scrambling down the muddy incline, clinging to trees, stepping around debris fallen from above and washed down towards the river in the timeless churning of the forest. They seemed like strangers to him; leaden-footed, clumsy.

He hung behind fascinated by the ornamental beauty of his women.

Their easy grace made them appear weightless. In their downward flight they seemed to soar, as lovely as any butterflies he had ever studied; touching the ground lightly only to lift up again; now together, now apart: the sturdy grace of the woman, the quicksilver fragility of the girl; two exquisite day flyers.

Shafts of sunlight, piercing the roof of the jungle, gleamed briefly on their hair as they glided downwards through the dappled light and shade.

Down, down they flew and Oshima followed them, discreetly distanced so that he could observe them without frightening them; without causing them to lift up, soar up out of sight, out of his life.

But the joy of it was overwhelmed by regret. He knew himself to be their Nemesis. For all that glitter of life on them now, they were as doomed as all the other lovely creatures he had consigned to the killing flask. Their fate was an airless death; imperceptible decay; dust gathering on their wings.

Now he could glimpse patches of water rushing below. The roar of the river was loud.

The woman was shouting in his ear. Oshima cupped his hand to hear better.

Asking him to stay close to the girl. Oshima nodded vigorously to show that he understood.

The river surged past. As far as he could see in both directions, the broken water stretched out of sight, yet boulders showing above it indicated that it might be shallow enough to cross.

Coming this way was yet another mistake, Oshima knew. But there was no choice now. It would take hours to work their way along the tangled bank to find a less dangerous crossing and the enemy might already control the usual fords.

The women looked scared as they contemplated the forty yards of raging water before them.

He crossed to Nagato, impassive by the edge of the jungle.

'Stay together. You stick with the woman. Moritoh and I will take the girl.' Even shouting, Oshima was not sure the man had heard.

But Nagato nodded expressionlessly and, slinging his machine pistol over his shoulders to leave his hands free, walked over to the woman.

The girl seemed anxious. Oshima saw the woman shrug at her resignedly.

For a moment it occurred to Oshima to leave them. What was the point of taking them? But he was locked in; to shoot them was unthinkable, to leave them was possibly to consign them to another, maybe even worse, fate.

He walked across the narrow sandbank into the water, knee deep, feeling the amazing pull of the surge on his legs. Moritoh and the girl joined him.

'She's frightened, so stay close,' he yelled. Moritoh understood and nodded.

Oshima held out his hand. For a moment the girl hesitated, a look of fear and dismay on her face, then she grasped it tightly.

The soft, smooth texture of her skin! How vulnerable she was. Oshima looked Brandeis directly in the eye and gripped more tightly to encourage her; to reassure her that he would not let her down on this dangerous journey they were to share.

He jerked his head at Moritoh. He, too, took Brandeis in his grip, holding her high on the arm.

Together they edged into the deeper water.

Out of the corner of his eye Oshima saw the woman ignore Nagato's proffered hand. She waded into the water alone. Nagato stood for a moment, his hand hanging foolishly, then went in after her, a yard or so behind.

Although Winters was exhausted she was determined that she was not going to take any help from Nagato. She would cross, she vowed, without having his filthy paws all over her. She would stay as close to Sally and the other two Japanese as she could.

The anger showed on the squad leader's face when she ignored his hand.

Winters waded into the torrent. The malevolent power of the river shocked her. It was far rougher than she realised, and here and there frighteningly deep.

She edged and manoeuvred from rock to rock, making graceless lurches between the boulders. The water tore at her.

Keep your head. Take your time.

The panic came under control.

She was aware of Nagato just behind her. Winters felt resentment that he seemed to be having no difficulty with the current. She had

259

the feeling he was laughing at her desperate efforts to stay upright. He stayed close enough to intimidate her, yet not quite close enough to help, if she did get into difficulties.

Waist deep, chest deep; on an on, traversing one stretch of surging water after another.

From time to time she glimpsed Brandeis, obviously frightened, making slow progress with the help of the two soldiers. But Winters had enough on her hands surviving, without worrying about her companion.

Already Winters and Nagato were yards ahead of the others, who seemed to be making heavy weather of it.

Not even the earth tremor Brandeis had experienced on her first day in the Islands had the elemental force of this river.

To Brandeis it was as though the torrent was made vindictive by her fear of water. She was to be its special victim. It pulled and worried at her as a dog would a rabbit. It clawed at her legs and she had a surreal vision that the moment her feet were prised free of the river bed, she would be cast downriver like a flung spear to embed head-first in a rock.

The officer's iron grip and the shoulder of the young soldier, which she held on to with a frantic force, were her only lifelines, but the men felt weak and inadequate compared with the primal savagery of the water.

Oshima was waist deep now and moving slowly sideways, looking back at her, his face grim.

Yard by slow yard they edged across. About halfway Brandeis missed her footing and hung between the two men dragging like a flimsily anchored boat in a tidal wave.

Scrabbling desperately she at last found solid ground beneath her feet. Moritoh grabbed her belt. She could feel his knuckles biting into her back, and managed a fleeting smile of relief at him.

He nodded encouragingly. They edged on into deeper water.

Twenty-five yards upstream Brandeis could see Winters clinging to a rock. She and the squad leader were already much nearer the bank than they. Nagato was standing immobile a yard or so behind her with the torrent pouring around him as though he were a boulder solidly embedded in the river.

Brandeis felt angry at her own weakness and clung more tightly to her supporters.

They inched forward, Lieutenant Oshima now chest deep in the surge. He reached forward to grab a boulder standing high out of the water. Suddenly he was gone in a white flurry of foam.

Brandeis screamed.

For Oshima, the river crossing was a metaphor of all the irresistible forces which,

261

lately, had caught him in their grip.

When he lost his footing he became mere debris to be flung about by the fates. To be completely at the mercy of wild nature seemed appropriate. Somewhere along the way he felt he had lost whatever right of authority he might have had.

He resigned himself almost gratefully to the whim of the river. Whirled around in a vortex of water, he was conscious of a series of vivid impressions; the great vee of the valley pointing down to the sunstruck, broken rapids; the steep walls of the jungle, on the one side, then on the other; the woman – her arms wide, balancing like a slackwire walker – and behind her Nagato (afterwards Oshima was to think of the squad leader at that moment as a hawk poised for the kill); Moritoh standing helpless with his arms reaching forward in a gesture of despair; the bobbing head of the girl, a yard away.

As Oshima sluiced downstream great rocks seemed to slide apart before him like iron gates. He saw Moritoh dive after the girl.

Then, independently of his mind, Oshima's survival instincts began working again, battling against the crazed, wilful force of the river.

His feet touched bottom. He caught at a rock and his world stopped spinning.

Oshima worked his way towards the bank. For a moment there, as he summoned up the strength to haul himself clear, he saw the four of them for a frozen moment: the woman by the bank; Nagato close behind her; Moritoh and the girl, clinging like lovers. Spray hung over them all as though the river were covered in a mist of butterflies.

Moritoh braced himself against the flood for a moment, dismayed by having the girl dragged so effortlessly from his grip. Then he plunged into the channel after Brandeis.

He careered almost joyfully downstream. Ahead he could see her half-surfing in the torrent flailing her arms, trying to regain her footing. Ten yards further on, caught in a wider channel, Lieutenant Oshima was out of his depth, swimming desperately.

She was closer now. As she twisted round on the flood she shouted something. Her words were drowned by the roaring of the river.

Now, reaching for her hand Moritoh grabbed and missed; grabbed again. Then he was off balance and helpless with his back against her legs and both she and he jammed against a boulder. Then Brandeis was supporting him as much as he supported her.

They steadied together. The panic left her eyes. Moritoh was acutely aware of her beauty. The river had washed the mud from her face and hair. She looked fresh and her skin was as smooth as a child's.

She looked back over his shoulder and Moritoh craned around to see Winters, fifty yards upstream, scrambling up the bank. Nagato was behind her.

Downstream, the lieutenant was still struggling, sometimes on his feet, sometimes caught by the bucketing water.

Moritoh took Brandeis tightly around her waist and they worked their way sideways, letting the current carry them towards the shore.

Behind them Oshima was using the same method to gain the bank.

It took ages, alternately surging downstream then edging shorewards until they manoeuvred close enough to grab at branches and vines.

Ten yards downstream the lieutenant was pulling himself up the bank, then crabwise, along the top of the tangled bank, he came back for them.

Brandeis reached up and was grabbed. Moritoh pushed hard from below and she was clear of the river. With his last strength Moritoh dragged himself up the bank after her.

The three of them stood together on top of the lunatic tangle of roots, creepers, fallen branches and debris that crowded the bank and hung over the edge of the river. There was barely room to stand. The noise of the river was deafening.

Moritoh unslung his rifle and pack. Water poured from it. He saw that Brandeis was close to exhaustion. Doubled over, she hung on to a creeper with her head bowed and her chest heaving. She looked small and fragile.

He gripped the shoulder straps of her pack and dragged its weight from her. Brandeis nodded her thanks, unable to speak.

'Will you tell her that her friend is safe,' Moritoh shouted the words into Oshima's ear. 'Saw them make the shore.

Oshima nodded then spoke to the girl, his mouth close to her ear.

For a moment she looked at him uncomprehendingly but then, suddenly, her expression changed sharply to one of fear.

Moritoh saw her move quickly to the overhang. Holding onto a branch, she leaned out, looking back upriver anxiously.

When she turned, her expression was horrified. Moritoh saw her shout something at Lieutenant Oshima.

Suddenly, Oshima was gone, crashing his way through the undergrowth, Brandeis hard on his heels.

Moritoh, caught up by their fears, grabbed his rifle and the two packs, and went after them.

When their configuration of three sundered, to Winters it was like seeing the links of a chain part in slow motion.

First she saw the officer go. A moment later he reappeared clear of Brandeis, one yard, then five. Then Brandeis went. The young soldier grabbed at her and missed.

Distracted, Winters herself was caught by a surge and temporarily ducked under. By the time she regained her balance Oshima and Brandeis were being swept downstream at terrible speed. Moritoh was still upright, but shoulder deep.

Must help Sally! Must get to the bank!

Desperately Winters thrashed towards the shore still ten yards away.

She slipped and fell half a dozen times; half-drowning in the surge, then she was thigh-deep, then hanging on to exposed tree roots and dangling creepers overgrowing the steep bank.

Winters clung there, frantically scanning the river. She caught sight of them all, clinging to rocks in the middle of the stream.

Scrabbling up the bank Winters felt as though she were caught in a slimy spider's web of foliage. She was almost clear of the water when something tore agonisingly at her hair, dragging her head back. For a moment she thought her hair had tangled on a branch, but the she heard Nagato's heart-stopping grunt of triumph.

Chapter 16

Oshima ran blindly through the tangle, oblivious of the tear of thorns and branches, more angry with himself than ever before in his life.

It seemed to him that his brain had ceased to work properly. It worked only in snatches. In the past days, each time a vital decision had to be taken, it seemed to switch off, leaving him with an uphill struggle to reorder events; a struggle for which he no longer seemed to have the will, the strength, nor the intellect to win. He had become a sad blundering creature, a night flyer without an antenna. Everything was coming asunder. His mistakes, coming one on top of the other, seemed to him to be the loss of some fundamental control over himself; over his life, and the lives of those under his command.

How could he have been so stupid as to trust Nagato with the woman's care? Nagato, that mindless, venal thug.

He charged on parallel to the river, now invisible behind the dense screen of trees. Had he run far enough, or was he already past the place where he had seen them climb up, with Nagato close enough behind her to touch? He slowed uncertainly for a moment, then ran on again.

Oshima practically fell over them.

The scene at first did not register. The woman, her clothes seemingly ripped from her body, face down on the ground as though impaled. Nagato, half reared up, gripping her shoulders, his naked back arching as he thrust at her, head back, teeth bared in an agonised rictus of lust.

Oshima's roar of anguish and rage sounded above the sonorous, muted boom of the river. All reason gone, he smashed his gun, two-handed down across Nagato's head and shoulders. The squad leader's reflexes enabled him to half twist away, but the blow was a terrible one.

Nagato cried out and fell sideways to the ground on the other side of the woman's body.

Oshima leaped across her and raised his gun high overhead to batter the life out of his squad leader.

Nagato struck upwards in a great backhand arc of steel.

Oshima's motion was arrested as though he had run into a wall. A searing pain caught under his arm. He felt as if he had been cut in half.

As he stood there, his shirt metamorphosed scarlet before his eyes. Terrible surges of pain agonised through every part of his body, then he began to stagger backwards. His feet caught the legs of the woman and he fell, his gun still in his hands. He lay there, nerve ends shrieking in protest. Nagato reared up slowly against the dark green background of the trees, holding his head in agony.

Oshima's mind seemed to have changed down into slow motion. If only, he thought, he could change grip on his weapon he could shoot Nagato. But his arm was useless. Although there seemed to be all the time in the world, he knew he'd never be able to do it.

The squad leader was directly over him now, still clutching his head, but his expression had become one of savagery.

As Oshima watched Nagato eased himself down and picked up something. His knife.

He stood there swaying for a long time then casually, contemptuously, he kicked the gun out of Oshima's hand.

He came closer and with his knees together speared down viciously on to Oshima's chest with the full force of his massive frame.

The white agony slowly cleared away. Oshima could feel Nagato's breath on his face. His hair was grabbed painfully and his head jerked to one side.

'Cutting the throats of queers has always given me special pleasure.' Nagato's face was twisted by an agonised grin of triumph.

At that moment, before he was about to die, Oshima was no longer in pain. The first tormenting shock of his wound was past. It had never occurred to him that death would be like this: cold-blooded and deliberate, with time to think about it. Most of the deaths he had witnessed, or inflicted, had been quick, anonymous endings, impersonal and over in a moment. In this jungle war the victim seldom saw the face of the man who separated him from his soul.

But Oshima was seeing everything with extraordinary clarity; the pores on the smooth skin of Nagato's face, the wispy beard and moustaches falling on either side of the fleshy mouth, the superb teeth, the way the eyelashes lined the brown, gleaming eyes.

Nagato fixed Oshima with an almost rapturous gaze. Oshima felt as though he were a human sacrifice watching the High Priest choosing the place into which to drive the obsidian knife.

The blood he could see on the knife-blade was his own. Another mistake. Oshima thought coldly about that. His brain really must have ceased to work. He could have so easily shot Nagato. But to come within range of Nagato's knife! He was not the kind of enemy you tackled with anything less than a bullet.

Dying did not matter to Oshima at that moment, but he regretted having failed his matched pair. He wondered if the woman was dead.

Nagato must have sensed the question by some tiny, instinctive movement of Oshima's eyes.

He grinned down at Oshima.

'She was good,' he said, 'and she'll be good again.'

Oshima felt a surge of disgust and closed his eyes.

Nagato slapped him lightly on the cheek with the blade of the knife. Oshima opened his eyes again.

'Perhaps you would have preferred it, sir,' he said, 'If I had fucked you instead?'

There was a sharp crack behind them. Nagato half raised his knife. He continued to look down at Oshima, but his eyes lost focus; a film glazed over them like the sum on milk. Out of his forehead he had grown a thick, scarlet column. A unicorn's horn.

The column spouted for a few seconds before it twisted and collapsed. The squad leader pitched forward like a wrestler butting his opponent, and his gouting brow smashed into Oshima's face.

Oshima cried out in horror and pain as warm blood spilled over him and filled his eyes.

What Moritoh saw when he burst through the thicket was a preconception; rapist and victim. He saw Nagato straddling the woman, the woman spreadeagled on her

271

back. He shot from the hip and, in that moment realised that Nagato's victim was not the woman, but Lieutenant Oshima.

As Moritoh ran forward he saw Nagato sitting perfectly still above Oshima. Something odd about the scene stopped Moritoh short; a curving column of red arched from Nagato's head to the ground a yard or so beyond the lieutenant.

Abruptly the smooth, solid-seeming curve lost its geometry. Nagato pitched forward to lie forehead to forehead in Oshima's arms like an exhausted lover.

Dazedly Moritoh moved forward. Then it was he saw the body of the woman lying on the ground beyond the two men. He wondered if she were dead.

Moritoh dragged the squad leader's body sideways. The head and shoulders came clear, but the heavy bulk of the man resisted his efforts.

The lieutenant opened his eyes; the whites showing startlingly against the mess of scarlet that covered his head and shoulders. They told of shock and agony. Oshima closed them quickly against the blood.

Angrily Moritoh pulled at the dead, unresisting weight of Nagato until Oshima was free of his macabre burden.

The front of Oshima's shirt was covered in blood. For a moment Moritoh thought it was Nagato's, but then Oshima clutched at his chest near his right armpit and his face crazed in pain.

As Moritoh knelt he saw the girl come crashing through the scrub. She ran past him to crouch beside the still figure of the woman.

Again the lieutenant tried to open his eyes, then clawed agitatedly at the blood that covered his face.

'Hold still, sir.'

Moritoh reached across and pulled some of Nagato's shirt free. The fabric was half rotten with sweat and damp, and tore easily.

Gently Moritoh began to mop the blood clear of Oshima's face and eyes, but it was hopeless; the warm, sticky, glutinous mess would not come away.

'Sir.' This, urgently, to calm Oshima who seemed to be panicking. 'Keep your eyes closed.'

Moritoh unslung his water bottle and uncapped it. Slowly he poured water over Oshima's face, wiping away the blood, this time, effectively.

Frantically Oshima was opening and closing his eyes. There was a look of terror about him and he was making strange, animal like whimpering sounds.

'Steady. Steady,' said Moritoh. At last the blood was clear of Oshima's eyes. 'Try that.'

Oshima opened his eyes. They were bleak with pain but his breathing steadied.

Moritoh began to unbutton the bloody shirt pulling it clear of the sticky mess underneath.

'Hold still.' He cut the shirt free around the shoulder using Nagato's knife. When he lifted the lieutenant's hand there was a surging of blood. Oshima gasped with pain.

The cut began deep under the armpit, the bicep was practically cut in half, as though by a sword. The razor-like knife had passed between the arm and the thick vertical muscle down the trunk, then continued in a deep sweep across the ribs and the muscles of the chest.

Moritoh ripped the rest of the shirt from Nagato's back.

He made a thick pad and wedged it over the deepest part of the wound. He eased the lieutenant's arm over carefully to hold the pad in place and pressed down gently trying to staunch the pulsing flow of blood.

'You'll be all right.'

Lieutenant Oshima's eyes were closed once more. He nodded. His teeth showed as he gritted against the pain. A gasp of agony escaped him.

'Anywhere else?' Moritoh asked, feeling helpless.

A slight shake of the head.

'The woman?' Oshima's voice was low. The words had cost him dear.

Moritoh saw that the woman had not

moved. The girl was crouched over her trying to give comfort.

She stared at Moritoh with an expression of cold hatred. Assaulted by the force of her anger, Moritoh looked away, knowing that something personal between them had been sundered irretrievably.

'She's all right. At least, she's alive.'

'It was my fault.' Oshima gritted it out. 'Damn Nagato.' He attempted to sit up. Moritoh supported him. The shirt was red to the waist. The lieutenant looked over at Winters and closed his eyes against the pain.

'Give her your shirt.'

Moritoh stood up and stripped off his shirt.

Brandeis, kneeling with her arms around her companion, looked at him coldly as he did so, unsure of what was going to happen.

The woman looked as though she had been in a bomb blast. Her clothes were in strips. Moritoh could see the smooth white skin of her naked back and shoulders. Her boots and gaiters looked pathetic on her bare legs. Some of her underwear was crumpled on the ground nearby.

He proffered the shirt to Brandeis. Her expression did not alter.

Moritoh felt annoyed that she might believe he meant her harm and gestured towards the woman irritably.

Finally she comprehended, and took the shirt. When she had draped it around the woman's shoulders Brandeis turned back to him with a wan and regretful nod of thanks.

He bowed his head formally and curtly then returned his attention to the lieutenant.

His thoughts were angry. Was he to be blamed for Nagato? What could she have thought as he removed his shirt? Did she think him some kind of unfeeling beast? The barrier of language had never been higher than at that moment.

A great cloud of droning flies were already at Nagato's bloody head. The implications of the squad leader's death struck Moritoh. He was finally free of his tormentor. The intention he had formed to kill him when he got the chance, was something he had known to be a dream; something that could not happen. And yet it *had* happened.

Nagato was dead and he had killed him. But, for all that, Moritoh felt a deep sense of failure. Had it been the girl whom Nagato had raped, then Moritoh would have failed in his sworn purpose of protecting her.

It was not just the woman whom Nagato had attacked, he had ravished them all with that irresistible, primitive power of his. Moritoh stared down at the body, an inert lump of fibre and tissue; so much compost. At that moment, he wanted nothing more than to fire bullet after bullet into it.

'How does it look?' Oshima asked.

'Deep. It's bleeding a bit.' Trying to keep

the panic out of his voice, Moritoh eased Oshima back on to the ground. How much blood can he lose? he wondered.

'The woman have some bandages,' Oshima said weakly. 'First aid box. In my pack. Find my pack.'

Moritoh bit his lip. Hs cursed himself for not thinking of that. After casting about, he found Oshima's pack near the spot from where he had fired the shot.

Kneeling beside Oshima, he tore the wrappings off several dressings, but when he removed the blood drenched pad from the wound, he felt helpless. The task of staunching the flow from such a huge cut seemed, to him, impossible. His lieutenant was going to bleed to death and there was nothing he could do about it.

Winters did not want to look up. She did not want to know what was going on, who had fired the shot, nor why.

She did not want to face anyone again, not ever. An overwhelming feeling of shame and anger consumed her. She could never be clean again, not after that.

The pain of it etched acid thoughts into her brain. Fear had immobilised her, but would it not have been better to die? Oh, she had struggled, but that glittering knife-edge at her face had turned her fight into impotent tokenism. She had been more afraid of that knife than anything else.

That, and his silence had been the terrifying things. As he had dragged her from the riverbank he had said nothing; made no sound as he had cut and slashed her clothes from her body. She had screamed, but the river had masked her cries; looked around desperate for proof that she was not alone, but there had been no one to help her.

She was not alone now, but she had been when it had mattered. Someone was there; someone had fired a shot; someone was dead. A few moments ago someone had said something. But what did she care? What did it all matter now?

If she were to look up, it would all begin again; all that humiliation and pain.

For her, pain and sex had not gone together before, except perhaps for memories of trivial discomforts during those clumsy first efforts with poor, dead Ian, when neither of them knew anything about anything. With David sex had been only the purest pleasure.

But not this. This had been pain all the way.

She had been pitched forward on her face and, when she tried to twist around to stop whatever it was he was doing with her clothes, he had smashed her on the back of the head with the hilt of his knife.

She had clutched her head and lain like a child trying to shut out a nightmare vision, her face in the mud, the broken skin of her scalp under her fingers and her blood coursing through her hair.

She had hoped that it wouldn't hurt too much, but then the pain had begun and she had been disgusted by what he was doing to her and appalled by the force of him as he drove himself into her anguished flesh.

Then he was gone, abruptly.

Now her flesh felt as if it had been torn open and she knew that this was what it was going to be like, if she lived, wherever it was the Japanese were taking her. And she hated the officer and the boy, for, with their protection, they had given her a false sense of security. They had left her vulnerable with no warning of this; no warning to steel herself to bear such abuse and hatred and brutish lust that was worse than any beast, for even they court and have rituals of excitement and prepare themselves for the act, but not that act, that filthy act she had only heard of, although some of the girls said they couldn't see anything wrong with it oh how could they bear it and there were hands on her.

Hands on her. Winters cringed away from them, for hands were fear and pain and power.

Brandeis' voice.

'He's dead. They killed him. The bastard's dead.'

And Winters turned her head away from her friend, because there was no one who

279

could comfort her, or repair her, or make her the same again, not Sally, not any woman, nor any man. Not even David. No one.

Her life was over, for that filth had destroyed something in her, she knew it. And Winters wept in deep racking sobs for all the sin she had committed and all the hurts she had inflicted on her parents and on Sally and on Ian whom she had not loved enough and poor Chuck whom she had failed and for Sally, above all for Sally, whom she had led on this journey and whose fate she knew only too well.

Now there was nowhere to go but out. There was no future for her, nor for Sally. Tomorrow would only bring them something as bad as this, worse than this, and it would be better to be dead than to be used and abused and hurt and humiliated.

And how was she going to be able to move with her clothes shredded on her back like so many rags? She felt again the knife point touching her skin and her clothes being hacked, slashed; felt again the brutal power of his hands ripping and tearing down the walls protecting her body's gates.

Her clothes were being replaced. Winters sat up, not looking at Brandeis but aware of arms around her, gentle and comforting; and the texture of a shirt covering her. Winters buried her head against Brandeis and cried because she was ashamed of not having resisted more, for not having been prepared to die by his knife. She felt that she had surrendered her body too readily in exchange for her life. He had made her feel like a cheap and worthless whore.

Winters lay there choking in self-disgust.

'You're all right now.'

Winters drew away sharply from Brandeis' embrace. Angrily she sat hugging her bare legs with her cheek laid against her knee. Holding herself together, feeling the pain down there where he had torn her flesh, and not seeing anything.

Her bitterness poured out: 'How the hell would you know?'

It was all right for her.

'It's all right for you. It didn't bloody well happen to you! You're not fussy. You'd probably have liked it!'

Brandeis' shoulders drooped in despair.

It was a rotten thing to have said, but Winters had never disliked Brandeis more than she did at that moment. *What does she know? Mouthing that rubbish. She's not feeling this pain. How does she know it'll be all right? What makes her think that?*

'Don't you know, you silly little bitch, this is only the beginning?'

Winters began to weep.

Brandeis ignored the outburst. She understood Winters' anger. She felt only pity for her companion and agonised about her own helplessness.

If only there was something she could say she thought, some way to comfort Mae; to reach out and try to bring her back.

Winters sat there staring into the darkness buttoning the shirt over her body obediently like a patient in shock, hostile and remote.

Brandeis saw Moritoh fetch the first aid box. He knelt beside the officer looking dismayed.

'The officer's wounded.'

Winters did not reply.

'Looks pretty bad.' Brandeis said. 'He's bleeding like a sheep. I'd better take a look.'

'No!'

Winters looked towards the wounded man with an expression of loathing. 'I hope he bleeds to death!'

Winters grabbed Brandeis' arm and shouted into her face. 'To hell with him! Why should we help them? What have they done to us, but this...' She encompassed herself, the two of them and their world, in one hopeless eloquent and pitiful gesture.

'He looks bad, Mae.'

'Don't you dare help him.' Winters cried, furiously. 'If he needs help, then tell him to let us go!' There was an increasing hysteria in her voice. 'That's it! That's the price. We'll save his stinking hide if he lets us go. Tell him that!'

Brandeis said nothing for a moment, then

she shook Winters' shoulders gently.

'I'll be back in a minute.'

'No. That's an order.' Winters' voice was brutal.

Brandeis ignored this and knelt beside Oshima. She took the bandages from Moritoh and addressed Oshima.

'Please send your man for water.'

Oshima's face became oddly calm and peaceful. He passed on the order to Moritoh who looked at Brandeis in astonishment that she would render aid. Already she was concentrating on the wound.

Obediently he went to the river with all the water bottles.

Brandeis glanced back at Winters who was angrily tearing her shredded trouser-legs clear of her gaiters. She got to her feet wearing only the soldier's shirt.

'Did you tell him?' Winters' face was working. 'Did you tell him?' She seemed deranged with anger.

Oshima looked up at her, his face filled with sorrow.

Brandeis went on dressing the wound.

'Let the bastard die,' Winters said and began to cry, her sobs racking her body.

Moritoh returned, gave a water bottle to Brandeis and stared concernedly at Winters.

'Hand me one of those rolled bandages,' Brandeis said, looking steadily at Winters.

Through her tears Winters regarded her

coldly. 'It's all right for you,' she said, sullenly.

Nevertheless she reached into the box, tore the wrapping savagely from a bandage and handed it across.

With a surge of relief Brandeis turned back to the task.

The hideous wound should have been stitched, but there was no chance of that. Tight bandages and dressing would have to do, she decided.

Gently Brandeis eased Oshima half on his side, then she laid dressings along the whole length of the cut.

Winters knelt down beside her and squeezed Brandeis' shoulder briefly.

'Sorry I said that,' she said. Her crying was under control. She shook her head in resigned disbelief. 'But we're a pair of bloody fools just the same.'

They worked together to dress and tightly bandage the wound. Moritoh helped them sit Oshima up so that they could wind the bandage around his body.

'He's in shock.'

'God knows how much blood he's lost.'

At length, they eased Oshima on to his back and sponged the last of the blood away from his face and hair.

Oshima closed his eyes.

'Thank you,' he said.

Brandeis and Winters smiled ruefully at each other across his inert body.

Part 5

THE CAMP

Chapter 17

Winters thought of Nagato's body some-where downstream, bumping its way to the sea.

She had watched impassively as that lump of dead meat, a thing that had been once all fear, all aggression, all terror and pain, was dragged by one foot across to the edge of the river and levered over the tangle on the bank into the grip of the torrent. The body had been heavy, awkward and had snagged a dozen times, but at last Moritoh had kicked it clear and the river had taken it.

She had watched it carefully – a black shape in the black-green water, bobbing and float-ing obscenely on the rain-swept surface – to make sure that it was really gone; that its evil, destructive force was out of her life forever.

The body moved faster and faster as the river asserted its claim; the further from the bank the faster it moved. It slammed against a boulder, was caught in a race of broken water, disappeared under the surface to re-appear seconds later, fifty yards down-stream. Finally it passed out of sight behind some great rocks and did not reappear again.

When Moritoh had left her, Winters had

stood staring across the river to the trackless forest on the other side. A sense of hopelessness brimmed over. That far, unattainable country on the other side seemed to her to have been their last possibility of escape.

Her attacker had died, but nothing had changed, it seemed. Her flesh still ached down there and she knew she would never be the same again. Even if the officer died from his wound, they will be prisoners under the implacable command of guns and knives.

Later Brandeis examined her and used a dressing and some sulpha powder to dress the wound. The cuts on her head had coagulated, but without cutting the hair away, there was not much Brandeis could do except sponge the blood off.

They found their packs. Clean clothes made Winters feel better. They were wet, but here, everything was wet, so it did not matter.

The three of them ate in silence. Before the rain began, flies swarmed around the cuts on Winters' head. The young soldier took of his cap and gave it to her. She shook her head at first but he insisted gently and she took it. Later Moritoh, looking much less fearsome without his cap, gave them each a piece of sugar cane.

Moritoh pulled out his tobacco tin and offered it to Brandeis. She came close to smiling at him for that, and rolled a smoke for each of them, two-handed, no longer bothering to show off.

The rain began about one o'clock in the afternoon, a relentless, cleansing waterfall dropping straight out of a bruise-grey cloud of mist that pressed halfway down the slope of the valley. It drummed mightily high above them on the treetops and spilled own through layer upon layer of foliage, forming solid silver cables of water that jetted down on them as though from spigots.

The great river, which had so nearly destroyed them all, boomed on behind the screen of trees. The rain hissed down on its angry surface turning it black.

Winters and Brandeis sat together facing Moritoh under the shelter of a leafy lean-to he had constructed expertly from branches and the leaves of a ginger bush. Next to him, Oshima lay flat on his back on a spread groundsheet.

When, some two hours later, Oshima opened his eyes he refused food, but drank a lot of water.

It was obvious to both the women that he was in shock. They laid him back.

'We will rest here,' he murmured, and immediately lapsed into unconsciousness again.

Winters felt cut off, detached from the others, as though she were observing them through a soundproof glass screen. She saw Brandeis, preoccupied with her own thoughts, sitting blank-faced, cupping her thin hands around her cigarette; the anxious face of the handsome young boy concentrating on his food, and the thin, bloodless face of the wounded officer, inert as a corpse. She gazed at their captors.

How ordinary they seemed, these two Japanese soldiers, so unthreatening compared with the other who had died. The boy could have been eighteen, twenty-five or thirty. It was impossible to tell. There were great fatigue shadows under his eyes that aged him.

Now it was he, with his striking face and his oddly formal manner, who held the power of life and death over them. At that moment she hated him for it. She was overcome by bitter thoughts. Why do we not have guns? They put us in uniform and bring us here to this stinking, primitive place and then cast us loose like lambs to the slaughter. If we had guns we might have had an even chance, instead of being helpless; able to be shoved about, ordered about, abused and tortured without being able to fight back.

If ever she got out of this, Winters vowed, she would never again allow herself to be in a position where everyone else could dictate her destiny.

It was hard enough to resist the power of men whose ways you knew, who spoke the same language, fought on the same side. To resist these aliens was impossible. *Next time*

I'll come back as a man. Next time.

Winters turned her face up towards the rain, seeking solace from it, as though it might cleanse her, act like some tranquillising drug, soothing her wounds, calming jangled nerves and smoothing the edges of her terrible anger.

Oshima regained consciousness. He lay, trying not to breathe too deeply. To breathe was agonising.

If I keep perfectly still, he thought, it doesn't hurt so badly.

He wondered if he had slept, or fainted. It seemed to him that all the blood in his body had spilled out. Had any arteries been cut? He could not remember enough of anatomy.

What time was it? Impossible to tell. The sun was hidden behind the rain mist. His watch was on his right wrist and the whole of that arm felt as if it were no longer attached to his body. Oshima tried moving his fingers.

Somewhere under the sheet of pain there seemed to be a slight movement. He felt inordinately pleased about that.

'Akiro.'

It was as if someone else had spoken; someone far away. It did not sound like his own voice.

Was he asleep, he wondered; dreaming this?

'Sir.'

A handsome, concerned face was above

291

him. Kurosumo Akiro.

Oshima wanted to reach up and touch that face haloed in light against the dark green background of the leaves. His hand was drawn to that lovely remembered face but it was Moritoh not Kurosumo, who gripped Oshima's hand strongly with both his own.

Moritoh? Of course. Kurosumo was dead; long since.

Moritoh, who had saved him.

Moritoh Senjo.

Senjo. Senjo. Senjo.

His hand feels strong and comforting.

To Oshima it seemed that a smooth balm flowed from the boy, flooding into his own body as though through a thick conduit. The pain was suddenly bearable.

'Is it bad?'

Oshima shook his head, content to look at that young anxious face; to look deep into those soft concerned eyes.

'Put my watch on my left wrist. What time is it?'

Moritoh held up Oshima's left arm so that he could see his watch face.

'Three o'clock. See? Your watch is already on your left wrist. The women changed it over when they dressed your wound.'

Senjo. The sound of the name reverberated pleasingly in Oshima's mind. He had never used Moritoh's given name before. Senjo. In real life he would have been able to

292

call him always by his given name.

What a waste war is! It had taken all that death and all that blood before he could say it.

'Senjo.'

Talking hurt badly. He must take his time. They might have been loving friends, Moritoh and he, if things had fallen out another way. He could be one of my students. Another Kurosumo. How alike they were in the eagerness of their youth, in their confident, arrogant beauty. Akiro, Senjo: two men, one rhythm.

Get a grip. They must move. Must warn command. There was no possibility now that they could make camp by tonight, but if they could get halfway up from the river, they could sleep the night and maybe he would feel stronger in the morning.

Must tell him; tell Senjo, must push the words up through the pain.

'Sir?'

The boy's eyes were soft with pity.

'We must move. Now. Get as far as we can.'

Why is he shaking his head? He thinks I'm too weak to move. He thinks it is the wound that causes me to lie here. He does not know of the force that pins me here to the ground; the implacable weight of a man without resolve, of a man who has no volition for anything. He does not know that once, I, Oshima Eeji, was like this for a

293

whole year.

'You've lost too much blood.'

Blood? What is a loss of blood? How does that compare with losing your purpose, or having it taken away from you? What does something so trivial matter put alongside being caught in the field of force of nothingness; no direction, no purpose, no work allowed, no supporters, no students. Even his beloved Kurosumo gone.

Maybe I'll lie here for a year to show him what it means to be nothing, to want to do nothing, to simply exist.

'Help me up.'

Moritoh's arms feel strong about my shoulders, his chest solid against my forehead. If he could only stay there, not take the conduit away, the pain would be bearable.

Must move. They won't know the enemy is coming.

If I breathe in shallow fashion the saw-blade seems to stop slicing at my chest.

The women sat watching.

What curious enemies we are given to fight. They are standing close now, spinning in whiteness.

'Sit down. You can't possibly go on.' Winters' words had immediate meaning. There was no delay as ancient linguistic circuits, sharpened by pain, instantly connected.

Three faces above him. He was surrounded by beauty. Three beautiful courtiers in attendance. They could have been hatched from the same egg, Senjo and two lovely captives. Oshima felt strong and happy.

'No.' This in English for their benefit. 'No. We must go on.'

The women were speaking, arguing, telling him he could not go on. Had they forgotten that they were prisoners? The pain was sharp now, clearing his head with its insistence.

He would give the orders.

Senjo was searching his face. Oshima wondered: was the embryo of a special friendship contained in his look of deep understanding?

'We would be safe here, sir. And tomorrow you'll feel stronger.'

Oshima shook his head. If he continued to lie down he might not want to get up again, not ever. What would be the point of climbing that ridge, going back to camp with a piece of useless intelligence they probably knew already? It would make no difference to anything. But if he continued to lie there the futile answers to all these futile questions would pin him there, like a flight of arrows, forever.

'You take my pack, Moritoh. I'll manage my weapon. Help me up.'

Moritoh considered him for a long time.

'Sir.'

Leaning back against the tree Oshima watched them collect and don their packs.

Their faces were closed. He felt like a patient who made his nurses angry by ignoring their advice.

He tried a few steps. The pain caught him halfway through a breath and the sear of it stopped him. In time, it subsided. If he took his time he might be able to stand it.

Oshima lowered himself gingerly, supporting his weight with his thighs, and picked up his gun. It felt heavy, inert and unbalanced. The white-out cleared.

He nodded to Moritoh. He, in turn, gestured to the women. With one last backward glance, Moritoh led off slowly up the slope.

When they came to the track the boy went off alone, scouting ahead, presumably to see that it was all clear. Oshima stood with his eyes closed, leaning against a tree. He seemed about to collapse.

Brandeis and Winters stood opposite him; feeling awkward. Not knowing whether to suggest he sit down, or not.

They had not come two hundred yards and already Brandeis was feeling that she could not go another step. A crushing tiredness weighed upon her.

It would be better if he did fall down. He wouldn't keep going for too long, not with that wound.

Brandeis had been constantly amazed by the incredible resilience of wounded men.

They could put up with the most intense agony for hours without morphine. They would be carried in with shattered bones, or great hunks ripped from their bodies, lying on stretchers gritting and grinding their teeth; something inside them, some steel armature of courage, holding them together. She had known men who had gone twenty-four hours like that; it could take longer to get back to a dressing station. After that, of course, they fell apart. Then, only morphine worked, if it were available. Or, if it were not, the oblivion of madness, or death.

And here was this thin, white-faced man, who had lost God knows how much blood, walking around with a knife wound that would have put a civilian on his back for three months.

The poor bastard. Putting up with all that pain. Probably standing there because he daren't sit down.

She was aware that Winters was staring at him, too. There was a distracted expression on her face. She looked bad: the same angry, withdrawn expression she had worn ever since the rape. So bewildered and shocked at having suffered so much fear and pain.

An overflow of compassion caused Brandeis to put her arms spontaneously around her.

'How d'you feel?'

Winters leaned her head down on Brandeis' shoulder.

'OK.'

The acceptance of her gesture of comfort pleased Brandeis greatly. If only there was a way to erase time; to take out the ugly bits and throw them out; to excise the bitter words that had passed between them, to start afresh first thing in the morning.

'I'm frightened, that's all. I don't know what we should do any more.' Winters spoke softly, introspectively. 'I've been thinking ever since...' she shook her head as though fighting off a troubling vision, 'that we should try to get away. I don't think they could stop us with him wounded. And somehow I don't think that boy would shoot us.'

'I wouldn't bet on it.'

'I doubt it. I think he...' Winters searched for the right word 'fancies you.'

Brandeis shrugged, well aware of Moritoh's attention to her.

Winters went on: 'But then I think we'd simply get lost, or what's worse, run into another lot of Japanese. He said they didn't have far to go, so their camp must be near. This side of the river is probably swarming with them and what scares me is that the other ones might be just as bad as that swine who's floating down the river. I just feel safer with this pair. But God knows ... they could be leading us into something a lot worse.' She began to cry deeply and pain-

fully against Brandeis' shoulder. 'I just don't
know what to do.'

It took a long time before the heaving of
Winters' shoulders ceased, and the muttered
words of apologies and curses subsided.
Then she got hold of herself, her face a wreck
of tears and bruises and muddy streaks.

She looked at Oshima who was standing
swaying as though asleep.

'We'd better take a look at that wound of
his,' she said. 'It's bleeding badly.'

Oshima's bandages were bright red from
the blood welling through. When he felt
their hands on him he opened his eyes dully,
and for a moment they flashed with
suspicion. Then he stood quietly.

'The devil you know,' Brandeis said, very
quietly.

'Something like that,' said Mae. 'Sit
down,' she ordered, in her best, no-non-
sense Senior Sister's voice.

He did not resist them. They removed his
shirt and cut away the soaked bandages.
Blood flowed steadily from under the dressings.

Brandeis fetched some of the bandages,
fresh dressings and sulpha powder from the
first aid kit.

Carefully they lifted off the dressing. The
open cut looked like a slice out of a melon.

'Shit.'

'Bandages won't staunch that, not if he's

going to be stupid enough to keep on going.' Winters tentatively pushed the gaping flaps of flesh together.

'Safety pins?'

'Have to be. He'll bleed to death if we don't. Take them off the spare bandages.'

Brandeis found the safety pins and pushed the edges of the wound together as Winters expertly caught the wound with a crude lacing of steel.

Oshima winced in agony, but made no sound.

Brandeis found him looking disconcertingly into her eyes. He tried to smile, but it failed to form as the last pin hooked through his flesh.

Winters laid the dressings along the length of the wound.

'You shove those two ... hard.'

Brandeis obeyed and for several minutes they concentrated on pressing the dressings against the wound to stop the flow.

As Brandeis began to wind the bandages around his chest, Winters took his useless arm and bent it against him so that it was, in turn, bound into place.

'All right?' Brandeis asked.

Oshima nodded, then turned his gaze directly to Winters.

'Sorry,' he said. 'My squad leader an evil man. You are kind. Very sorry.'

Oshima's apology angered Winters.

Sorry, was he? Damn him.

She pressed hard against the thick bulge of dressing under the bandages. Oshima drew in his breath sharply.

It was all very well being sorry, but it was a bit late for that. If this man had been her attacker, Winters thought, she would have watched the blood pour out of him and she would have laughed. But this one is being sorry. Being someone with feelings and some kind of decency. Oh, God, why is it so bloody complicated? He was the slant-eyed enemy, wasn't he?

Sorry. Oh, yes.

It occurred to Winters then that they should simply take his gun and go, but her train of thought was interrupted when Oshima said something in Japanese. Moritoh was standing behind watching. She had not heard him return.

Oshima smiled painfully at Winters. She recognised the kind of smile it was – one of embarrassed gratitude. She had seen it a thousand times in the long, thatched wards back on the coast; somewhere she had worked once, in another life, a long time ago.

Brandeis held the water bottle for her and Winters washed the blood off her hands. She in turn, held it for Brandeis. Already the pile of blood bandages and dressings on the ground had been claimed by the flies.

Winters damped some bandage and used

301

it to mop the blood off Oshima's skin. Their handiwork looked impressive. The fresh bandages gleamed white against the smooth, ivory-brown skin. His body was thin, but functional and well-proportioned.

'It might hold if he'd lie still,' Winters said for his benefit.

They both looked anxiously at the bandages. Very slowly a red patch appeared.

'Bugger,' said Brandeis crossly. Once more, she leaned against the wound firmly pressing with both hands.

'You must rest. Stay still, or you will bleed,' she said insistently to Oshima. 'Do you understand?'

'Sorry. We go now.' He held up his hand to prevent argument. 'Very careful. Slow.' He nodded to them. 'Thank you. Now much better.'

Moritoh handed Winters a shirt he had dug from his officer's pack. They cut away a sleeve then buttoned it over his body.

When they had Oshima back on his feet, Moritoh gave him his gun which he hefted tentatively. Satisfied, Oshima began at once to walk up the steep slope.

Some time later Brandeis looked back at the wounded man. With the fresh shirt covering the bandages he looked remarkably normal, but his face betrayed him. It was clear to her that only willpower was keeping him going.

Brandeis wondered how long he would last. She looked up ahead. The slope seemed to rise forever.

Chapter 18

Lieutenant Oshima had fallen half off the track over a low clump of ferns, face down.

Moritoh turned him over on his back.

His face had the whiteness of death. The wound must have worked open as they climbed. The once white bandage was dark red.

Winters scrambled back down and knelt down beside them. She took his pulse, her slim hands white against the darker skin.

Moritoh looked anxiously at her. She answered his unspoken question by taking his hand and placing his fingers against Oshima's wrist.

The pulse murmured strongly enough under his fingertips. He nodded, then, anxious about them exposed out here on the track, began to lug the lieutenant back into cover.

Winters shook her head and indicated by pushing her two hands, palm downwards, towards the ground, that he should leave the wounded man where he was.

Moritoh pointed determinedly towards the forest, then she understood.

Together, the three of them carried Oshima gently off the track into the deep cover.

Moritoh watched as the women cleaned and redressed the wound. They were almost out of dressings and left a couple of the less bloody ones one. The safety pins had held save one, which had torn through the flesh. They replaced it.

When they sat Oshima up to wrap the bandages around his chest, Moritoh braced himself against the lieutenant's back. The man flopped like an unstrung marionette.

At length the women laid Oshima back gently and Moritoh saw the girl put her pack under the lieutenant's head.

How gentle she was! Moritoh wished it were he who was feeling the soothing touch of her hands.

The woman took Oshima's pulse, but Moritoh could not tell from her expression whether the unconscious man were better or worse.

With a start he realised he should be keeping a lookout. First, they would eat.

He took some biscuits and three cans of beef from his pack, and opened them. He gave food to the women, indicated that they should stay with the lieutenant, and headed back to the track.

Moritoh sat a yard into cover eating out of

the can. His tongue touched the cuts in the inside of his mouth, now nearly healed. He had forgotten about them long since. He thought with some satisfaction of the way the river had dragged Nagato's body out of his hands as though hungry for fresh meat. For those blows he had been revenged many times over.

The squad leader would not be terrorising anyone, ever again, nor spreading his malicious stories about the lieutenant when they got back to camp.

Moritoh was convinced now that Oshima would make it to the camp. He was, more than ever, in awe of Oshima. How could he bear such pain? His courage and endurance were incredible; that of a true samurai.

Perhaps after this they would be closer, Oshima and he, maybe with the closeness of two samurai who had shared a great battle. Like brothers.

If only just once, Oshima had unbent towards him, but Oshima never had. Indeed, if anything, it seemed to Moritoh that he had been treated more stiffly than the other members of Section Seven. At first Moritoh had thought it was simply because he was a new man, yet to distinguish himself. Yet, even after half a dozen missions in which he had proved himself to be as good a soldier as any in the Section, Oshima had not softened. It seemed to make no difference that his lieutenant had more in common with him than with the raggle-taggle group of wharf labourers, shop assistants, clerks and farmers. The reverse was true. In time Moritoh had come to think that the lieutenant must have misjudged their common background of education a disadvantage; something awkward that Oshima rejected as a matter of Section politics; to prevent favouritism. Within the Section, Oshima's cool treatment of him had always puzzled. And yet there were times when Moritoh felt that Oshima had some special regard for him; treated him with warmth, as though he were a special protégé.

Perhaps, thought Moritoh, things would be different now, after all that they had shared on this patrol.

Moritoh felt strangely peaceful. He did not wish to move. It was quiet and still here with the late afternoon sun slanting through the trees, and the lulling drone of insects and the cries and chitterings of birds. There was no war here; no tension, only the lush sound of the jungle and the soothing, moist-green foliage all around.

Perhaps they could simply stay here, never to return to the conflict; just the four of them. The fighting would go on out there somewhere in that futile and murderous world of ambush and counter-attack.

The lieutenant, the woman, the girl and he could live off this teeming land; would be

306

written off simply as statistics, their names as forgotten as those of the dead whose corpses were buried in this land and whose smells caught the throat when you passed along some nervous native track.

Moritoh could now think almost fondly of the old tyrant. (*'You and your friends have drunk and whored your way to expulsion from the university. By your failure to obtain an engineering degree you have brought dishonour not only to yourself, but to me. You can no longer evade your responsibilities. The Army...'*)

Now his father would assume that he had died, would regret his harshness and boast with fond pride how his only son, Moritoh, had died like a samurai in the service of his Emperor. The thought pleased Moritoh. In this place he could be free of his father forever.

There would be no complications in such a life. No need to make another day's journey in peril of your life, never knowing when you were sighted along the barrel of a gun, to have your flesh torn and sundered into a bloody pulp; no need to think about what would happen to her, if and when they did reach the camp; that straggle of sacsac huts and smoky campfires on the other side of the ridge. The camp: his sanctuary, the girl's prospective hell.

Moritoh thought of the men there, lying about, bored, frightened, lethal. Writing letters home, bathing in the river, foraging for fruit and vegetables from the native gardens for miles around.

In Moritoh's mind: memories of night sounds when native women were brought in for sport.

How would the lieutenant explain about taking women prisoners? The men back there would assume he had captured them alive for one purpose. If they were lucky, they would only be shot.

Perhaps Oshima would point out their usefulness as nurses. There were sick and wounded men there rotting with malaria, beri-beri and dysentery, without any medical care at all. But even as that rationale crossed his mind, Moritoh realised how unlikely it was. Half the officers were no better than Nagato. How long would it be before the women were simply used as camp playthings?

The thought of this beautiful girl so defiled made him sick.

How would he have felt if it had been the girl who had been raped? The woman was older; would have known many men; would recover from it.

Had it been the girl, would he have been content merely to shoot Nagato?

Moritoh knew that there would be nothing he could do to save her once in that festering camp. He decided he would rather shoot her than allow her to suffer such torment. She was too fragile to bear such things. He would not let it happen. He could not. He would persuade Lieutenant Oshima to let them go.

Judging by the way Oshima looked, he had the courage and the will to make the journey, but how much blood can you lose? That wound of his belongs in a butchery; great flaps of pink flesh, white sinew and tendon.

How expert the girl seemed to him. She was the one who had been most willing to help Oshima. Moritoh knew that, without the women, there would have been nothing he could have done to save Oshima. He would not have been able to dam that waterfall of blood.

Moritoh found himself nodding. He shook himself awake, scared of his vulnerability. He would require all his vigilance to survive this disastrous patrol. Travellers in ancient times had made long detours to avoid what they believed was an unlucky direction. On this journey Moritoh felt they had been travelling in an unlucky direction from the start. And there was still a long way to go.

His food finished, Moritoh checked the track carefully and picked his way back through the tangle to where he had left the others.

Oshima had regained consciousness. He was sitting, pale and weak, propped against a tree. His gun was on the ground several yards away. Moritoh knew he should have taken it with him. He should have been vexed but, somehow, such things no longer mattered.

Winters had a water bottle to Oshima's lips. By her hand there was a half-eaten can of meat.

Moritoh sought out the girl's eye when he returned but there was nothing in her expression. They had all become used to each other. No emotions were being wasted.

He stood watching the women.

What if he should let them go? Moritoh had thought much about that in the past hours. Let them go. But what would happen to them, having been dragged this far? Perhaps Lieutenant Oshima would allow him to take them back where they might have a chance of being found by their own people; maybe back across the river, as far as the native village where they had been attacked. There they might be safe until they were rescued. He determined that he would ask.

'All clear?' Oshima was having trouble speaking. The pain was obviously bad.

Moritoh nodded. He was about to broach the subject of the women when Oshima attempted to rise. His face was riven by the effort.

'We must go.'

'You can't, sir. We'll go tomorrow. What differences does it make?'

The lieutenant's expression was agonised.

'They may not know about the enemy ... at the camp.' He looked away from Moritoh and there was a long silence. Then he said, as though speaking to himself, 'I don't want another slaughter of our men on my conscience.'

Moritoh carried all three weapons; his own rifle, the guns of Nagato and the lieutenant. Brandeis carried Oshima's pack. Winters supported him as they made their slow way towards the track.

It was near vertical, broken and slippery. For every two yards they made upwards, they slipped back one.

Their grim journey up the steep trail was uncannily silent, save for their harsh breathing, and an occasional gasp of pain from Oshima.

Not a word was spoken – partly from a learned response to danger, but mainly because they understood instinctively that one single word from any of them might open up the processes of thought and they could not afford to think about the futility of what they were doing.

Heavy rain fell at one stage, but briefly. They ignored it and kept on going up towards the top of the ridge far above them, as though the existence of that hidden crest were reason enough for their madness. They seemed caught in a dreamlike frenzy.

A half-illusory force mesmerised them. It

was as if the jungle heaved with some disease that incubated in the feral rot all around them.

Winters felt oddly disembodied. The pain in her chest and the leaden fatigue of her limbs seemed to belong to someone else. It was as though her body had melted and begun to fuse with the jungle. She was at one with it, simply a part of some incomprehensible indifference. All that had gone before in her life, all the pettiness, the guilt, fear and anger had been burned away to a white ash by the green furnace that held her. She felt pure. She simply was. Mechanically, she moved towards that elusive and weightless moment when nothing would ever frighten her again.

Sometimes Moritoh took the weight of the lieutenant, sometimes the women supported him. They lost count of the number of times Oshima fell, or had to stop because the pain was too great to bear. Eventually, it was not only the wounded man who could not continue. All of them had come to the end of their physical resources.

The last time Oshima fell, they carried him in off the track and slumped to the ground together, unable to move.

The hushed jungle around them echoed with the constant chirr of insects. Near them a giant, sweet blossomed tree grew a rainbow crop of butterflies.

When, at length, they awoke, Winters felt a crushing, bone-deep exhaustion. What must it be like for the wounded man? she wondered. She looked at her watch. They had lain there for at least an hour.

Oshima was unconscious where they had left him, his bandages completely soaked in blood.

Moritoh, squatting beside his officer, questioned them with anxious eyes.

Winters took the pulse. 'We're gong to have to take a look,' she said to Brandeis, who nodded tiredly, her face gaunt with fatigue.

They knelt down on either side of Oshima and began to strip the bandages.

Winters nodded encouragement to Moritoh. He looked relieved, stood up and walked away quietly to disappear in the direction of the track.

Oshima was now half-conscious. His teeth showed in a grimace of pain as Winters pressed against the bloody dressing to try to stop the bleeding. She looked at Brandeis and gave a worried shake of her head.

They shared a memory of hopeless cases in wards they had worked in; times when only habit and hope had kept them going.

They knew that if Oshima lost much more blood he would be finished. Not even the safety pins would be much help if he insisted on walking any further.

'We'll have to use the old dressings. There are none left,' Brandeis said. 'Just a few bandages.'

But Winters had thought about that.

'Yes, we have.'

She rummaged deep down into her pack and found the sanitary towels. How ironic that it should be his bleeding that was to give them use, she thought. She had brought them along in the superstitious hope that, somehow, having them with her would bring on her period. How trivial the complications of an unwanted pregnancy seemed to her at that moment.

Brandeis grinned tiredly at Winters when she saw the dressings.

'Use your initiative, girls.' She mimicked Winters. 'Senior Sister Winters' first lecture to tyro nurses.'

'I won't be needing them.' Winters concentrated on unwinding the blood-soaked bandages. 'I'm two months gone.'

Their eyes met across the wounded man. Brandeis' face filled with concern.

'Oh, Mae. I am sorry.'

Winters shrugged and went on stripping away the dressings. She felt released, like a convict whose fetters have been struck off.

'It doesn't matter. Not now.' She caught Brandeis' eye. 'And I don't regret it; not one bit. Nor do I regret my ... "hypocritical behaviour" ... wasn't that what you called it?'

Brandeis looked grieved.

'I'm really sorry about that. That was someone else talking.'

'I know.'

There was silence for a time as they focused their attention on the wound. It seemed free of infection, but the flesh had torn away from the pins in three places.

As they replaced them: 'Do the girls really call him that?' Winters coloured slightly as she spoke.

'Your David? "Balls of Fire"?' Brandeis gave an embarrassed grin. 'Yes.'

'Good God!' Winters suddenly laughed outright. Her laughter chimed magically in the jungle; seemed to let in the light; seemed to push back the trees.

'He would be flattered. Here...' Winters placed the thick napkins along the length of the wound. 'Press down.'

They worked in a curiously light-hearted harmony winding the bandages around and around their unconscious patient.

'One thing,' Winters said. 'The little bugger's not having a boring start to his life.'

Chapter 19

Something was making Moritoh uneasy.

He looked down the trail, back in the direction of the river. A long, careful look. Nothing. Then the other way, up the native pad to the left in the direction they would take in a few minutes. Again, nothing, but still he was not satisfied. He had learned long since to trust his instincts.

Then, as he drew back, he saw it; a flicker of movement. The momentary blocking out of a thin shaft of sunlight.

Moritoh froze. The saliva dried in his throat.

Again the movement; then again.

Ours? he wondered.

A minute passed. Two. Then, totally silent, a black passed the spot opposite where they lay.

Forward scout.

For a time there was only the normal racket of the jungle. Then, as though at some given signal, all the jungle creatures had held their breath, the sounds of the forest abruptly cut out.

The point soldier passed; green uniform, beret. The enemy.

Moritoh took a deep breath to steady his racing heart and very carefully drew back. With great care he went back to where he had left Oshima and the women.

They had, in his absence, propped the lieutenant against a tree. Oshima's eyes were open but he ignored Moritoh. He kept looking into the gloom somewhere to his right. He was clutching his shoulder.

Moritoh knelt beside him and breathed the words into his ear: 'Enemy Patrol. Tell the women to keep quiet.'

Oshima did not seem to hear, but then, staring in the same direction, he groped one-handed for his weapon in the manner of a blind man and automatically, he checked the magazine.

Moritoh eased the safety catch off his own rifle. He picked up Nagato's weapon, saw that it was ready to fire and laid it down on the ground at his feet.

He was aware of the women watching him. There was a tense, volatile look about them, as though they were about to bolt, or cry out. They looked back towards the track, at him and the lieutenant, then at each other. He gained the impression that, at any second, they would act.

Still Lieutenant Oshima gave no signal; said nothing. Moritoh was puzzled. Was he going to tell them to remain silent, or not?

Oshima continued to stare off into the

trees. Moritoh followed his gaze.

Twenty yards away there was a tree covered in brightly coloured flowers. But, as Moritoh looked, the blossoms moved. The tree was swarming with butterflies: a vivid mosaic of them like a living stained glass window.

The lieutenant seemed spellbound by the sight. His gun was held loosely in his one good hand, its butt resting on the ground by his hip. There was a distracted expression on his face. Moritoh wondered if pain had taken Oshima over the edge into madness. He caught the girl's eye. She was staring at him with a bright, expectant look that disconcerted him. Once more the focus of Moritoh's attention returned towards the trail. He strained to hear, but there was only the eerie, expectant hush of the silent forest.

With his left hand, palm down, he indicated that they should get down slowly. He put his fingers to his lips, but they stood looking at him blankly as though they did not understand.

It occurred to him with a shock of anger that they were not going to obey.

He swung his rifle up at them. The eager look in their eyes changed into something sullen, disappointed.

They sat down facing him; both looking grim. He pointed his rifle at the woman and stared over, slowly shaking his head at them in warning.

He slid a glance at the lieutenant and was shocked to find that he had closed his eyes. It was as though Oshima had lost all interest in the proceedings.

A sound.

With his eyes back on the women, Moritoh half turned his head to hear better.

Silence. He thought that the enemy soldiers must be about opposite their hiding place by now. How many? How long would they take to pass?

There came the sound of a voice; very quiet, very near. Another; replying.

Had they seen him, and stopped?

The lieutenant's eyes were open again, but still he was staring over at the swarm of butterflies as though hypnotised by the strangeness of it.

Moritoh heard the swishing of legs against foliage. Instinctively, he reached down to ensure that Nagato's machine pistol was by his hand.

The prisoners' faces were turned eagerly towards the sounds. Moritoh jerked the tip of his rifle at them and scowled. They reacted nervously; their faces darkening with frustrated anger.

There was silence again, but then suddenly Moritoh was profoundly shaken by a new sensation, the meaning of which came to him slowly: the smell of tobacco smoke.

The men of the enemy patrol were no more than five yards away. They must have stopped to have a rest and smoke!

Moritoh could sense nerve ends quivering all over his body. He gripped his rifle fiercely to stop his hands trembling.

Have to take a chance.
I'll go when I get to ten.
One...

Winters had been certain there was something scaring Moritoh when he had come scuttling back, his face drawn and tense. Her heart had leapt. She guessed he had spotted someone on the wrong side, for him; perhaps natives, but maybe even another Australian patrol. She was certain that, had it been a mob of Japanese, he would not have returned looking so agitated.

After a few words to Oshima, Moritoh had signalled urgently – sit down and shut up – and had backed the order with his rifle.

In the agonising minutes that had passed since, Winters' mind had been racing. This time, she determined she would do something. But what?

She tried to read the expression in Brandeis' eyes and wondered if Sally understood that this might be a real chance to make a break for it; attract attention, anything that would cause them to be rescued.

Moritoh, all the while, was aiming his rifle

320

directly at her and she was disconcerted by the agitated look in his eye.

Smart, mind-reading little bastard.

He knows I'm just looking for a chance.

If we do get away, he'll be one very dead little Japanese. Both of them will.

Two...

Winters glanced towards Brandeis, but the girl was staring hard at the young soldier as though trying to exert her will on him.

To Winters, Moritoh looked really troubled. His eyes were darting about in a panicky way and he kept looking towards his officer who seemed only half-conscious.

Three...

He's no use to you, mate. He's about to fall over. He's no longer with us, by the look of him.

Four...

Probably just an ordinary bloke in Civvy Street. Poor devil. If he does get out of this lot, he'll have a useless arm for the rest of his days. All that sinew and ligament cut like so much butcher's meat.

Winters was worried about whether, when the moment came, she would have the courage to make the break. Would Moritoh miss his aim if she were to roll over and over the way she had seen the officer do when the natives had ambushed them? She looked at Oshima staring at the butterflies swarming over the tree.

He was really sorry about that animal attack-

ing me.

The tobacco smoke registered with her. She saw Brandeis' eyes widen as the implications of it struck her too.

Oh, God! Our own blokes. Having a smoke. Close enough to spit.

Anguish rose in Winters. Just a few yards away there were unseen men who could save them both and end their ordeal. She felt nauseous with tension.

Why didn't they take their break five yards nearer?

Got to go now. Soon.

I'd be mad not to try.

Held in the thick coils of the jungle's atmosphere, the smell of tobacco smoke was strong now. Moritoh could feel his heart pound.

Occasionally there would come to him sounds at the last threshold of his hearing; murmuring voices, near imperceptible noise of movement in the bush. He wondered how long it would be before one of the intruders stumbled over them all.

Moritoh was acutely aware that the women kept glancing at each other, as though trying to reach some understanding.

If they made a break, or cried out, they would die for it, he vowed. And yet how pointless that would be. He did not hate these enemy women. He could kill them, but then he would die too, and Lieutenant Oshima.

Moritoh thought of the four of them rotting in this unmarked place, so much mulch in the jungle's ever-evolving process of life, death and decay.

What if the lieutenant were to bargain? What if he were to tell the women that we would hand them over unharmed, in exchange for our lives? But even as he thought it, Moritoh knew how absurd such a pact would be. The enemy soldiers, sitting somewhere out of sight, but almost close enough to touch, were no less unyielding and pitiless than he and his own comrades.

The girl was biting her lip nervously. Moritoh saw the woman take her hand.

Sweat was trickling down his back. He stared at the faces of the watches crowding his wrists. The sweep hands crept around in slow parallel.

Oshima sat like a praying monk staring across at the tree with its strange, living decorations.

Suddenly Moritoh had had enough. If Oshima were taking no interest in living, why should he? What was the point of going on? They were not going to make it back to camp; not now.

Any decision to act would have to be his. Moritoh knew now, with perfect clarity, what he must do. Sacrifice his life, the ultimate gesture. He may not have yet earned the right to be a samurai, but he was not afraid to die like one.

His father would understand and be proud of him. Myoko, were she ever to learn of his proud death, would forgive him.

Moritoh look a deep breath and composed himself. He looked across at the girl. She was no more than two yards from him and looking intently at him with an even, penetrating gaze.

How beautiful she was, thought Moritoh. One day she, too, would remember his sacrifice.

Moritoh lowered the tip of his rifle until it was pointing at the ground. All the while staring into Brandeis' eyes.

With a brief smile of resignation, very deliberately, Moritoh put his rifle down on the ground by his side, gave a slight bow and folded his arms.

It was over.

Winters counted on.

Six...

He's nervous.

She watched his eyes as they flicked back and forth between the officer and them, then over to the place from which the tobacco smoke and those sounds came.

A low voice; then another. She could not pick up the words, but the rhythms and

324

cadences were the familiar sounds of her own language.

How long will they sit there?

The boy was staring at Sally with a strange look on his face, as if he wanted to tell her something.

Winters wondered if she should make her break now that his attention was on Sally.

But what'll happen to Sally? Will she move too? What if he begins shooting? It's an awful chance to take.

Seven...

Suddenly Winters was aware that Moritoh's rifle was no longer pointing at her. He was lowering it from its steady aim.

...eight...

Her stomach was churning. Her mouth was dry. Winters saw him smiling at Sally, a curious inward smile. He put his rifle down.

For God's sake what's he doing?

That weird expression on his face!

Moritoh folded his arms and Winters felt herself go still inside.

He's can't have done that!

He's given it away!

Winters was puzzled and deeply troubled by Moritoh's action. As she watched he bowed his head. He looked like someone resigned to the executioner's axe.

If it is our blokes over there, he'll get the chop for sure. Both of them will. He must know that.

Brandeis looked bewildered and was

about to say something, perhaps even call out, when Winters, on an impulse she was never after able to explain, put her hand on Brandeis' arm to restrain her.

Their eyes met. Winters could see the same grim realisation had dawned on Sally too.

'If we give them away they're dead meat.' Winters breathed the words into Brandeis' ear, keeping her eye on the boy all the while. He did not react.

Brandeis leaned back against her tree and looked directly at Winters for a long time. Her face registered the conflicting emotions that were flooding in on her.

Brandeis looked away over to where the butterflies swarmed, aware of a slight upsurge of voices from the unseen intruders.

She had grasped at once the astonishing implications of Moritoh's action. Had seen the prison gate swing open. They would be saved.

Now Winters' words had wrecked the simplicity of it all.

Brandeis turned back and tried to read the meanings in Winters' troubled expression. There overcame her a feeling of profound sadness. She nodded almost imperceptibly.

They sat staring at each other in mutual disbelief at having made this strange, unspoken compact.

After a short time there came the sounds

of discreet movement; the swishing of leaves; a click of metal. A single, smothered laugh. Silence.

Everything became perfectly still. The sun had shifted half a yard across the sky. Through the trees; chinks of blue.

Then the first sounds of a cricket, and, as if that had been an all-clear signal, the jungle whirred into life again.

Whoever had been there had gone.

They sat in the void of jungle, the four of them: the officer, staring off into the trees, seemingly uninterested; the young soldier, his head in his hands looking down at the ground between his knees; Brandeis and Winters restless, agitated, close to tears.

Winters, above all, felt a deep sense of anger. It was not directed at the Japanese who had made them captive; but at the indifference of the universe; at herself for her own puny and ineffective efforts to make sense of this impossible, unwinnable situation.

They lay there in the fragmenting hours of the forest afternoon.

Four stone figures on a living plinth of green.

Oshima allowed his mind the luxury of blankness. Stillness. In stillness lay some kind of answer to it all.

They would become as one with the forest. Lichens, mosses, vines and succulent

327

creepers would grow over them as if they were the stone statues of some sacred city hidden in the jungle, passed by Time and man. The sun that now angled sharply through the vaulting trees would melt their atrophied bodies until they had fused with nature. It was all so clear.

Oshima was filled with a great warmth. For the first time he could surrender to the random chaos of this wild nature.

For that brief time he had opted out of decision-making; cast his fate to chance. Now, having made every mistake in the book, having been responsible for the things he had inflicted on the living as well as on the dead, these women of his had rewarded him for their pain and suffering by letting him live.

He was glad for Moritoh. The boy would survive now. At the crucial moment his humanity and compassion had triumphed.

Moritoh would be free of any guilt after all this was over for, when it had come to the moment of truth, Moritoh had taken the action that he, Oshima, was incapable of: he had offered them their freedom by offering them his life.

There was hope for him who could act so selflessly, for whatever reason.

As they sat together in the painful vacuum of silence left after the enemy patrol had faded into memory, Oshima had seen Senjo's shoulders bowed with shame. Superior Private First Class, Moritoh, Senjo; Koiijama Corps, Murazumi Company. Warrior.

His sacrifice had been turned back on him by the women and he was too young to know that there was no shame in that.

A boy had reappeared through the steel mask of the soldier.

To Oshima's astonishment and wonder, the girl had risen silently and crossed to Moritoh and put her arms around him and comforted him. She had stayed there for a long time, not moving, just holding him as though he were a child.

Oshima had felt the tears within him brimming towards the surface. All this waste!

The woman sat on the ground opposite him with her head down between her knees, her hands clenched in despair as though in deepest depression. When she did look up, it was with an expression half resigned, half disbelieving.

Oshima felt deathly tired. The small force left within him drained out. He slept. In his dream a swarm of butterflies sucked the life from a tree. Some time later Oshima opened his eyes to find the two women crouched over cans of liquid fuel, heating food and boiling water.

Moritoh had not moved. His back was half turned away from the others and he stared of into the forest, looking lost.

Winters, seeing Oshima awake, came and knelt down beside him, peering closely at his bandages. Squinting down Oshima could see that there did not appear to be any bright red patches that would have shown fresh bleeding. Winters touched the bandages lightly with her fingers and seemed satisfied.

Oshima examined her face. There was dirt and mud on her skin and dark bruises on her cheekbones. But her expression was calm. There was no trace of the terrible fear that Nagato had elicited in her on those first days.

How long ago that seemed to Oshima. Time had ceased to have any meaning. Besides, he thought, all that was in another life; another, more brutal place than this.

'We'll leave that,' Winters said. 'We have no more bandages anyway.'

Oshima wanted to speak to her; wanted to tell her something; anything, but he remained silent.

Later Winters brought him some food and he watched the young girl take some to Moritoh.

Poor Senjo. No doubt he felt unmanned and dishonoured by her. Oshima felt pity for him. He watched as Moritoh took the food like a blind beggar, not looking up, not acknowledging her.

Oshima ate slowly and mechanically, his one good hand moving to his mouth as though he were underwater, moved by unseen tides.

The darkness under the jungle's canopy anticipated the night. Swatches of pale sky made random patterns in the blackness above. Here and there, a star glimmered.

Brandeis felt numb. It was as if she and Mae had become the captors: the soldiers, the captives. And yet it was more complicated than that. They were captors who could not act; only react.

Why had they sat there? she wondered. Made no move, when they could so easily have cried out, or run for it?

From the beginning Brandeis had never doubted that these two Japanese would have killed them without scruple if they had had to. Yet the young soldier had put his rifle down.

Had she misread that? Over and over again Brandeis replayed that scene and that sequence of events, and each time she had arrived at a different answer.

She thought about Moritoh as she had held him, his shoulders heaving with grief as, many times in hospital, she had comforted some wounded kid who had temporarily found himself with no further resistance to the pain and terror he had experienced.

Giving comfort to the enemy. That was the phrase they would use about her, but, at that moment, the young soldier was simply someone who had been broken by too long a proximity to fear.

She could sense that Winters was awake. What was Mae thinking, she who had been so vilely treated by these enemies? How could she have decided to let them live?

'Why did he do that?' Brandeis whispered. 'Put his rifle down?'

'Don't ask me.' Winter's voice was no louder than the breath it was borne on. 'Maybe it all got too much for him. He's only a kid.'

'Why did we?'

'What? Just sit there?' There was a long pause before Winters went on. 'No guts, maybe? Didn't want their deaths on our conscience? God knows, I'm sure I don't. I feel as if I can't do anything right any more. It doesn't matter what you do here, it's always wrong.'

They lay once more in thoughtful silence. Brandeis took Winters' hand. It felt warm and comforting.

'In a way I'm glad. They haven't been too bad, these two.'

'Maybe.'

Later when she heard Winters' breathing change subtly into the slower rhythms of sleep, Brandeis lay staring up into the blackness, listening to the night.

She slept fitfully. There was a confused and

broken dream. The smell of cigarettes and a half-familiar sound she could not place.

She was wide awake. The sound came from somewhere nearby. Scared, her mind frantically sorted through a thousand memories of night sounds, seeking some reference point.

Two o'clock, according to the glowing green hands of her watch. Brandeis looked around fearfully and thought of nameless jungle creatures; of snakes and crawling things, spiders and blundering moths and all those things of slime and web that slithered and spun eternally in the jungle's night.

Then she identified it.

Mae?

She eased herself closer. Winters was lying on her back, half turned away. Brandeis had to lean over her to know that the sobbing was not coming from her.

She would ignore it. Brandeis decided. Lie there. It would end soon.

But it did not.

If only she had a light. Was the officer in pain, perhaps? But, even as she sat up, she knew that it was not Oshima. She crawled forward on her hands and knees. Then, fearful that she might put her hand on some scuttling horror, she rose to her feet.

She moved forward; one yard, two.

The sound stopped. Brandeis could sense the expectant stillness of the young soldier somewhere in front of her in the blackness.

Cautiously she put out her hand. Touched the fabric of his shirt, his shoulder, his arm, hard with muscle. His neck, his hair, his face. His cheekbones were wet with tears. He lay rigidly still.

Gently she eased herself down so that she was sitting with her arm around Moritoh. She held him close and the feel of the smooth skin of his face and the silk of his hair calmed her own fears of the dark.

After a time she felt his hand close gently over hers and the trembling of his body subsided into quietness.

Chapter 20

Morning. As they climbed up out of the valley Moritoh's mind was in a turmoil. Had it all been a dream, he wondered, a memory of Myoko?

When like some invisible wraith, the girl had eased herself backwards into the darkness, he had felt the soft touch of her lips against his cheek; a gentleness such as he had never known.

Twice in the past few hours he had wept. All his discipline, all his soldier's shield of unfeeling, so carefully erected in the face of death and danger, had fallen away like plaster from a wall, leaving his fears exposed; those that entered his mind in the few moments before an ambush, or when some unseen enemy was probing his cover with shafts of jagged steel; and those in dreams that left him sweating in the dark, unwilling to return to sleep, where nightmare rules.

Moritoh felt at once dishonoured and exulted. He had been dishonoured when the girl had thrown his samurai's gesture of sacrifice back in his teeth, and further shamed by his tears in last night's all-too-transparent cloak of darkness. What kind of women were these who would so unman a warrior?

Yet he was glad. If only tears could always summon up such gentle solace!

Moritoh glanced back yet again at the girl but she was concentrating on helping the lieutenant, steadying him as Oshima struggled to keep his balance. He was making heavy weather of it, lurching painfully up the steep slope, the two women hovering close, like courtiers attendant on an ancient king.

In another minute they would stop, take cover and rest. Then he could look at her, study the lovely face he had not been able to see in the night.

Moritoh pushed up the narrow track cautiously.

He wondered how Oshima could go on

driving himself up this killing slope towards the camp that lay beyond the crest of this enormous valley. They could have halted for another day at least. Moritoh had tried to persuade Oshima to rest until they felt stronger but, at first light, they had set out.

Perhaps because of the intense pain he was suffering, Oshima had been icy and angry, had refused to discuss it. They would march on, he said; get back to camp as soon as possible; make their report. He rambled on, half delirious, about duty.

And maybe he was right, thought Moritoh. They had heard no sounds of battle from the direction of their camp. Maybe there was still time to warn their comrades of the enemy threat.

But he was puzzled. He wondered why Oshima persisted in taking the women. What was wrong with him? Did he not care what happened to them, who had certainly stopped him bleeding to death and then, incredibly, had saved them both from their own soldiers? Did Oshima really think he could protect them when he got them back to the camp. What force would he represent, returning wounded, his shoulder useless, with one survivor from his Section and two women prisoners?

Above all, it was the fate of the women, particularly the girl, that concerned Moritoh now. He knew that there would be many men there willing to treat enemy women worse than any prisoner or wounded soldier they made sport of on the lonely and pitiless trails they were all forced to tread.

Equally worrying to him was the thought that they might run into one of their own patrols any time now. What would happen then? The women might never know the horrors of the camp; their ordeal might begin right here in some unmapped clearing in the jungle.

Some of the men in the other sections were animals. What would her fate be before release by bullet or knife?

And what would he be doing? Standing there apologising? I mean you no harm. Would she believe that he would be powerless to interfere? Moritoh felt ashamed just thinking about it.

Was Lieutenant Oshima so weakened by his wound that he had lost the capacity to feel? Did he not understand he was leading his captives into hell?

They must be allowed to go free. He would persuade Oshima. Plead with him. Tell him. Oshima must be made to see, even if by force.

Behind him Moritoh could hear the wounded man gasping with pain.

Moritoh turned to see Oshima slip, sag wretchedly against the support of the women, then straighten up again and

337

struggle on.

Minutes later Oshima was unable to continue. He lay on the ground, his face a chalk-white 'No' mask.

Although bright blood was showing again Winters decided to leave it. There was nothing she could do. She glanced at Brandeis seeking confirmation, but the girl was nearly out on her feet, leaning against a tree with both hands, her chest heaving.

Winters knelt down and pressed gently against the bulge of dressing. Maybe digital pressure would hold it for a while, but she doubted it.

Oshima lay watching her face.

'Where are you taking us?' she asked looking directly into his eyes.

Oshima shook his head as though the question were too difficult.

'Your camp?' Winters insisted.

He closed his eyes, perhaps against the pain, but Winters had the feeling that he was simply avoiding her gaze. There was a long silence then: 'Yes ... camp.' His voice was low and hoarse.

'How far is it? How far from here?'

Something about the extraordinary way the wounded man had been pushing himself had suggested to Winters that they were coming close to the end of this journey. Since she had awakened in the chill, dripping dawn, a feeling of dread had mushroomed within her, painful as a cancer. It was fear: the fear of something unknown, something silent, armed with a knife. Something worse than she already knew.

Oshima opened his eyes.

'Not far now.'

Winters searched his face for some indication of what was in his mind; for some reassurance that her fears were groundless and that their plight would be assuaged in some way. There was nothing in his expression to give her reason for fear, or for hope. But she knew that whatever lay ahead would not be good.

'What will they do to us?'

'Please?'

It's no good pretending you don't understand, mate.

'What'll happen to us there?'

Oshima seemed to be gathering together his thoughts and feelings. He made as if to say something but, in the end, did not answer.

Winters felt angry enough to want to press hard against his wound, jam her hands against the torn flesh and the open nerve ends to try to force some kind of acceptable answer from him.

'Tell us, damn you!' She no longer bothered to keep the anger from her voice. 'What will they do to us? Will they kill us?

Will they treat us properly?'

'You are war prisoner. Wear uniform. Proper treatment.' He closed his eyes against her rage. 'Geneva Convention,' he said.

Brandeis was listening to the exchange. Winters looked at her in frustrated anger. 'He doesn't even believe it himself.'

She rounded on him again.

'Do you? Your sergeant didn't exactly treat us properly.' She was shouting now. 'Is that what you call "proper treatment"?'

Oshima's face was closed when he looked at Winters again. He made to get up.

'We go now.'

Winters stood up abruptly and walked away from him. Brandeis stood watching as Moritoh helped his officer to his feet.

Oshima stood swaying. His face set against the pain, as though he were waiting for it to sink to manageable proportions.

'I should have shot the bastard when I had the chance,' Winters felt herself shaking. 'Can you imagine what it'll be like with a campful of them?'

'Why don't you let us go?' Now Brandeis was urging Oshima fiercely. 'We haven't done you any harm. We've helped you. Saved your rotten life, that's what we've done.'

Oshima shook his head angrily like a sleeper trying to shake off a bad dream.

Moritoh guessed what the women had been saying.

'We're no more than an hour from camp, sir. Can't we let them go?'

Oshima's face contorted with anger.

'Silence!' He stood for a moment clutching at his chest. 'The prisoners go with us.'

Bowing his head in acknowledgement of the rebuke, Moritoh picked up the three guns and Oshima's pack. He jerked his head to show the two women they were to start moving.

Brandeis shrugged resignedly and began to sling her pack, but the fear was on Winters now and she could not control the trembling in her legs. Brandeis crossed to her, deeply concerned, and put an arm around her shoulders.

'Steady,' she said. 'You all right?'

Winters took a grip on herself and nodded. Brandeis helped her on with her pack.

'Sure?'

Winters nodded dolefully. 'Geneva Convention. Christ!'

Run.

As they struggled up the trail near the top of the valley the thought repeated itself in Brandeis' mind again and again.

It was a grim irony. The rain, falling steadily for the past half-hour, had turned the earth into a glutinous brown paste which sucked at her ankles obscenely as she moved.

341

The Japanese could gun them down before they had gone three steps and Brandeis knew it.

Even while she thought of escape Brandeis' mind was seething with anger against their captors.

How can they do this, these two, after all Mae and I have done for them? Taking us to their camp. God knows what'll happen to us there. Run. There must be something I can do. Must be.

She looked back at Winters' closed and grim face as she slogged along a few yards behind.

She's really scared. Does she know something I don't?

Brandeis thought of Winters shouting at the officer, and wondered if Mae were getting close to the edge. Was she, too, filled with the crushing foreboding Brandeis now felt, that made it difficult to think?

Run. But where to?

Brandeis tried fruitlessly to reassure herself that these two Japanese would somehow protect them against harm when they eventually arrived at this camp of theirs.

He's an officer. He'll protect us. He'll make sure we get decent treatment.

Surely he will.

They couldn't all be like that animal, could they?

Great lines of pitiless men...

Oh, God don't let it be like that.

Oshima opened his eyes at last. Moritoh had been content to let him lie where he had fallen fifteen minutes before. Anything that would give Oshima a respite from his agony.

The rain coursed down Oshima's corroded face. His black hair was plastered against his scalp. The eyes were huge in the dark sockets of his head. The bones showed. It was as if the skull was coming through the skin like a death mask.

To Moritoh, Oshima's eyes looked fevered and oddly out of focus.

'How far now?' Oshima asked.

'About a mile.'

Oshima nodded.

'We leave in fifteen minutes.' His voice was barely above a whisper.

'Lieutenant,' Moritoh said hesitantly. 'Let them go. Let the women go.'

Oshima considered him for a long time, listening to inner voices. He turned his head away without answering.

'You know what will happen to them,' Moritoh insisted.

'What will happen to them, Moritoh? You tell me.' Oshima's voice was glacial.

Moritoh had never felt so distant from him as at that moment. They should be able to talk, he and Oshima; discuss, debate. They had something in common now; more than just their background and education.

'The camp is no place for these women, sir,' he said. 'And we won't be able to ... at least, *you* won't be able to protect them.' Moritoh glanced down at Oshima's bandages. 'Not wounded, like that.'

'They are prisoners of war, Moritoh. They wear uniforms They will be treated accordingly.' Oshima spoke woodenly as though he were reciting a creed in which he no longer believed.

'Nagato knew what they are, sir. They are women. And in the camp, we're all Nagatos.'

'Silence!'

So great was Oshima's fury that if he had not been so badly wounded, Moritoh knew the wounded man would have struck him.

His anger at Moritoh's remark had cost Oshima dearly. The death mask showed gritted teeth. He groaned with agony.

'They wouldn't last a day there,' Oshima said, at last, 'back in the forest.'

Oshima seemed to be talking to himself rather than to Moritoh, but clearly he was considering the idea.

'Sir,' Moritoh pressed on eagerly, 'could I take them back, at least as far as the river? They'd have a chance once on the other side.'

The lieutenant closed his eyes. The rain hammered on the trees far above their head.

'Information.' Oshima's voice sounded as though it had echoed up from some deep well in his mind. 'They might have useful information.'

Information! He can't believe that! Oshima's reply filled Moritoh with despair. What on earth could these women provide in the way of intelligence that Oshima did not already know? What was the matter with him? How could he simply deliver them into that den of beasts?

'Let them go.'

'No!' Oshima looked up at Moritoh with a wild, covetous expression in his eyes. 'No. Fifteen minutes, private,' he said.

Oshima gasped in pain and once more closed his eyes.

Moritoh stood up, deeply angered.

He walked over to where the women sat like pair of bedraggled cats. Exhaustion and despair were written on their faces.

He opened a can of meat for each. As he handed it to them he avoided their gaze.

Chapter 21

'Can't make it any further.' Oshima lay on the ground gasping with agony. He gripped Moritoh's shirt front. 'Moritoh.' His voice was a whisper. 'You go on. Report in. Tell them about the enemy coming. They can send out for me … and the women.'

'You're not going to let the women go, are you?' Moritoh was filled with despair and bewilderment.

Oshima did not reply, preoccupied by his pain.

'Don't you care what happens to them?'

Oshima's eyes were empty of expression as though he were uninterested in the question.

'You don't!' Moritoh's anger was in his voice. 'You don't care about anything!'

'No!' Oshima was anguished. He clutched at Moritoh's hand. 'Senjo!' He gathered himself. 'Don't say that. I care about *you*.'

At that instant Moritoh might have killed Oshima. Instead he had stood there, impotent with rage until the habit of obedience prevailed.

He turned and, unable to look at the women, set off in the direction of the camp no more than a quarter of a mile away.

He did not obey Oshima's order.

He did not keep to the track, nor take the familiar paths that led to the camp.

Instead, he used all the stealth and skills that had enabled him to survive for the past months to avoid the keen eyes of the sentries posted wide out all around and the lookouts high in the trees.

He arrived, finally, in a deep patch of cover, busy with insects, to observe, unseen, the place to which Lieutenant Oshima was determined to deliver his prisoners. For half an hour Moritoh hid on the ridge that quartered north and south, overlooking the camp that had been their destination for the past days. To Moritoh, his sanctuary now seemed alien; a foreign country, glimpsed in fragments through the tangle. He peered down at the sagging brown-thatched roofs of three huts, and over to the right, parts of two others.

From time to time, in the cleared spaces between, he could see men walking about, or lounging in the shade cast by the huts as the sun tilted over finally into evening.

Camp sounds: the clink of cooking pots: the familiar gutturals and sibilants of his own tongue; occasional bursts of laughter carried clearly in the steamy tropical air.

Moritoh swung Oshima's field glasses slowly around the perimeter of the camp. Heaps of refuse; tin cans stacked by the edge of the clearing, washing draped over bushes and on the lines stretched between the huts: the sea of trampled mud glistening.

He stared hard at the soldiers below. These men; these comrades of his, lounging in the sun looking so young and relaxed, knew nothing of pity. Or if they did, they had long since set it aside. They knew nothing now but death and survival and taking what was in front of you for tomorrow did not exist for you. Tomorrow you were dead.

347

As Moritoh watched his plan formed complete in his mind. He would not report in. He would go back. Now.

How stupid, he thought, to have taken so long to make up his mind. He should have done it before, but fatigue, and the ingrained reflex of obeying orders without question, dulled the mind. They could have been halfway to the river by now, the women and he.

He would come back for Lieutenant Oshima when they were safe. There was nothing Oshima could do to prevent him releasing the women and Moritoh no longer cared if he got into trouble over it.

With extreme care, Moritoh started back the way he had come.

In his delirium Oshima was not sure how long Moritoh had been gone, whether for five minutes, or an hour, he could not tell. But he knew he must be ready for him, for Senjo, when he returned.

Red and white waves of nausea, distorted images, faces, sounds dizzied his mind.

He thought of firm hands tending his wounds, feeding him, supporting him when the trees had spun sickeningly. Of beguiling low voices, the gentle cadences of concern heard through scarlet veils of pain.

The sun, blazing through the dripping trees, burned the sweat trickling down his neck and off his cheekbones.

He leaned back against a tree, favouring his right side against the pain that tore at his flesh with iron hooks. Felt again the cruel cutting edge of Moritoh's rage, keen as any knife.

Moritoh. A boy who should have been at his studies, the better to take his place in his father's rich world which he had not yet had the time to discover. A boy who might have been friend, lover, drinker of kisses.

Instead, he was here on this killing ground, skulking and scuttling to survive in this formless, pitiless anarchy of jungle. And likely, before it was over, if this war were ever to be over, to finish up like his comrades from Section Seven. The food of wild pigs, ants and maggots: fresh meat for this man-eating cauldron of vegetation.

Surely that would not happen to Moritoh Senjo?

Senjo. Oshima thought with regret of the boy's beautiful face twisted with anger as he argued fiercely to let the women go.

Let the women go?

To Oshima it seemed incredible that Moritoh would suggest it. Were they not his precious matched pair? Did not he, Oshima Eeji, possess them? Could he not look after them as lovingly as he tended all the specimens in his great collection? Did Moritoh imagine that he would allow such rare creatures to be destroyed? They had information

349

didn't they? The enemy build up.

The women sat opposite, glazed with exhaustion. His captives. Their pale, questioning eyes had fear in them now. Oshima wondered why.

Above Oshima and to his right, he saw a flash of black, green and gold.

An enormous and exquisite butterfly settled on a leaf near his head. The twig bent sharply under the great weight.

Wings of black and green. Body of gold. *Paradisae*. Kurosumo's gift; but alive. Ravishingly alive.

It flew a yard or so, big as a bird, then suddenly there was a pair of them: two glorious birdwings, like brilliant kites jousting in an eddy of wind.

They settled no more than two feet from his head. Oshima watched their wings shimmer and shiver as they drank in the sun's warmth.

With luck, he thought, they might live out their brief lives without fetters; without adorning anyone's hair.

Oshima knew what he must do and he felt a sense of delight at having reached such a decision. Above all, it would please Senjo. And Senjo would be back with him soon.

A tremor of pain. As his head spun he groped blindly into his shirt pocket.

Ah, they were there; the treasures he had taken from the pocket of the girl's discarded shirt after Nagato's attack on her.

He must look his best for Senjo. Oshima thought it a pity he had no mirror.

When Moritoh had been gone some time, Brandeis had begun to feel more than simply apprehensive.

The officer seemed only half conscious. Sometimes he looked at them, but mostly his eyes were closed.

'Something's on,' she ventured to Winters in a whisper.

'We're close to their camp. I'm sure of it.'

'No, it's more than that.'

There was something oppressive about the jungle around them. Brandeis was reminded of the hours spent beside the planewreck; the same feeling that the jungle was an animal made of eyes.

Perhaps, she thought, Mae was right and it was simply that they were conscious of being somewhere close to the Japanese camp. Yet the feeling seemed stronger than that. She felt the rank air of the jungle's rot pressing in on her face, her chest, her back. The trees seemed to be weaving the coiling intricately all around her. This fantasy became so strong that she felt growing within her an overwhelming need to cry out. Just when it seemed she could restrain the impulse no longer, Winters touched her arm.

Brandeis followed Winters' shocked gaze.

351

The officer was doing something odd to his face, all the while grimacing in the rictus caricature of a smile.

'Good God.' Winters sounded aghast.

Brandeis saw what Oshima was doing.

'Oh, the poor bastard,' she said, horrified.

Moritoh appeared, as if he had risen out of the ground. One moment he was nowhere to be seen, the next he was in their midst.

The women were facing him, both staring at the lieutenant who was propped against a tree with his back to Moritoh. Something in their expression, a look half of horror, half of pity, made him wonder if Oshima had died. Then he saw that Oshima's face seemed to be covered in blood. Had they killed him? This shocking thought made Moritoh tighten his grip on his rifle.

He knelt in front of Oshima. It was only then that he realised what it was that covered the lower half of Oshima's face. Lipstick. Oshima had crudely outlined his lips with a vivid scarlet rouge. It was thick around his mouth and coated his front teeth obscenely. Moritoh felt sick.

Oshima smiled at him grotesquely. 'Oh, Senjo,' he said, his voice oddly shrill and fragmenting with the effort of speaking. 'I meant to be ready.' Weakly he pushed Brandeis' tiny green comb through his lank hair; once, twice. He stared foolishly at it then let it fall from his grasp on to the ground beside a red bakelite lipstick container. His gaze travelled slowly back to meet that of Moritoh. 'You are just like him,' he said. 'Exactly like him.'

'Sir?'

'Akiro,' Oshima said, as though amazed that Moritoh did not understand. 'He died, you know. I missed him when he was gone.' He clutched Moritoh's hand and suddenly pressed it hard against his mouth. 'So badly.'

Disgusted, Moritoh jerked it away. Immediately he regretted that act. Oshima looked deeply hurt. As he stared at the grisly mask before him, Moritoh was filled with an overwhelming sense of pity for Oshima. How could he desert his lieutenant now? he agonised.

He looked helplessly towards the women. they were watching, their faces gentle and filled with compassion.

He had no choice, he knew. He must get them away.

'Sir,' he said, 'the women. I'm taking them back. I didn't go to the camp.'

Oshima's dazed eyes were glittering. He reached again for Moritoh's hand and grasped it weakly. This time Moritoh did not resist.

'Yes. Take them back,' Oshima's eyes were soft. 'Yes. Whatever you want to do. You see, I have always favoured you, Senjo. Always. You did not know it, but always you were the one.'

'I'll be back soon for you, sir,' Moritoh felt like a traitor, 'and take you to the camp.'

Oshima nodded. 'Yes. That's it. Let them go. Give them the food that's left. Show them the track.' He smiled an agonising, epicene smile, baring lipstick-covered teeth. 'Now, you will be my true friend, Senjo.'

Moritoh looked at the scarlet travesty of Oshima's face and knew that he could not leave his officer with his deepest instincts so revealed. He ripped a piece from his own shirt and moistened it with water from his own flask. Urgently he began to wipe the lipstick away from Oshima's face. Oshima did not resist.

'You'll be all right until I get back,' Moritoh was conscious of Oshima's disturbing gaze.

'The reds and yellows are the worst,' Oshima's voice was faint. 'They fade so quickly.'

'Sir?'

'Yes, go on. Release them. You must see now, Senjo, that I favour you.' Oshima smiled wanly. 'My matched pair. Dryness and dust. In the end they fray into dust.'

He struggled to sit up.

'Help me, Senjo. Ask the women to come here.'

As Moritoh helped Oshima sit up, the women came close. Winters took over wiping away the rouge, but Brandeis hung back, distracted still by her feeling of apprehension.

Oshima spoke in clear English as if he had rehearsed his words carefully.

'Moritoh will take you back to the river.'

Winters paused for a moment, glanced at Brandeis with excitement in her eyes, then went on cleaning the last of the lipstick from Oshima's pale face.

Brandeis began to tremble, half with excitement, half with fear. She was at once amazed and uneasy. The implications crowded her mind. Take you back? He was going to let them go? Why? What had happened? To bring them all this way, then let them go? It didn't make sense.

Oshima was calm now. The pain had drained from him with the woman's gentle touch.

His brain cleared. Suddenly everything was lucid, magnified larger than reality as though he were observing truth through a drop of distilled water.

Moritoh was right. To deliver these women to the camp was to sentence them to a thousand deaths.

Inside himself Oshima had known this truth all along. His obsession with them, not as women, but as trophies, had blinded him to the reality of the terrible fate towards which he was leading them.

'Very sorry,' Oshima said quietly to Winters. 'Perhaps we meet again in better times.'

Winters finished wiping his face clean and threw the rag on the ground. She reached forward and pressed her hand gently against the dressings bulging redly under his swathe of bandages.

'What is your name?' she asked.

His face twitched briefly, then almost shyly: 'Oshima,' he said, 'Lieutenant Oshima.'

'Oshima,' Winters repeated the name as if it were some kind of incantation.

'He is Moritoh. Moritoh Senjo.' Oshima looked over towards Moritoh. Winters was aware of the tender expression on his face like that of a man looking at a favoured son.

Moritoh was hurriedly stowing rations into their packs. He was suddenly desperately anxious to get clear of Oshima and distance the women from his camp.

Brandeis was only half aware of this exchange. Suddenly she was scared; really scared.

There was something wrong with this, she knew *It's too good to be true. It's a trap. A set-up.*

'I learn English in USA,' Oshima said. 'I am student. You understand?'

Brandeis now felt angry. She was going to die and soon. That was it! She and Mae were simply going to be taken back down the track and shot.

Now that the officer was back near his own kind, now that they were no longer useful to him, no longer needed for dressing his wound, supporting him, carrying his pack, picking him up every time he fell down, and after letting him off with his life, now the rotten bastard was going to get rid of them.

It was all a charade, all this; a cheap trick.

She half-heard Winters saying her own name then, looking over to her, say 'Brandeis'.

There Mae was, she thought, talking to this man with the same look on her face she always wore in the wards; a mixture of concern, compassion and warmth. She was too good, too decent, too stupid to see through all this deceit. Couldn't she see? Did she not realise what was really happening?

'Long life,' Brandeis heard him say. *What sort of macabre joke is that, you bastard?*

Moritoh's feeling of agitation was now acute. He slung his weapon hurriedly and pushed the women's packs at them urgently. He knelt beside Oshima, and slipping off the binoculars, hung them once more around his officer's neck.

'An hour,' he lied.

Oshima looked at him, eyes sombre, knowing it was a lie. He nodded.

They were off, walking slowly and cautiously through the mazy shadows of the trees, single file behind the cat-graceful boy.

The trees seemed to whirl fearfully around Brandeis. Questions crowded. Where was he taking them? The river? To free them? To shoot them?

She was certain now it was nothing but a trap.

Must warn Mae. Must tell her.

Brandies turned to tell Winters of her premonition.

And the trap sprung.

Oshima lay watching them go.

First the jungle blurred their shapes, fragmenting them into patches of light and shade, then dissolved them abruptly.

His captives, his matched pair, were gone, lifting in flight, soaring up through the intricate camouflage of the jungle. Above him the evening mists fumed, absorbing light.

Oshima felt weightless. They were free of him; free of his killing habit, of his destructive, obsessive fascination; of his labels and classifications; free from the airless death of his laboratory's vacuum pump.

Those creatures of his could now coruscate in the sun, glisten, flirt with life, swoop and soar and glide, touch down where fate would have them touch down. They were free to be.

And he, at last, was free of them.

Loneliness and fear rushed in to fill the vacuum they left behind. Oshima felt as though the bony armature of his body had melted. A crushing tiredness pressed on his brain and the pain of his wound took him and shook him like some pitiless interrogator.

A sob of agony escaped him and he gritted his teeth to prevent himself from crying out.

Oshima was sure there was something important he had to do, but he could not remember what it was. Some report to make. Senjo would remember. And he would be back in an hour.

An hour. He would need an hour, Oshima knew it; a lifetime, to find the will and the strength to make that last journey to the camp.

Oshima pictured the shocked faces there as he described the death of their comrades, his charges. He heard their questions, saw the lust blooming like a virus in their eyes as they looked at his prisoners (butterflies tethered to his hair). The coarse remarks; all of that.

But then he remembered he had let the women go. For Senjo's sake. Senjo, who would be back soon.

A single shaft of sunlight pierced through the treetops. Its warmth felt good on his face.

It seemed to Oshima that he could feel the smooth, cool bamboo of his catching net by his hand. He hefted the thin, balanced shaft, feeling its familiar contours; the knuckled surface. But this weapon had a stock, a breech, a barrel. This was the most efficient of all catching nets; one that cast an implacable steel mesh of bullets.

Oshima let its weight down on to the ground. He was finished with it now. There was no further use for it, not for him; not any more.

If only he could summon up the strength to break it over his knee as he had broken another net, once, long ago.

Something nagged at him. Something was missing; something had to be done. The report! Of course.

The jungle had gone deathly still. The silence seemed to contain a profound question.

Oshima raised his head, alert.

In a moment the question was answered.

From the direction of the camp, the terrible saw of steel. Then a succession of explosions. Mortars? he wondered.

Oshima knew he must delay no longer. Command had to know about the enemy coming to attack the camp.

Oshima tried to rise.

A burst of gunfire swept across his thighs and jack-knifed him back against the tree.

Oshima heard the sound of the gun echoing a long way off. He hurt badly. In his nostrils the laboratory's familiar and subtle smell of dust. Thin grey dust settling over him like a shroud.

Oshima knew now that an hour would have been too long. He would not need to deliver his report. The enemy were at the gates.

Two men were watching him; vague broken-shaped, green impressions of soldiers. One of them disappeared behind him somewhere; the other crouched, gun in hand, watching him.

Something agonising at his throat. He could no longer breathe. Oshima felt the mesh of netting. A flurry of wing's beat. Frantically he clawed upwards, but the golden fetters were too heavy. Great wings thrashing themselves to shreds; the hissing sound of the vacuum pump; somewhere near, the sound of children shrieking with excited laughter.

Silence.

All around, the clatter of gunfire. Brandeis cringed fearfully anticipating bullets, feeling only anger and disgust. They had fallen for it. It had been a trap.

She saw Moritoh with his face turned towards her, laughing at her; a shout of derision on his lips.

Then he was twisting and diving into the tangled undergrowth at the side of the track, all his lithe grace gone as he crashed half across a clump of bushes.

Seeing their betrayer so clumsy nearly

made Brandeis laugh, until she saw the blood gout from his body as though he had exploded from within; come apart, disintegrated.

Brandeis stood there, puzzled, watching Moritoh kicking at something; some nameless invisible thing that seemed to be tearing at his legs.

And then she heard a high pitched and terrible screaming.

The sound went on and on; walling her in. She saw Moritoh's face was no longer beautiful, but jerked and grimaced in a series of grotesque and agonised masks.

Brandeis heard his voice. He was saying something she ought to understand, for he was saying it in English.

'Get down! Get down!' he was saying over and over again.

The screaming went on drowning his words.

She ran a few steps towards the low clump of dark green bushes into which he'd fallen.

Moritoh was thrashing about like a landed fish. The green leaves around him were covered in vivid red flowers. There was a roaring sound. Before her eyes the leaves were flailed into red and green confetti. A crop of scarlet flowers bloomed on Moritoh's body. He became still.

Brandeis heard his voice again: 'Get down!' She was with the dead boy now and felt once more the texture of his shirt, the hardness of his muscles, the silk of his hair. For a moment there was a trembling of nerves, then nothing. The memory of screaming; that insistent voice: 'Get down! Get down!'

A young Australian soldier with startled eyes was staring down at her in astonishment. 'Get down!'

Hands pulled at her. Brandeis stared into dark green fabric and caught the reek of sweat and dampness.

'For Chrissakes, you could've been killed!'

An arm around her. On her feet.

'You all right?' the soldier kept asking as he dragged her in off the track. 'What the hell are you doing here?'

Brandeis did not hear the babble of questions. She turned back and looked down at the dead face of Moritoh.

His face was calm. And you could see he had been beautiful.

Frozen on the screen of Winters' mind: a picture of the boy writhing on the ground and Sally standing there with her hands to her mouth.

Then Winters was running back, searching for Oshima. Ahead of her the terrible din of battle as the Australians attacked the Japanese camp.

She felt the shock wave of one explosion

after another; the hysterical chatter of guns; the cries of men somewhere up ahead.

Blindly Winters ran on. Behind her, screaming. Overhead, the crack of rifle bullets, the deadly whirr of steel scything down showers of leaves.

To her right, the brief image of a man crouching down firing. The white of startled eyes, then she was past him, running hard.

Oshima was sitting facing her. Behind him a green-clad soldier supporting him, as though helping him sit up.

Sickeningly Winters felt as though she had seen all this somewhere before. She heard herself cry out in horror. She saw what the soldier was doing to Lieutenant Oshima.

The bloody mess that had been the throat of Oshima. The blood pumping, then slower. The body fell sideways.

The soldier crouching behind Oshima met Winters' eye, then looked away as though embarrassed. He wiped the blade of his knife on Oshima's shirt, leaving broad swathes of red; left and then right; one side of the blade, then the other.

Winters became aware of another soldier to her left watching her. He stood up abruptly and grabbed her arm.

'Get down, lady, for Christ's sake!'

She shook off his grip furiously and walked on.

She stopped in front of Oshima's body.

The soldier who had killed him pushed the blade of his knife into the ground several times to get the last of the blood off.

Winters crouched down beside the body and hugged her knees with her arms and stared at the dead face, unable to speak.

With the Japanese sentries and lookouts disposed of, the noise of battle had diminished around them. Firing went on in a desultory way to left and right. The action had swept past them and raged fiercely several hundreds of yards away around the Japanese camp. Bullets whined and cracked, short bursts of gunfire and explosions reverberated damply in the forest.

Three young soldiers hurried up the track escorting Brandeis.

She ran to Winters, knelt down on the ground beside her and held her close.

Neither of them spoke and neither of them looked at the dead body of the lieutenant. The soldiers crouched, staring at them in disbelief and asking a deluge of questions which they did not hear.

'They kill the boy too?'

Brandeis nodded numbly.

A young officer appeared at the run. He looked angrily at the soldiers crouched on the ground.

'What the fuck is this? A Sunday school picnic? Get on with it.' Then he saw the women.

'Shit! Sorry!' He stared at them incredulously. 'Are you from that plane?' he asked.

Brandeis said, 'Yes.' Winters said nothing.

'You three. Get these sisters to hell back out of here. The rest of you get moving.'

'Right, boss,' said one of the soldiers.

The officer disappeared up the track followed by some of the soldiers.

The three soldiers hovered near them, unsure of themselves.

'Jesus, ladies, you'd be a bit lucky. We heard about that plane going down,' said one.

'Did it come down near here?' asked another.

The women did not answer.

'We'd better get going,' said the first soldier.

'Just a tic,' said the soldier who had killed Oshima.

He squatted by the body and dragged at the bloody binoculars around the dead man's neck.

The strap snagged underneath Oshima's head.

He jerked at it irritably.

Winters began to shake.

'Leave him alone!' she said, her voice trembling with rage.

The soldier looked at her, surprised.

'He's not going to be looking at anything, lady,' he said, then jerked the strap savagely so that it snapped.

Winters flung free of Brandeis' arms, got to her feet and walked quickly towards him.

'Leave him alone,' Winters said, 'You disgusting animal.' She was on him now, pushing him away from the body.

'Jesus,' said the soldier. He scrambled to his feet, alarmed. 'What the hell are you talking about, lady?'

Winters kept at him. 'Leave him alone, you animal.' She smashed at his face and chest. 'You rotten fucken' animal.' She screamed the words she had never used in her life before.

Awkwardly the man tried to restrain her, but Winters kept on battering at him and shouting at him frenziedly.

Finally he grabbed her by the shoulders and began to shake her, his face white with bewildered anger.

'Cut it out!' he snarled. 'What the hell's wrong with you, you mad bitch? He was a Jap, wasn't he?'

'Take it easy, Gerry,' said one of the other soldiers.

'Yeah, don't act like a bastard,' said the third. 'Can't you see she's had a bad time?'

After a while Winters stood quietly, staring down at the dead lieutenant and Brandeis felt her own tears begin.